The Exile of the Glen

The Glen Highland Romance

Michelle Deerwester-Dalrymple

BOOK THREE

Bonus Ebook

DON'T FORGET TO GRAB your bonus ebook about Gavin and learn what happened before he and Jenny met! Go to the webpage below to receive *The Heartbreak of the Glen*, the free Glen Highland Romance short ebook, in your inbox, plus more freebies and goodies!

https://view.flodesk.com/pages/5f74c62a924e5bf828c9e0f3

Contents

CHAPTER ONE

A Long, Cold Ride

THE MINCH, LATE FALL 1306

The coastline of western Scotland drifted away into the dusky horizon as the oarsmen worked the birlinn farther west toward the open waters of the Minch. Though the sky was cloudy and rain fell in a steady drizzle, the waters were thankfully calm. Light winds caught the sails, propelling the boat and easing the work of those on the oars. The mood aboard the sturdy wooden boat was energetic and jovial.

At least, that's how the scene appeared to Alistair, who sat bound and freezing in a barreled alcove near the stern of the birlinn. After his wet ride to the port of Gairloch with the MacNally's, his plaid wrap was sopping wet. The chilled air of the Minch settled into the rough tartan and through Alistair's tunic, and he could not stop shivering. Every part of him shook with damp and cold — his clothes, his hair, his skin, his fingernails even — and he wondered if he would ever feel warm again. He flexed his bound hands to revive and warm them as best he could.

The seamen handled the birlinn with ease, stepping easily over Alistair, ignoring him altogether. Most of the oarsmen abandoned their posts as the boat caught full sail, smooth and clipped with the wind. The Minch at midday filled Alistair's view, a seemingly endless gray sea against a lighter gray sky. The clouds swept across over the water in shades of grays and whites, the overcast light reflecting on the iron gray waves. He had never seen such a wide and expansive view and felt even smaller than he had when he boarded the boat.

The panorama, the emptiness of the sea, so comfortable to the sailors, struck a wedge of fear in Alistair. Never more than knee-deep in a local loch, the vastness of the seas presented an unknown adventure he did not wish to embark upon. The seamen moved confidently, secure in the seaworthiness of their vessel, and Alistair marveled at them. *How did they feel safe with nay solid ground under their feet?* A crisp wind blew across the hull, flapping the sails and loose tarps. Alistair tucked himself tighter into the alcove near the barrels, trying to retain what body heat he could in the crisp air. He thought the chilly ride on horseback to the coast was long, but his trip on the birlinn lasted an eternity in comparison. Alistair shivered again.

He rested his head against the damp wood of the boat and closed his eyes. Braced on both sides by barrels, the cutting wind did not reach him. Alistair warmed a bit in his hidey-hole, out of the range of sight from most of the seamen. His body still shivered, but weakly, and he was slipping into a light doze when he heard several men at the stern chatting loudly, oblivious of the spray of the sea.

"We have t'deliver the ass to the MacDonald in North Uist. Just what we need after this late jaunt," one deep-throated man said.

"Can we nay deliver the lad to MacRuaidhrí instead? He is right in Lochmaddy. Then we can find our whiskey and ride some women instead of having empty bellies and riding a horse," another man chimed in.

"Aye, I agree, Archie," yet another man responded. "We dinna have any obligation to the MacNally. Hell, he does no' want the lad as 'tis, exiling him like this. What did the lad do t'deserve banishment to the Hebrides? Might as well have kilt the lad instead, save 'im the misery."

Alistair's head hung at hearing the man's assessment. He had known that the Isles were nothing more than the last bastions of civilization, a word that is nay taken lightly in the Isles. If he had accused the MacColloughs of being wild men, they were courtly knights compared to the men of the Isles, if the rumors were correct. And if the men elected to dump him with some clan other than his own? Where would that leave him then?

"Weel, I dinna care either way," the first man told the others. "I dinna want to drag myself halfway across Uist just to deliver an unwanted man somewhere else he is no' wanted. Your idea is sound, Archie. We will drop him with MacRuaidhrí and let them deal with the bastard." The deep-voiced man, obviously the leader of this small troop, made the final decision.

This canna get much worse, Alistair thought aggrieved. *If I did no' have bad luck, I would have no luck a'tall.*

The birlinn struggled over the rough, freezing waters of the Minch well into the night. While Alistair was unsure how long the ride would be, he was certain they would likely arrive sometime the next day. He needed to prepare himself for these unanticipated changes to this trip.

The strange men wandered away, leaving Alistair to wallow in his own blistering cold misery. He shifted slightly, moving his head out from under the alcove to catch a view of the dark sky. A few glinty stars glimmered out from the patchy clouds. A pale moon strained to provide its muted luminescence, lighting their path over the water. The winds favored them, blowing continually throughout the evening, cutting through the fabric of Alistair's tartan.

A flapping sound attracted his attention, and he found a scrap of tarp billowing near one barrel. As he tugged on it, the tattered tarp slipped free, and he wrapped the dense cloth around himself to fend off the cold air of the night. He huddled under the tarp as feeling began to return to his fingers and toes.

Alistair felt small under the wide, dark sky, smaller even than when he was under the rage-filled scrutiny of his uncle. His thoughts drifted to the past few weeks and how his life had changed so abruptly, so miserably. Just a few months ago, his future was secure, set to be a leader and husband, active in his clan, beloved by his family. Now here he sat, freezing on a flimsy vessel on the even colder

Minch, his future uncertain, any hope for leadership or a wife gone. No clan, an embarrassment to his family.

He did not want to imagine his father's reaction when he learned Alistair's fate. His mother would never forgive her brother, no matter how justified MacNally was to demand his exile. Tears formed in the corner of his eyes, and he had to blink them back lest they find their way down his cheeks. Most likely to freeze as they fell. *The plan seemed sound. How did it all go so wrong? What happened to me to take it all that far?* His stomach churned worryingly, and he had to swallow several times to stop the vomit from rising. Whether he was sick from the cold voyage on the sea or from the depth of his regret, he did not know.

Regret is a painful awareness of a misguided reality. And under the shadowy skies on the small boat on the Minch, Alistair could do nothing but wallow in the regret that overwhelmed him. A part of him harbored hatred and anger over the loss of his position, his family, his life as he knew it, but the farther out to sea he traveled, the less space those emotions occupied. Instead, the weight of regret pushed those thoughts to the side. He had learned a hard lesson at the hands of his cousin Elayne and his uncle Laird MacNally, and he hoped that, in the future, he would not act in such a rash, crazed manner as he had for the past month.

He formed the idea into a prayer, asking God for clarity and guidance, and sent his prayer up to the mysterious stars above him. Perchance this trip to the Isles could be an opportunity for a new life, a rebirth, to become the man he knew he could be, not the broken, disturbed man he left behind in the Highlands.

Alistair blinked his eyes open to the incandescent glow of morning settling over the Minch. His tunic and trews had dried as he dozed under the tarp, so he felt moderately better and had stopped shivering. He folded the tarp to the side and lifted his hazy green eyes over the edge of the boat, trying to surmise their location. Some land masses in the distance seemed to surround the birlinn, and Alistair guessed they had entered the Little Minch that lapped at the shore of North Uist. Hopefully that meant they would be on land soon. A sailor he was not.

Sunrise peeking through the clouds alighted the water in a reflective steel gray, a smoother journey now that they had left the more open water of the Minch. His stomach settled while he slept and now grumbled loudly. Alistair adjusted himself back between the barrels, wondering if any food could be found on the boat. Surely dried mackerel or herring? A dry bannock? He could not remember the last time he ate.

His attention on his hunger was interrupted by two sailors who stomped down the hull of the birlinn, dragging a dense, rough rope. They joked with each other as they worked.

"Ach, I'm just glad that the Blue men of the Minch did nay climb aboard yestereve." The second man laughed at his portly mate.

"Christ's blood, Angus, are ye afeard of imaginary Blue men? I would think ye abandoned childish fears afore ye climbed aboard a boat!"

"I dinna fear them," the man named Angus responded sheepishly, a rosy blush rising over the beard covering his heavy cheeks. "And my brother told me his boat did encounter 'em last season! The Blue men are real!"

The other sailor only laughed harder. "Ooch, ye are a weak-minded lad, Angus. There is nay such a thing as a Blue man. Your brother dinna see anything other than waves on the Minch."

They worked the rope past Alistair, who popped his head out and called to them. Both sailors dropped the rope, their expressions altering from levity to seriousness.

"What do ye want, ye rogue? Ye have a bold tongue on ye to speak to us," the fellow named Angus spoke.

"My apologies." Alistair tried to make himself appear as contrite as possible. "I have nay eaten in several days. Could ye find a wee bannock?" His stomach growled as he spoke, confirming his request. The other man smirked at his situation.

"Your uncle did no' finance this trip for ye to have luxuries," he scowled, but Angus elbowed him. They leaned their heads close to one another, speaking in low tones that Alistair could not hear over the crashing of the water against the hull of the boat. They returned their attention to Alistair.

"Angus will find ye a bannock. He pointed out that it would no' do well t'have ye die of starvation in our care." The man looked over at Angus. "Christ knows that this one here would die if he missed even one meal."

Angus snorted in response.

The other man disregarded Alistair, resuming his work with the rope, looping it so it rested on the stern, ready for use. Angus disappeared to the far side of the vessel and reappeared with a lump of crusty, brown bread in his hand. He held it out to Alistair in a large, grimy hand.

"Ye are in a bad way, aye?" Angus probed, looking for the details that Alistair was not prepared to give. He nodded vaguely, grasping at the bannock. His throat was parched, but Alistair still gobbled at the dry bread, swallowing as fast has he could. He smacked his lips and tried to produce some saliva to wash down the cakey remains from his mouth.

"Aye, quite a bad way," Alistair finally managed.

"Did ye really try t'kill your cousin?" Angus continued.

"No' exactly," Alistair responded, unable to look the man in the eye. "'Twas more like a misunderstanding."

"A large misunderstanding if ye are now banished to the Isles."

"Mmmphm," was all Alistair responded, and Angus took the hint.

"Well, ye are in for a change on the Isles. They are tight knit people, mostly all related, and they hate outsiders."

Angus opened his mouth to speak again when the other man hollered for him to quit dawdling and get back to work. The heavy man lumbered away, leaving Alistair once more alone.

"*Talamh ho*!" a voice near the bow carried throughout the sails and over the crashing waves. While land was visible to the west since they entered the Little Minch, from Alistair's view when he peered over the edge of the boat again, the man meant he could see the port of Lochmaddy proper.

As they approached, the port, for what it was, became clearer. 'Twas nothing more than a long wooden dock extending far over the shallow, craggy fjard. The rocky shore itself appeared empty, not a croft or a keep nearby, nary a boat to be found. The tiny port stood out in stark relief, a mark of life in an uninhabited expanse of water and rock. Alistair's shoulders slumped. The distinct lack of civilization meant more travel, and he was sick of this voyage.

They sailed in a smooth motion to the dock, the calm waters mirroring the rare bright autumn sky. Alistair hoped the weather would hold if more travel was forthcoming. Noting the dusky trail leading from the docking up the hill to the west, Alistair studied the horizon, searching for a hint of his next destination.

A strong clap against his backside sent Alistair stumbling over the side of the birlinn. He would have ended up swimming to the shore had Angus's monstrous hand not grabbed his tunic and pulled him back on deck, ripping the already threadbare material. All the strength left Alistair's body, and he swooned. Angus held onto him, laughing.

"Ooch, weel lad. Ye nay have sea legs, for certain." Angus shook Alistair as he laughed, and Alistair tried not to scowl in return.

"Ye are no' going to the MacDonald, at least no' right away," Angus continued, hefting himself to the edge of the boat. "We need to attend the MacRuaidhrí first. We will let him ken ye are on his land, then he will decide when ye best continue t'the MacDonald. Let's get moving, aye?"

Angus joined the other sailors to leap over the side of the boat as it pulled alongside the dock. Thick ropes flung over the edges to the dock where the bulky men strained against the pressure of the boat as it rocked on the water. Bulging muscles flexed and shone with sweat as they looped the ropes over the docking poles, securing the vessel. The scarred, wooden dock threatened to buckle under their thick feet.

"Come, lad!" Angus hollered to Alistair. "Time to jump ship!"

Sighing heavily, Alistair chanced one last look back to the east, as though he could see mainland Scotland from this far shore. Despair hung about him like a worn cape, and he stepped over the lip of the birlinn onto his new homeland.

CHAPTER TWO

MacRuaidhrí

LOCHMADDY, NORTH UIST

Marching up the dusty trail to the interior of North Uist worked his under-used legs which cramped as he climbed. Rocks and loose stone littered the pathway, and Alistair seemed to find each one and trip over it, drawing harsh glares from his escorts. The only refuge he could muster was at least he was no longer stuck on a boat. If nothing else, he felt more confident now that his stiff, leather-clad feet were on solid ground once more.

As they reached the peak of the rolling hill, the trail opened to a glen below, ringed by sparse thin trees, brush, and a valley on the south, with sprawling grasses and low purple hills to the west. To the north, marshlands stretched back to the sea. There in the marshlands and in the east behind them, several inlets from the sea reached toward Lochmaddy, these fjards like watery fingers from the hand of the Little Minch. Delicate rays from the thin sun shining on the trees and grasses created a serene, enchanted glow over the village. The chilled air did not stop the villagers and crofters from bustling about their duties. A braying of cows echoed over the glen and a heady aroma of fish renewed Alistair's hunger. The MacRuaidhrí stronghold proper ran to the north, most likely backing to the secure, rocky shore of Loch Maddy itself.

The men continued down the trail, past the village, to the castle of MacRuaidhrí, approaching the outer bailey. Several kinsmen raised their arms in greeting. Others welcomed the men in a strange Scots-Gaelic accent. Alistair struggled to understand their words, and his heart sank even more, if such a thing were possible. Not only was he now a strange man exiled to an uncivilized land, 'twas a land where he barely understood the language. The large sailor from the boat spoke truer words than he realized; Alistair surely would be better off dead. His head throbbed in agony at the prospect.

The late autumn wind rolling from the west over the grass and rocks chilled him to the bone. A strong stone barbican opened to the small inner bailey, where armed clansmen bustled about. Once inside the inner bailey, the winds cut dramatically, but Alistair still shivered under his tartan until they entered the cavernous main hall where a towering hearth fostered a blazing fire. Alistair wiggled his way toward the flames, as far as his captors would allow, and began to feel warmth spread through his body for the first time in almost a fortnight.

Angus, Archie, and the third man (whose name Alistair learned was Malcolm), left him by the fire to take an audience with the MacRuaidhrí.

The MacRuaidhrí let Alistair abide in the main hall for several hours. While inconvenient and downright rude, to be honest with himself, Alistair was bone tired. Having spent the last several days hog-tied, then riding awkwardly on a horse to the shore where he was loaded onto a boat like no important riff-raff, sailing for a day and night on stomach-churning waters, to be unceremoniously dumped onto this scrub-covered pile of rocks these strange people called an island and walking to the MacRuaidhrí castle, Alistair desperately hoped this strange clan would let him take a nap. As it was, the hard-wooden bench would have to do. Rearranging what remained of his tattered plaid, he wrapped the wool around him, reclined on the bench, and fell into a deep sleep.

Sunlight ebbed from the window slits of the main hall when Alistair next opened his eyes. Someone was slapping at his cheek. Alistair sat up quickly, his head swimming with effort, and he groaned. Perchance now he could get supper and a decent night's sleep in a real bed?

"Get up," the grating voice above him commanded. Alistair lifted his weary head, hoping to see Angus, and was dismayed to see Malcolm before him. His feet planted and stance formidable; Alistair's spirits sank. A hot meal and a comfortable bed were not in his immediate future. Alistair raised his fatigued eyes to the man.

"Ye ha' ta leave," the immense man grumbled, grasping Alistair roughly on his upper arm to yank him to his feet. Alistair complied like a rag doll.

"Leave?" Alistair wrangled his arm away. "Where am I to go?"

"Your kin? The coast? Back to the Highlands? My Laird doesna care. I dinna care. Ye must leave MacRuaidhrí land."

"What, now?" A heady panic overwhelmed Alistair, a light sweat breaking out all over. "'Tis almost evening! How far is it to MacDonald land?" Alistair asked in a desperate voice, trying to make sense of this inhospitable island.

The ruddy man shrugged. "Dinna ken. From here, walking? A few hours south? Aye, go south. Ye will find it."

With those final words, Malcolm gave Alistair a powerful shove through the doorway. Stumbling down the stairs, Alistair caught himself just before he landed in the cold mud, the hall door slamming with finality behind him.

The sunlight was naught more than a thin purple blush under a pink and gray sky to his right. Darkness and stars had already closed in on his left, capturing the east of the Hebrides in a shadowy net. Alistair rubbed his aching neck (*Christ's blood, was anything NO' aching on him?*) and peered down the pathway extending south into the diminishing light. With nary another option in sight, he took a labored breath and stepped forward onto the path, making his way to another foreign land.

"Do ye believe the lad? That he is just an exile and hoping t'find a place with his kin here?" Lachlan stroked his ebony beard as he pondered this new development.

Lachlan and his brother Rudy, the Laird of the clan MacRuaidhrí, reclined on cushioned chairs in front of the fire of the study, and each man clutched a stout mug crowdie ale. A rough desk covered in parchments and trinkets littered the space behind them. The hearth with the blazing fire, however, was clear and welcoming. And while Lachlan did not typically consider himself a man to let irritations and inconveniences of others weigh on his mind, the strange lad from the Highlands would not leave his thoughts. Rudy responded with his typical sense of certainty.

"The lad is a mess. I dinna believe him to be more than an errant fly. Did ye see 'im snoring in the hall?" Rudy guffawed at the memory. "If the lad is an English Spy, I will eat your shoe."

Lachlan's gaze moved to the worn leather strapped to his feet, one corner of his mouth pulled into a slight smile. Unlike his brother, Lachlan struggled with uncertainty regarding the MacNally.

"They are ripe for the picking," Lachlan said, meaning his shoes. "'Twould seem I stepped in a pile of cow shite earlier today. Ye may no' want t'eat it."

Rudy's laugh increased, his own black hair, streaked with specks of gray, shaking with amusement. He wiped a lather of froth from his nearly gray beard.

"Weel, we dinna need such associations further complicating our position. Where do ye think he will go?" Lachlan continued, the matter of the lad nagging at the back of his mind. His deep-set eyes blazed with the fire. "Will the MacDonald's take him in?"

Rudy shrugged with one shoulder. "They are more loyal to the Bruce than ye are, brother."

Lachlan could not deny his brother's words. With the continued animosity between the Bruce, the clans, and with England in general, the MacRuaidhrí's loyalty to the Bruce was shaky at best. Though few knew the full truth, Lachlan and his brother, ever the opportunist, kept communication to each side in balance. The MacRuaidhrí brothers walked a fine line between keeping themselves in the good graces of the English while maintaining a supposed loyalty to the presently absent Robert the Bruce. The MacRuaidhrís wanted to come down on the side of the winner, with their coffers full and land intact.

"They will no' accept him. An exile from the Highlands? He may as well have "traitor" stitched on his forehead," Lachlan stated, raising a questioning eyebrow toward Rudy. "Where do ye think he will go then?"

A shadowy figure removed itself from the recesses of the doorway that led to the great hall. Having eavesdropped long enough, the figure stepped forward, asserting its own opinion regarding the exile.

"So ye dinna ken the lad? He is nay one of your *associates*?" The feminine voice filled the hall and brought a moue of ire to both men's dark faces.

"Ahh, dear sister, o'course ye would have t'put your coin into the game," Rudy commented dryly.

Christina MacRuaidhrí, their slender yet forceful sister, was not a woman to be reckoned with — something both brothers had learned early in their lives. Their father favored her, granted her an education far beyond that of a woman of privilege, and they mocked her for it. Regardless, everyone on North Uist knew who had the real power, and 'twas nay the MacRuaidhrí brothers. And much to their chagrin, they knew it as well.

"Coin or nay, it behooves all of us t'ken the man's intentions."

Christina tried not to sound patronizing as she pulled the cowl off her light roan braids. She pulled a third cushioned chair near the hearth and settled into serious conference with her soused brothers.

"Man's?" Lachlan guffawed. "If he is more than a score of years, *I* will eat my own shoe, shite and all."

Christina raised her chin at her brothers. Once again, she despaired that she was not born a man and thus Laird of her clan. As it was, she had to play her brothers' game, one in which they believed themselves savvy, but truly came across as nothing more than lack wits. She waved away their slights.

"Do ye ken who he is?" she pressed. She would not leave the keep until she was satisfied.

"Nay, dear sister, and ye can report that back t'your man. As far as we have been informed, he is naught more than a banished Highlander, sent to distant MacDonald kin as punishment for some prescribed atrocity," Rudy admitted.

"Where will the lad go, then?" Lachlan wondered aloud.

"I dinna care, brother. Once he is off our land, I doubt we will be troubled with the lad further. We must keep our focus on MacRuaidhrí concerns," Rudy claimed with authority.

God save me from Scottish politics, Lachlan thought. Nonetheless, Lachlan agreed and nodded his head toward his brother. They may want to keep their options open regarding an English alliance, but that door was slowly closing as more clans, the MacDonalds to the south included, and even their own sister, sided with Robert the Bruce, wherever the supposed King of Scotland was hiding. Lachlan felt more certain than Rudy that the MacRuaidhrís could come down on the side of the Bruce, especially if his sister had any say in the matter, which she did. He tipped his head to his sister, then lifted his sterling chalice up and toasted this wisdom.

"*Slainte*, brother, sister."

Christina returned the salute with her own nod of recognition, then replaced her cowl and retreated back to her shadows. Rudy's teeth gleamed in a confined smile at Lachlan as he raised his own chalice.

"*Slainte.*"

CHAPTER THREE

Falling Ill

THE LONG AND LONELY walk to the MacDonald clan lands was only made worse by the relentlessly increasing rainfall. Sunset robbed him of both light and heat, temperatures dropping with every step he took. And each of those steps meant a struggle of mucking his feet out of the cloying mud. The leather of his boots was caked in the thick mud, making each step heavier and more difficult. He had walked most of the day, and the muscles in his legs trembled. He sneezed, spraying water droplets and a string of snot out of his nose. Alastair wiped his drenched hair off his forehead and wrapped his travel-weary tartan more tightly around him. 'Twould be of no use, though; not only was he cold, he was bone-achingly tired, and now it appeared he was sick to boot.

He had hoped that the reception he received at Clan MacRuaidhrí would be a welcome one, that perhaps he would be invited to stay a few days to recoup from travels and fill his belly with warm meat and mead. His short stay and abrupt dismissal belied something else. What happened to Scottish hospitality? Was his reputation so tarnished? What did his uncle write in the message he sent with the sailors? Fury at being turned out from the MacRuaidhrí keep with no basic courtesy simmered beneath his skin, truly his only source of heat on this miserable journey.

All too soon his head began to throb, a steady pounding ache. Alistair checked his surroundings. He thought he was close to the MacDonald keep, definitely on their land, but thus far civilization was naught. He could see nary a croft or a campfire in the dismal weather. Now, on top of being cold, tired, and sick, he would have to walk for half the night to find shelter. The MacRuaidhrí had not even granted him victuals or extra cloth to use as a tent this evening when they sent him away, so camping for the night was not an option. And even if he did, what would he use for kindling? Every stick and leaf in this rocky land was more soaked than he was.

Alistair halted his movements and looked up at the darkening sky. Clouds obscured any light from the moon or stars, and Alistair felt wholly alone in the world. As an exile, what would become of him now that he landed on the Isles? He turned his head to the left. The rocky shore of the Little Minch was surely only a short distance to the east. Perhaps a dive off a rocky cliff to his demise below would be in everyone's best interest.

But he shuddered at the thought of taking his own life. Inasmuch as he was a coward, he was too afeared of the afterlife to bring his life to an end. His uncle had not granted him any audience with a priest, and there had been none on the boat, for certain. The thought of dying unshriven, and even more so, dying in a way that God would not forgive, gave Alistair pause. Life, even as miserable as his was in this sopping, fatigued, sickened moment, had to be better than what anyone would encounter in the depths of hell.

He took a deep breath to resume walking, and a dull pain in his chest flared. Coughing painfully, Alistair looked again to the south and, lifting his foot out of the sucking mud, resumed his voyage to Clan MacDonald.

In what seemed like a short time (but who would know by this point? He had lost all sense of time), a tenebrous light flickered in the distance to the west. Alistair blinked several times, wiping raindrops out of his eyes, trying to focus on the light. Was it a distortion of the weather? Only a reflection in a small parting of the clouds? Ghost lamps? Was he seeing things? Alistair took another heavy step in the direction of the light, then two, and when it seemed that the light was not a trick or a mirage, he tried to run.

A braying sound close by startled him. He made it near the edge of a rough lean-to before he collapsed, his sickened body spent.

A slight banging sound roused Alistair from his stupor. As he peeled open one crusty eye, the brightness in the air assaulted his sight, and the painful throb in his head pounded harder. For a moment, he feared he had died and that the bright light shone the gates to heaven. Slowly, the actions over the last fortnight came back from his memory, and he knew he was not dead. If he were, it would not be the brightness of heaven in his view.

The second thing he noticed is that, for the first time in days, he felt both warm and dry. Deep, soft fur and heavy woven tartan surrounded him as bedding. Was this a dream? He tried to sit up and assess his location, but a hammer of pain came down inside his head, and he flopped on the furs, grimacing in agony.

"Do nay sit up so quickly, lad. I can only imagine the headache ye have."

The soft voice of an angel filled Alistair's ears. Perhaps this was heaven? Then why did his head ache so much? His mind spun in a crazed fog. Unable to focus his thoughts or keep his eyes open, he turned his head to the direction of the voice.

"Where am I?" he croaked.

His parched throat would not give rise to his voice, and he coughed at the effort. The pain in his head thrummed all the more, now matched by the pain in his chest. No, not dead, but well on his way if he had to continue his travels in this condition.

The soft voice responded. "Ye are on MacDonald land. Ye collapsed near my croft nigh two days ago. I did no' think ye would make it."

A cool hand rested on his head. Warmth pressed against his lips, the smell of broth accompanying it. A wooden ladle of soup?

"Open your mouth," the angelic voice spoke again. "Take some broth. Ye are fairly parched and hungry, t'be sure." The voice was accented, Scots and Gaelic and something else. Perhaps 'twas an isle dialect? He parted his lips, as much as his chapped skin would permit, and the broth dribbled in, giving succor to his poor throat. She gave him another spoonful, then waited to see if he could keep the nourishment down.

"Thank ye," he croaked at her.

She grumbled a deep-throated response and continued spooning thin broth between his lips. Just a bit more to give him substance before his breathing slowed, and he fell back to sleep in the pile of wool and fur.

He had fevered dreams and nightmares as he slept. Much of the time he didn't know if what he heard or saw was real or imagined. Some of the visions were horrors — monsters from the sea or the swamps. Other visions, luminescent images full of warmth and light, where ones that rivaled those of the heavens. In his stupor, he heard another voice in the cottage, this one clearer than those from his dreams. Wiggling his eyelids to dislodge the crust that sealed his eyes and blurred his vision, he managed to open one eyelid in a narrow slit. Shifting his throbbing head to his right, he saw shadowy outlines of two people, both sitting near the fire.

The voice of one was that of his rescuer and nurse, a delicate, blonde, fairy-like woman in his distorted eyesight. His mind wanted to describe her as "bonnie," but she was so much more beautiful. The other voice was also female, but she was a black silhouette against the fire. She spoke in hushed tones as if not to disturbed him.

He closed his eye to focus on his hearing, their whispers louder in his infirm darkness. The other woman sounded concerned. His healer, however, never lost her controlled tone of voice.

"Ye dinna ken this man, Elle!" The other woman's whisper tried to be forceful. Who was Elle? His nurse?

"*Haut yer wheest,* Muira. Have ye no' seen the man? He canna sit on his own. I dinna fear he will try to hurt me. I could tap his head, and he would fall back into his sleep."

"The herbs may help, Elle, but if the man is as sick as that, he may be too far gone. What will ye do wi' a dead body? Do ye want a corpse in your home? What will they think —?"

"He yet lives. With the right treatments, he will continue t'live. Do ye have any blessed water or healing candle that may speed his recovery?"

A low chuckle floated across the croft. "Elle, I dinna think ye followed Alisa's old ways."

"Nay Muira, I do nay follow the ways of the Druids," his nurse said with a bemused but compassionate note to her voice. "But what can help the man regain his health, I will try."

A fumbled rustling sound replaced their soft conversation. The other woman, Muira, continued, her voice a whispered lecture. "Here are some herbs. Mix it wi' goose fat and rub it all along his chest. Then, ye need to recite this prayer: *Tui gratia Iovis gratiasit cures.* Alisa says she has seen naught about him. 'Tis the best I can do," Muira sounded resigned.

"'Tis Latin?"

"Aye, from the priest. The herbs are from Alisa."

"Thank ye, sister," his nurse responded.

Alistair strained to hear more, but they fell silent, and his brain followed, sleep overwhelming him once more.

Blurry light popped into his vision as he awoke with a start, the cool cloth on his head dripping little splats of water onto his jaw and trickling down his neck. He swallowed a few times, phlegm gurgling in his throat. His blonde angel-nurse appeared over him, her hair pulled back in a kerchief, and she held a limp rag toward his face.

"Spit," she told him matter-of-factly, and he spit.

His throat and coughing calmed as he inhaled deeply, the slightly stinky scent of the herbs on his chest filling his lungs. It was as though he could feel the compress healing him from the inside out. The woman moved to toss the rag into the fire.

"Was it a dream?" he managed to croak.

"What?" she asked, as she hovered over him again. Her marine blue gaze returned to his face, a sharp focus like the sea cutting through rock.

"Who is Muira? Was she a dream?"

"Nay, ye are sick, and your dreams are likely tortured. But she was real. Take a sip," she neatly dodged the question, placing a wooden cup to his lips. He worked his dry lips to drink as much without dribbling it down his chin like a helpless baby.

"Now go back to sleep," she commanded.

Alistair slept.

Again, strange dreams haunted his sleep. This time, he dreamed of a life that was no longer his, of a home he could never return to, of a land he would never see again. To Alistair, they were both the best of dreams and the worst dreams he could ever have.

Several hours passed before Alistair gained consciousness again. This time, when he managed to open his eyes, the light had dimmed in a smoky haze, and he could easily hear the fire popping at the hearth. The pounding in his head did not diminish with his sleep, but his throat felt much relieved. Focusing better in the dull light, Alistair estimated the sun had set and ushered in evening, while a peat fire burned low. He eased his aching head toward the sounds at the hearth.

The owner of the angelic voice bent over a black pot, almost a small cauldron, that hung across the flames, stirring with a large spoon as the firelight danced over her small form. She was tiny, almost fairy-like (*was she a fairy? An angel?* he thought madly), her shockingly long, flaxen hair tied back with a piece of fabric. The whitish-blonde coloring caught reds and golds in the light of the fire and glowed like a halo around her head. Her coarse skirt reached the dirt and straw floor, and a wool tartan of fawn and forest greens hung loosely about her shoulders.

"Ye sound better at least."

The flaxen fairy's voice carried through the cramped cottage. She did not turn to him but continued to stir at the fire. The scene before him swam before his eyes as he struggled to focus past his aching head. Everything seemed to hurt, even his hair seemed to throb in agony.

"Your breath, I mean." She kept her back to him, intent on her work. "I have bone broth for ye. 'Tis the best for illness the like of yours. Ye had a few sips earlier but nay enough t'see ye through to healing."

"Will I heal?" he managed to whisper. "I would have thought I was awaiting death."

A swirl of platinum cascaded across his wavering sight. Facing him, she held a small wooden bowl in hand. "Ye were close. Ye were knocking at death's door when I found ye," she admitted.

Her crystalline eyes bore into his, like rays of blue sun, and he squinted under her gaze. Concern etched her face and lingered in her voice. It would take a lot of work for this diminutive lass to remove his corpse from her small cottage if he *had* died, so her worry was well earned.

"And now?" he wheezed.

"Your outlook is fair. I do nay think ye will expire this day."

"Weel," he drawled as best he could, "'tis probably the best I have heard in the past several months."

His voice drifted off as speaking spiked the pain behind his eyes. He closed them as his fair heroine spooned broth to his lips again.

This time he remained conscious for his entire meager meal. As the lass intimated, the broth seemed to work a wonder. The unending ache in his bones abated enough for him to focus on the persistent headache. Keeping his eyes closed helped considerably.

He felt her move away, the wooden bowl banging when she placed it away from his bed. Alistair ventured another question, bracing himself for the exploding pain in his head.

"Who are ye?"

"I am called Lioslaith MacDonald," the lilt of her Isles accent thickening as she pronounced her name. "Ye are in my home."

"Mmm," was all Alistair could manage, trying to arrange his thoughts through his fever.

He made it to MacDonald land — at least he didn't lose his way in the rain. His mind spun as he evaluated his position, his headache notwithstanding. Now that he had arrived here, he didn't know what to do next. Would the MacDonalds welcome him? With the missive from his uncle, the answer was most likely no. Where would he go from here? What would he do? The unending barrage of questions pounded his already sensitive head. He heard the fairy Lioslaith speak.

"Pardon?" he asked.

"Who are ye?" she raised her voice, and he cringed at sound. She must have noted his grimace because a feathery touch alighted on his temples. Alistair stiffened at first, then relaxed as her fingertips massaged those pinpoints of pain, chasing the throbbing away.

"Alistair. Alistair MacNally," he mumbled in answer to her question.

He groaned in relief as her fingers caressed around the hairline of his ears. She rubbed his earlobes, tugging gently, her fingers doing more to bring him back to health than the broth did. And the pinpricks of his throbbing head lessened as she worked.

But more than alleviating his headache, her kindness made him wonder about the last time he was touched so intimately, with such care. Since he was a lad? By his own mother? He had not seriously courted any women while in the Highlands. His conquests were local girls or comfort women at best, nary a loving touch from the handful of women he had lain with. His failed attempt to wed had not included any romantic interludes. Relishing in Lioslaith's light touch was a new sensation, one for which Alistair was grateful.

He slipped back asleep as her hands worked their magic on the back of his neck. Another day passed before he woke again.

Firelight danced off the walls as his eyes blinked open and pale light filtered in from the small, square opening near the hearth. The hazy light did not assault Alistair's eyes and the painful fog of the last several days had retreated. Having a clearer mind, he could better assess his current state of health. His muscles finally wanted to cooperate, and he wiped his face with his hand, trying to take in his surroundings, now that he could see it clearly. Lioslaith sat in the same place as she had the evening before, keeping guard over the pot on the fire. She bent low, her hair dangling dangerously close to the flames, her whole body on a precipice of disaster that never manifested. The woman appeared charmed.

Pushing away his damp, tawny hair from his forehead, he adjusted his gaze, taking in the rest of cottage. A second pile of tartan and fur bedding was tucked against the wall close to the hearth. On the far side of the hearth sat a narrow side-table covered with pots and bowls. The rich scent in the room emanated from swaths of dried herbs hanging across a wooden beam above their heads. Two rough-hewn chairs sat back from another table on a woven mat covering the hard-packed floor. Homey, simple, and perplexing. Did the lass live by herself? Was she a widow?

Lioslaith's hands moved by the fire, a light knocking as she ladled liquid from the pot into her wooden bowls. The scent of meaty stew competed with the scent of the herbs. She placed two bowls on the table, and cutting her hard, icy eyes to Alistair, she called out in a soft voice.

"Rowan, ye can sit for supper."

Alistair's eyebrows rose to his hairline as he watched a small girl child, her own flaxen hair covered in a dun kerchief, clamber over the stack of bedding from the other side of the room. The girl cast a worried glance at Alistair. She climbed up onto a chair, gracing her mother with a bright smile, and dug awkwardly into her soup.

Keeping her eyes on Alistair, Lioslaith seated herself next to her daughter, her voice sparkling as she spoke to the lass. *She has a daughter!* Alistair thought. And this scene answered part of Alistair's questions about Lioslaith; she evidently did not live by herself. Now a whole slew of new questions erupted in Alistair. Was the father absent? Or dead? How did Lioslaith care for a child on her own? Did the MacDonalds provide assistance for her? Noting Lioslaith's cold stare, he wisely kept his prying questions to himself.

Once Lioslaith finished, she wiped down her bowl and returned to the fire, spooning more broth into the bowl. This time she returned to Alistair.

"Are ye strong enough to sit up a bit, or do ye need me to feed ye again?"

While her words seemed harsh, her tone was soft, much like when she spoke to her own child. All that she had a random stranger invade her home and need her care, she was kinder than he could have expected. But the challenge to his manhood, sick though he was, could not be ignored.

"Nay, I can sit up and serve myself. Thank ye."

He shifted up on the furs, proud he could sit up almost fully. Lioslaith delicately placed the bowl in his hand, the heat emanating from the bowl comforting. He inhaled the broth, only to have his nostrils assaulted by an eye-watering stench. He had noted the odd smell from his chest again, but not this thick or smelly.

Lioslaith smirked at his reaction. "'Tis nay the broth, lad. 'Tis the rub on your chest. It's rosemary, lungwort, and goose grease. Ye can smell it better when ye sit up."

Alistair crinkled his nose.

"'Tis t'help ye breathe and heal your throat, laddie. Do nay grimace so." She chucked her fingers under his chin. "Eat up now. We need to get ye hale."

Fat, colorful vegetables and a wee bite of meat floated in the broth, added nourishment since he was finally conscious. He had to stop himself from eating it all in one swallow.

Lioslaith busied herself with the fair Rowan, wiping the child down after she finished eating and dressing her in a fresh shift for bed. They sat on the bedding across the cottage and, using an antler-bone comb, Lioslaith brushed tangles from the girl's feathery hair. Their similar white-blond hair painted a striking image, the two like tall, real-world fairy creatures. Alistair wiped dripping broth from his chin as he observed their ministrations.

"Tell me a story, Mama," the girl's slight voice asked. "A Blue man story?" Lioslaith set the comb aside, wrapped her arms around the child, and spun a tale.

"Once, a young lass and her husband lived near the rocks of the Minch," Lioslaith began. Rowan snuggled into her mother, obviously familiar with story time.

"And each day, the lass would walk the rocks, looking for eggs, seaweed, and mussels. Her husband often fished in the Little Minch, and between the two, their life was fair. Soon the lass was full with their first child, and the couple was happy.

"One day, the husband fished close to the Minch, and the water began to churn. A strange blue creature rose from the water, with the body of a man and the tail of a fish, a kelpie. It settled on the edge of the man's boat, trying t'overturn the vessel. The man begged the kelpie t'set him free as his beloved wife was home, carrying their babe. The Blue man took pity on him and crafted a deal. He promised to let the man return to his wife, but after the birth of the bairn, the kelpie would return to drag the man below the sea.

"The man, grateful for some more time with his family, returned home but remained quiet. He did no' want his wife to fret over him. A hearty boy was born t'him and his wife, and they celebrated. Each day, the man took the swaddled bairn to the edge of the sea, telling him of all the wonders t'be found in the waters. The man tried t'spend as much time with his wife and babe as he could, knowing his time with them would soon end.

"Soon after, the man was finishing in the Little Minch when the wily Blue man reappeared. The man hardened himself, ready to fight but knowing no man who fought a kelpie won. The kelpie again sat on the edge of the boat and spoke t'the man in his watery voice. He told the man he had watched him with his son on the coast, that his love for the boy and his pride in the sea was certain. The kelpie told the man that, so long as he continued t'respect the sea and teach his bairns t'respect it as well, then the Blue men would have nay dispute with the man and would no' drag him down into the sea.

"The man was again grateful for the mercy of the Blue men and sailed home t'his family. The man kept his promise to the Blue man and taught all his children t'respect the sea. Every so often, the man would see the Blue men, swimming below the surface, but no harm ever came t'the man's boat while on the Minch."

Rowan's head had slowly sunk into her mother's arm during the story, and now she curled up in Lioslaith's lap, breathing the sleepy breath of innocence. Lioslaith lifted the child over the side of the furs, tucking her in against the chill of the evening. The story similarly enraptured Alistair, who blinked to bring himself back to his bed once Lioslaith finished. Weaving a tale for the lassie was the most he had heard her speak since he awoke, the dulcet tone of her storytelling voice captivating.

His weary, sage green eyes followed her as she returned to the small table, clearing the bowls and tidying the room. Her shoulders slumped, and she looked back at Alistair over her shoulder.

"Ye can ask," she told him, her icy glare commanding an answer.

"Well, that she is yours is obvious," he began with caution. Lioslaith nodded, moving to seat herself near his bedding. "Where is her father? I can no' imagine he would let me recoup here with ye and your child otherwise."

Lioslaith flipped her hand to the door. Her crystalline focus never left him.

"I will tell ye what I tell others," she started.

His chest shuddered as he breathed in, taken aback at her strange sense of honesty.

"I will listen to whatever ye wish to tell me," he croaked, feeling the rush of sleep overtake him. He had not imagined that being awake could be so trying.

Lioslaith shrugged at his response. "I dinna ken ye, so there is nay difference. I say that she is the daughter of my husband who died."

She tossed her platinum hair, looking in adoration at the delicate form asleep on the other side of the room.

Again, her forward mannerisms surprised Alistair. He also knew that her words were lies. She showed no shame or embarrassment in her story, her reticent tone returning with her clipped response. The truth of Rowan's birth lay elsewhere, but at least she was willing to make him aware that she had no husband, that only she and her daughter lived at the croft.

"Thank ye for your explanation," he told her as his eyelids dipped low.

"I dinna ken ye enough to give anything otherwise," Lioslaith said as he slipped into oblivion.

CHAPTER FOUR

Send Me an Angel

ALISTAIR WOKE WITH A start, the pressure to piss waking him from a deep slumber. He glanced around the darkened cottage but did not catch sight of Lioslaith. The lass had done so much for him as of late, the prospect of bothering her to help him relieve himself while she was otherwise engaged, rattled him. He felt better, had eaten more in the last day, so clambering outside to piss should be no burdensome endeavor.

Bracing himself against the wall, he pushed himself up off the pile of bedding and wobbled to the wooden door, dragging a tartan blanket with him. As he managed to pull the door open, a blast of icy wind welcomed him to the dark outside. Having been stuck inside by a warm hearth for so long, he failed to realize that winter was rampaging across the Isles. Realizing that Lioslaith had worked by herself in this cold while he slept in a warm bed further insulted his manhood. What man allows a woman to do such hard work in this frigid weather? Though he had been ill, he had a sinking sense of failure as a man, a supposed Highlander. Exiled, relying on a young woman to survive, what manner of man was he?

He wrapped himself tightly in the plaid, a desperate attempt to ward off the cold. Alistair maneuvered near the side of the cottage, and the warm relief of pissing sent chills through his ravaged body. He felt as brittle as a dry stick and was certain he resembled said stick as well. Once his bladder was empty, he gave a final shiver in relief and turned to the door, when a strange sound caught on the wind.

Stepping back toward the edge of the croft, one hand on the thatched wall as support, he listened into the howling wind. When the air calmed, he heard it again, a struggling sound rustling in Lioslaith's lean-to barn. The animals did not make so much noise, and he feared reivers came upon her as she fed her few chickens and the goat for the night. In his weakened state, he was unsure what he could do to help, but Alistair could not let the young lass fend for herself. A burning need to repay her for her nursing and hospitality hung over him, even if it would amount to nothing. Searching in the dark, he found a thick branch on the ground and hefted it to his shoulder — a meager weapon wielded by a weak warrior indeed.

As he neared the worn door of the lean-to, the intensity of the rustling grew louder. A groaning sound accompanied the sounds of the struggle. Nearly blinded with fear for Lioslaith's safety, he burst through the lean-to door, hoping to take the invaders by surprise.

The surprise, however, was his own. Instead of villains thieving the livestock, Alistair found a lone man, bent over a bored-looking Lioslaith, panting and thrusting like a rutting bull. Lioslaith's skirts were rucked up to her hips, her pale legs glowing against the darkness of the stable. Alistair dropped this stick, the noise attracting the attention of the rutting man who barely glanced back over his shoulder.

"Get ye gone, will ye?" the man grunted, too focused on his work to care for any interruptions.

Alistair flicked his eyes to Lioslaith, who waved him off with a quick flap of her hand. His brow furrowed in confusion, he hesitated until Lioslaith flapped her hand more forcefully. Alistair tripped over his own feet as he stumbled out the door and into the icy winds of the Isles. His mind spun, and he feared he would keel over on the icy dirt at the cottage door.

He ambled back to the croft, trying to understand what he witnessed in the lean-to. The man appeared to be taking advantage, but Lioslaith did not seem to mind. In fact, she wanted Alistair to leave, not assist her. Did she welcome the man between her legs? Who was he? A paramour? A betrothed? Rowan's father, perhaps?

Lioslaith entered the cottage soon after Alistair, her platinum hair windblown and her cheeks flushed. Alistair had tiptoed inside, fearing any noise he made would wake the sleeping Rowan, who would call for her mother, and then where would he be? He returned to his space on the bed, feeling more like an interloper than he had when he was too sick to care for himself. Obviously, he'd become an impediment to Lioslaith and her life, and he wanted to rectify the situation as soon as he could.

Her rosy appearance when she returned, though, caught his breath. She had lain with another man, and his reaction should reflect that, but the longer he remained with her, the more enticing her looks became. The fairy-like aura she possessed attracted his attentions more often than he had cared to admit. And now there was the chance that she was betrothed or hand-fast to another man. Another missed opportunity for him, it seemed.

After bending over her bedding to check on her daughter, Lioslaith moved to the hearth, adding more kindling to fight off the chill of the night. She rested in silence by the fire, trying to warm herself. The lean-to was not warm by any means, and being exposed for any length of time chilled her to her bones. She also did not fancy a conversation with the man currently taking up residence in her home. Lioslaith knew so little about him but had enjoyed his company regardless. Just having another person to share her time with allayed much of the loneliness she felt in her isolated cottage. Now that he would know the truth of her, she feared he would leave abruptly, and her loneliness would again take hold of her life.

Fortunately, Alistair understood discretion. His intense green gaze burned into her backside as she occupied herself at the hearth, yet he remained quiet out of respect. She owed him no explanation, and he would not pressure her to speak.

He adjusted his bedding, nestling deeper like a burrowing vole, and allowed the comfort of the covers and the heat of the room to enshroud him. He had just begun to doze when she spoke.

"Do ye want to know who he was?" The lightness of her voice carried through the cottage. She posed the question like 'twas village gossip.

Alistair did not respond at first. He feigned sleep as he considered his answer. Who was he that she felt the need for accountability? He was a stranger living off her generous graces and healing abilities, and, keeping his eyes closed, he told her as much.

"But if he is your man, and my being here is an issue for him, I can leave," he continued. "The MacDonalds canna be far from here. Mayhap a clansman will grant me shelter." He paused before speaking again. "He seemed, um, familiar with ye."

"Aye, that he is," Lioslaith's voice was as icy as her eyes. For such a tiny woman, she commanded herself as though she were a goddess, commanding the earth itself.

"But he is no' the only one," she continued, and Alistair could not keep his eyes closed. His right eye popped open more easily than the left, so she was blurry in his lopsided gaze. But he could not miss her lips that twisted to one side.

"What —" he began, but Lioslaith held up her hand to cut off his words.

Glancing toward the sleeping Rowan in the corner of the room, Lioslaith moved her stool close to Alistair's head. The flare of the fire cast her in a back-lit glow, and once again Alistair thought of her as a fairy, too fair and bright and slight to be real. For a moment she appeared so ethereal, Alistair wanted to reach out and touch her to make sure she was here in the cottage and not a dream. Her voice, barely above a whisper, did naught but convey her as a fae creature all the more.

"He is no' my man. But he is a man, one who lacks a wife, so he comes to me when he has a man's needs." The surety in her voice held no shame. She knew herself and her occupation; she had no need to be coy. "I am a comfort woman."

Lioslaith allowed the weight of the words to settle on Alistair as she reached for her pot of stinky rub. Pressing the grease into his chest, she gauged his reaction. Some men harbored a firm disdain for women in her occupation, like fruit they could never eat. With those men, she had to be cautious, for they would have her run out of the clan, or worse. Most men cared little. Instead, they made a note of her for possible future use.

Alistair, surprised as he was, had no reaction. For the few hours he had been awake enough to engage with her, the woman presented more and more as an enigma. Why should her occupation be anything different?

"A comfort woman," he croaked out slowly, relaxing at the attentions she gave his overwrought chest. "A whore?"

Lioslaith's lips pursed at the word. "Mm, prostitute would be a more accurate term. I prefer comfort woman. I dinna care for the word 'whore,' ye ken," her authoritative voice scolded.

Chastised like a young lad, Alistair only nodded in understanding. As an exiled man too sick to care for himself on his own, he was in no position to judge her. Comfort woman or no, he probably would have died without her care. She could have been a lavender unicorn for all he cared; she nursed him back to health, and he was eternally in her debt.

A muffled rapping at the cottage door broke the stillness a few evenings later. Lioslaith's sick charge snored in the far corner of the room while her own daughter slept tucked away in their bedding near the hearth. The child was a staunch sleeper in the way only the very young or very ill can be. Confident that both were well into their dreamland, Lioslaith collected herself and answered the knock.

The blond giant who stood before her had visited her many times in the past. Though strikingly handsome, with deep azure eyes and enticingly defined muscles, his beauty was only skin deep. His boorish behavior and pompous words often suggested he had a claim to her, but that did not stem the flow of men seeking succor at her door. Lioslaith's stomach clenched at the sight of him now, fearful how he would respond to the stranger she was nigh hiding in her home. Since he was seneschal of the MacDonald Chieftain, Dougie wielded a measure of power in his clan, power he liked to lord over those he deemed less worthy. As a comfort woman, Lioslaith often found herself at his mercy.

She lifted her hand, pointing to her squat, lean-to barn. Her arm shook with apprehension.

"My daughter is within. Come."

"'Tis cold, Lioslaith," he said tersely.

"Aye, 'tis. Keep your tartan about ye. 'Tis nay much warmer in the barn." Lioslaith would not allow Dougie to pressure her; 'twas still her home, and she would or would not invite in whomever she wished.

Dougie's lips puckered with annoyance, but he said no more and followed the comfort woman to her lean-to. He despised the lean-to — the hard table covered only by a rough fur and old tartan blankets, the smell of the animals, the low beams that forced him to slouch, the cold or heat depending on the season. He felt like a rutting animal whenever she lay down for him in the barn. Despite all that, she was the fairest comfort woman in MacDonald's lands, one nearest to him, and he was nay about to traverse farther north to the MacRuaidhrí's land in search of a warm sheath.

Lioslaith's taupe and moss tartan skirt whipped about her hips as she led Dougie to the sloping barn. She pushed the worn slatted door open, and Dougie stepped over to a low bench to the left. Wedging the door shut, Lioslaith moved toward the bench with hesitant steps. Caring for both her daughter and a sick stranger wore on Lioslaith, and she was fatigued down to her bones. But Dougie paid in coin, and she was not about to turn the Laird's man away.

Dougie, true to form, did not wait for her to ready herself. He crushed his mouth on hers, grinding his lips on her chapped, delicate ones. The bulge under his plaid told her he was more than ready, and his aggressive kisses confirmed it.

His hands worked under his trews, freeing his cock from the folds of fabric as she reclined on the bench, trying to find a comfortable position on the tattered bedding. He tossed the front of her skirts up and leaned into her hips, grunting with effort and lust. The bench groaned under the weight of the two thrusting bodies.

Dougie was a rough and thoughtless lover. His sole quest was to dominate her, have her yield to his throbbing cock and achieve his moment. He thrust blindly and wildly, hoarse grunts escaping his throat with each movement. His hands clasped her shoulders, pressing her into the hard bench, and his fingertips often left subtle bruises on her translucent skin. The barn seemed an appropriate place for couplings with Dougie, as he rutted no better than an animal.

He also sweat horribly, working like a madman, and her thighs were sore for the rest of the evening after his visits. This night was no different, and she closed her eyes against the sweat droplets that flung about the bench as he pounded against her woman's mound. His grunting became more guttural, and she knew the best way to help bring him to his orgasm.

"Oh, my Lord Dougie," she whispered into his ear.

She allowed her hands to flit below his draping tunic, and she pressed her fingertips between the cleft of his buttocks, working as deeply as she dared. His thrusting became frenzied above her, the bench protesting loudly as Dougie strained in one final, long breath. His member spent, he collapsed atop her, his heavy form crushing her into the hardness of the bench all the more. Lioslaith breathed shallowly until he shifted away.

After catching a few deep breaths of his own, Dougie shoved himself off her, standing at the foot of the bench. He reached under his tunic, adjusting his satisfied member, and averted his flat, expressionless eyes. He never watched her fix her clothing after his carnal rampage. Lioslaith believed he felt guilt afterward but kept her thoughts hidden. She feared his wrath if she tried to engage him in an emotionally charged conversation. He did not seem the conversant or emotional sort.

Reaching into his leather sporran, he pulled out a small satchel of coin and tossed it to her.

"I should remove some of the coin," he bit out, "for the less than pleasurable chambers." His hard eyes glanced about the lean-to. "But ye were serviceable, as always."

Dougie gave her a final, cold wink, then spun on his heel and marched outside. The unnerving air surrounding the events in the lean-to departed with the man, and Lioslaith felt lighter. The brute of a man was gone, she had coin in her hand,

and the rest of the evening was hers. She tilted her head, listening to the light patter of rain on the thatch roof, which meant no more male visitors this eve.

Lioslaith rose from the poor, creaking bench and went into her cottage to wash the remnants of the man off her skin.

CHAPTER FIVE

The Long Road to Recovery

HE SPENT THE NEXT few days at the discomfiting mercy of Lioslaith as she resolutely nursed him back to health. Each day Alistair felt stronger, but his chest remained heavy, thick, and he fatigued quickly as his breathing was still labored. The best part of his early recovery was not relying on the fairy-like Lioslaith for his necessities with a chamber pot, a chore she undertook with grace; he could step outside like a man.

Which was something he had not felt like in a long time. Since learning he would not be Laird of the MacNally clan, followed by his exile for trying to usurp his uncle and his daughter, being bound and dragged across the Minch, and then relying on a wisp of a woman to help him remain alive, he had not lived up to his idea of what a man, let alone a Highlander, should be.

As he stepped outside to take care of business one bright, cold morning, he took a deep breath, the crisp air burning deep in his chest. He looked to the west, where the rolling hills and rough-edged rocks littered the horizon. Few trees and thatches of low brush grew between clusters of rocks and lines of marshy creeks.

Different from the snow-capped mountains that formed much of the Highlands, this sparse, windy chunk of rock was eerie, but after so much time sick, indoors, and unaware of his surroundings, he felt an immense appreciation for the beauty of the large island. Taking a final sharp, cleansing breath, he retreated toward the warmth of the cottage and noted a small stack of wood and tufts of peat near the door. The inadequate mound gave him a moment of pause.

His ill-rattled mind pieced together that the only one supporting the whole of the home, including harsher labors such as cutting firewood, was the dainty Lioslaith. This realization only added to his guilt — that she assumed the task of helping him when she worked unwavering on her own already. He cast his forest green gaze around the land again, aware of her isolation at this juncture of MacDonald and MacRuaidhrí land. She lived close enough for her men to visit, but those men surely did not help her chop wood. They came for one thing and moved on, leaving Lioslaith and her daughter to their own devices until need impelled the men to come to the croft again.

Yet still sickly, Alistair knew he must repay Lioslaith for her care. Exiled and a horrible excuse of a Highlander though he may be, his journey to atonement must begin. He needed to show he was still a Highlander of Clan MacNally, even if he would never return to that land again. He coughed and spit a wad of mucous onto the patchy earth by the door. Filled with conviction and freezing his ballocks off, he entered the cottage, ready to throw off the mantel of patient and assume the role of tenant farmer for Lioslaith.

As for Lioslaith, while her erstwhile patient may need nursing, she could not allow him to distract her from her larger duties. Although consorting with men offered her a bit of money and protection, much of her income came as a healer, working with her sisters to aid those who needed healing. Traveling to assist others became more difficult as the winter approached. Lioslaith made a point to visit those in dire need, icy nights like this one, notwithstanding.

She departed for the MacDonald village to the south after Alistair fell asleep, wee Rowan in tow. The child was a fast learner, already helping to retrieve items her mother required from the woven basket. And in truth, Lioslaith enjoyed Rowan's company. She felt less lonely when her lass was with her. And if some MacDonalds gave her the evil eye when she paraded into the village proper with her daughter, so what of it?

The miller's wife, Elizabeth, had burned her hand on a pot when a hole in her handkerchief exposed her skin to the hot metal, searing it into an ugly, weeping wound. She had done her best to tend the wound — Lioslaith was impressed at what she saw when she regarded it — but it had begun to suppurate. Lioslaith asked Rowan to hand her several herb jars from her basket and made a milky poultice to protect and heal the reddened, tender burn.

She left several more applications of the poultice with the relieved woman, instructing her how to care for the burn so it would heal quickly. The grateful woman slipped a coin into Lioslaith's hand and hugged her gently before Lioslaith stepped out of the cruck house with Rowan's wee hand in hers. Many MacDonalds may judge her harshly, but others, women like Elizabeth in particular, valued her. It may not be much, but the welcome of these women gave Lioslaith hope for her and her daughter. They trudged across the moorland toward home, the sound of Rowan's prattling chatter filling her ears.

Alistair's breathing slowly improved as days passed; his chest ached less and less as his energy came back. Lioslaith's patience ran long, as she continued her daily regimen of caring for Rowan, nursing him, all while keeping food and heat in the croft. Alistair had come to enjoy watching Lioslaith play with her daughter, usually from under half-closed eyelids. The little girl, an exact reflection of her mother, smiled throughout the day, as Lioslaith attempted to make even the basest chores a game. They counted the sticks of wood they brought in, made up songs about cooking broth, and sewed together by the light of the open door or, if it were too cold or late, near the fire.

The fairy-like girl was curious, though, and once while her mother was outside, she ventured close to Alistair while he slept. He awoke to her large, blue eyes peering close to his face, and he jumped back in surprise.

"Oh, lass. Ye caught me asleep, it seems."

Rowan gave no reaction, studying him with the same intensity her mother displayed.

"Why are ye abed so much?" she asked in her squeaky voice.

"Surely your mam has told ye I am unwell?"

"She says ye caught your death. Are ye dying?"

Alastair laughed silently, the effort aching his chest. "I dare say I hope no'. Your mam helped make sure that does no' happen."

"How long will ye stay abed then?"

Ooch, the curiosity of bairns. Alastair shrugged a shoulder.

"That I dinna ken. Hopefully no' much longer. I feel better with every day, thanks to your mam."

Rowan didn't respond, only pressed her lips together and nodded sagely. Oh, she was her mother's daughter.

Rowan had shied away from him, as though he were an injured animal her mother took in, one that could rise up against her at any time. Alastair found her reaction humorous. While sick, he couldn't rise up against his own blanket, let alone a person. But given her mother's occupation, perchance the lass' caution was nay unfounded.

Several days after his early morning pissing adventure, he gathered the strength to start earning his keep. God ken he had much to make up for. The first morning he felt well enough to stand and work, he surprised Lioslaith by taking up his bedding with the intent to air it outside.

"What are ye doing?" she squealed.

"Do ye have any pins or the like? I dinna think I am mistaken if I say this bedding smells worse than I do. I would air it out for ye."

Lioslaith narrowed her eyes, her pinched face telling him what she thought of that idea but moved close to him and lifted his shift.

"Ooch! Woman!" He called out in surprise as she shushed him. Pressing her ear against his chest, she listened to his breathing. She then reached up, placing her hands against his neck and face, then nodded her head.

"Well, ye have no fever, and the rattling in your chest is nearly gone. I dinna think 'twill kill ye to air your bedding. Do ye want some breeks to wear? Or are ye warm enough in a shift and a bare backside?"

Blushing, Alistair glanced down at his legs. He had forgotten he spent the last fortnight abed in naught but his shift.

"Aye, breeks would be welcome."

A sly smirk came to Lioslaith's face, and her eyes danced as she held back a bark of laughter at him. She pulled a pair of trousers from a basket, and he recognized the worn breeks he wore across the Minch. Lioslaith had graciously sewn some of the tears and worn patches, and while he was not exactly presentable, at least his backside would be covered.

She also tossed his tartan to him. "The weather has turned. The wind is icy, and snow will surely fly soon, if no' freezing rain. Wrap yourself well, afore ye spend another week in bed, knocking at death's doorway."

The tartan was mended well, and the heavy wool shielded him well from the cutting wind. Lioslaith had handed him several pins and directed him to a line that connected her cottage to the small lean-to. Shivering under the damp, gray clouds, he quickly draped his coverings over the line, pinning them in place so they would not blow away in the stiff wind.

Lioslaith was ready with a warm cup of herbal mead when he entered and sat him near the hearth. It was the first time he ventured to any other part of her home. Rowan watched him with her large, aquamarine eyes.

"I thank ye for that. I ken the coverings needed —" she started but he stopped her.

"Nay, ye have done more for me in the last fortnight than any has in a long time. I have lived off your kindness and generosity. Ye cared for me, a stranger, when ye did no' have to. The least I can do is earn my keep until I can travel to the MacDonald stronghold."

Lioslaith tipped her head at him. "I had wondered about that. What were ye doing out there in this weather? Ye are nay from the isle, that I ken well enough. Do ye have the energy to share your story?"

Alistair stared into the fire, watching the flames lick up in orange and russet hues. Fearful she would immediately kick him out if she knew the full truth, he considered her place on the island, settled in this remote croft between two clans, and thought she may have an understanding of his present turmoil.

"I am an exile," he began. Lioslaith's face revealed nothing — neither shock nor surprise — and he continued. He wanted to describe how he got caught up in the idea of power, aligned himself with a lunatic who had his own delusions of power, and almost killed his own cousin as a result, but feared her reaction too much. Instead, he spoke in general terms, only stating he had been banished. His tone became penitent when he told her about his uncle's banishment, his travels across the Minch, and his encounter with the MacRuaidhrí.

"I had spent the evening getting lost in the rain, trying to follow the directions to Clan MacDonald, where I have some distant kin. I dinna even ken if they will take me in or what my future holds with them. I am nay a good man, and they would be wise to reject me."

Lioslaith, for all the hard exterior she presented to the world, felt her heart breaking at Alistair's tale. She deeply understood the sadness and loneliness that came with exile, with not being accepted by one's own people. Since the birth of Rowan, she had become unwelcome with the MacDonalds, and the MacRuaidhrí tolerated her presence on the edge of their land for the purpose she served, and for her relationship with her own sister.

Lioslaith flicked her icy blue gaze to the strange man sitting by her hearth. He provided a comforting company in her croft, a male presence long absent. She had many men, but none in her home with her daughter. No man would have her, given her family history. But as she took in his form, his tawny hair alighted by the dancing light of the fire, she imagined what life would be like if a man like him did accept her and her daughter. She wanted to tell him he was a good man, to reach out and touch him, even raised her hand, then pulled it back and shook her head.

This man was nothing more than a stranger and exile himself who didn't know what his future held. What kind of man was that for her? God knew, when Lioslaith's sister made her next visit, if Alistair were still here, she would not hear the end of Muira's rantings.

Alistair began his tenant status the next day. With a bit more energy and stronger breath, he rose before Lioslaith and stoked the fire up against the never-ending frigid winds that blew across the rocky island. Alistair briefly wondered if he would ever be warm again. The Highlands may well be damp and cold, but the icy winds of Lochmaddy seemed never ending.

The stew pot from the evening prior still held heat from the banked fire of the night, so he pulled it over the fire, preparing to break their fast. He crept out the front door, trying to slip out quietly so as not to wake Lioslaith or Rowan, and collected firewood and dried grasses from the low pile near the door. The biting air chased him back inside. As he set the wood in a bin by the hearth, a rustling sounded behind him, and he tilted his head toward Lioslaith's bedding.

She was awake, sitting upright, her bright eyes wide with surprise, her fair hair lighter than the palest sunrise. His fairy nurse looked provocative and delicate, so unlike the hard-working Lioslaith he had seen since his arrival. Both his heart and his loins throbbed with wanton desire. She was like a dream, and he did not want to wake.

Lioslaith hesitated, blinking with bewilderment. Why was he stirring the stew pot?

"What are ye doing?" she whispered, tugging her furs to cover Rowan.

"I am preparing the stew to break our fast. Ye have worked much t'keep me alive, let alone provide for me, all while maintaining yourself and your little lass. 'Tis the least I could do."

She blushed at his gratitude, casting her eyes down. Then she returned her gaze to him, the intense blue fire burning under her eyelashes.

"And what was I t'do with ye? Near death and far from kin? Only a monster would've passed ye by."

Alistair kept stirring the stew pot, shrugging one shoulder. "I have met my fair number of monsters," he grumbled loudly enough for Lioslaith to hear.

She elected to ignore the comment and instead wrapped herself in her thick wool tartan, trying to ward off the morning chill as she moved off the bed. Gratitude infused within her, along with the heat from the fire — Alistair's attentions to the hearth already warming the cottage.

"Weel, I thank ye for your help this morn," she said.

Alistair shrugged again. "Ye have a goodish amount of foodstuffs on hand. I understand your, uh, business helps keep ye and the lass fed, but some of these items, are they difficult to find on the isles this time of year? Who helps ye keep the animals?" He tossed his light brown waves in the direction of the lean-to.

"Ooch, the —" Lioslaith peered at the tiny sleeping form under the bedding and lowered her voice, "gentlemen do help, aye? I take coin or vittles, and some men will help milk the goat or chop wood. My sister and —" Here she paused again, a look of concern passing over her face briefly, "weel, my sister helps when she can."

A flash of insight passed over Alistair. "Your sister. Was that the woman I thought I dreamt?"

Lioslaith dipped her head, a smile tugging at her lips. Alistair's heart fluttered at that smile. Her position as his nurse struck him in a baffling manner, and he experienced a gamut of emotions whenever he laid eyes on her.

"Aye, she is the one," Lioslaith responded. "She lives out here, no' far."

Alistair reached for the stew considering. His few ventures outside made it apparent that Lioslaith's croft was far from any other tenants. *Where did this sister live?* Lifting the stew pot from the fire, he opened his mouth to ask her why she lived so far from any village, when a small voice called from the bedding.

"Are we having stew to break our fast? Mama, I'm famished for stew!"

Alistair's mossy gaze caught Lioslaith's frosty marine one, both acknowledging their words would hold until later.

CHAPTER SIX

Family Matters

THE PIERCING WIND THAT had haunted their morning dropped away by midday. Collecting water and eggs and chopping wood in the rare bright morning air invigorated Alistair. When he completed his chores and entered the cottage at noon tide, his energy and attitude were high.

Lioslaith noticed the change, the color blooming on his cheeks and lightness returning to his hair. She felt a moment of vain pride in saving the handsome young man, then humbled herself quickly. She was in no position to flatter herself or fall for a rogue Highlander. *No' unless he's paying*, she thought dismally.

Trying to detract herself from his devilish handsomeness, she turned to the fire as he dropped onto the stool by the table across from Rowan. The wide-eyed child watched as he adjusted his plaid and removed his muddy shoes. Lioslaith dished broth into a bowl for the girl and set it at the table with some dark, nutty bread, then handed the same to Alistair.

The chilled air of outside emanated off his skin as he warmed up, his scent fresh and clean. *He must have washed in the barn*, Lioslaith thought. Her lips pulled into an unbidden smile, and she scolded herself for acting the love-lorn lass around him. She entertained men for a livelihood. Why was this young man so enchanting to her?

Alistair emptied his bowl in large gulps, swallowing loudly, his eyes cutting to Rowan to see if she would laugh. The lass did not disappoint, her giggles tinkling like glass. Alistair continued to make a mockery of eating, and Rowan mimicked him, laughing uncontrollably, piercing Lioslaith's heart. She did not hear that laugh often enough, but Alistair brought it forth with ease. Alistair's languid smile caught Lioslaith off guard, and she had to look away to stop herself from laughing along with them. Alistair failed to notice her discomfort, his own attention now on his pasty toe that popped out of his stocking. Both his stockings, in fact, were somehow more tattered than the rest of his clothing. Alistair sighed. How much longer before his shoes were as holey as his stockings?

From the corner of her eye, Lioslaith watched Alistair press the edges of the hole together. Wordlessly, she went to her small sewing basket tucked near her sleeping pallet and plucked out a needle and thread.

"Are these your kirk stockings?" Lioslaith asked with glowing eyes.

"What do ye mean?" he asked, perplexed. He only owned one set of stockings — what else would he wear? "I only have these stockings —"

"Weel, they must be your kirk stockings, then. 'Acause they are holy." Amusement flickered across his face, and it took a moment before her words fully registered. *A joke?* He gave her a sidelong gaze of utter disbelief.

"Are ye teasing me, lass?"

Touches of humor spread from his eyes to his mouth. A girlish giggle rose from her throat and she coughed to cover it, regaining her serious expression.

"Here," she said, holding out the sewing to him. Alistair took it in one hand and looked at it stupidly. The playful banter deserted her, and Lioslaith gave an aggravated sigh. Did the man not have a mam?

"Do ye no' ken how t'sew?"

Alistair bit his lip, hesitant to respond. Thus far, he had failed to make much of an impression on his stunning fairy rescuer; admitting he could not sew would only make that impression worse. Before his muddled brain could figure out a response, she snatched the sewing back.

"Ooch, *Highlander*, I'll show ye."

She grasped his foot and tugged off the frayed stocking. Her fingers wriggled against the bottom of his foot as she did so. The tickling sent him off the stool in peals of laughter.

"Oh please, careful," he begged with panting breath.

Lioslaith's mouth no longer held stoic lips, the terse line spread into a gleaming smile that took Alistair's breath away more than her tickling.

"Oh," the mischievous look on her face was unmistakable. "Are ye ticklish then?"

The subtle threat was followed by another run of her delicate fingertips against the sole of his foot, and he rolled to his side, trying desperately to pull his leg from her grasp.

"Argh, ye vicious wench!" he cried with laughter.

Rowan watched the two of them with absolute delight, banging her spoon against the table and cheering them on. A sudden forceful voice took them all by surprise.

"Sister, are ye well? Is this man abusing ye?"

All three heads swiveled to the voice. Lioslaith scrambled to her feet and dropped Alistair's leg, brushing at her skirts as she placed the valuable needle on the table.

"Muira! I was nay expecting ye!"

"Evidently," Muira responded tersely.

"This is the man who was sick. The man ye helped with your herbs? 'Tis Alistair." Lioslaith's closed countenance returned, her azure eyes once again cautious and hooded.

Alistair rose awkwardly, feeling the fool in one stocking-less foot, and bowed toward the woman.

"Alistair Lee MacDonald MacNally, at your service."

His compromised vision limited his view of her when he was ill. She was nothing more than a shadow on that day. Now, in the fullness of light and his health, he could see Lioslaith's sister well, and her appearance was almost shocking. The woman stood a hair's breadth taller than Lioslaith. Other than that difference, the fact they were sisters was obvious. They shared the same striking moonlight pale hair and fierce blue eyes that commanded authority. Alistair wondered if they were *leathon* — born together. He reasoned this may be why Lioslaith lived isolated from her clan — children born from a mother at the same time were often viewed as marked, or even cursed. One could easily mistake one sister for the other. The likeness was disconcerting.

"Hmm," the woman, Muira, intoned, flicking her iron gaze over him. She reached her dainty hand up to his face and peered closely into his wary eyes. She then stuck her thumb into his mouth and looked into it like she was judging a horse. Alistair whipped his head back.

"Mistress!" he protested. Muira shrugged, dismissing him, and turned her attention to her sister.

"Ye did good, Elle. The man lives. When I saw him last, I did no' think that would be the result." A light blush, again something new to Alistair, touched Lioslaith's cheeks. *She is flattered,* he surmised, suppressing a condescending grin.

"Weel, 'twas work, and I dinna believe he would have lived without the help of your herbs and cunning."

"Ye can thank Alisa for that," Muira replied.

"Your chickens are fair freezing, Elle!"

A second laughing voice called out as another woman entered the cottage, her wispy brown hair bound back with a leather tie, an engaging smile on her face. She drew up short at Alistair.

"Ooch!" She gasped, the basket in her arm swinging. "Ye are a tall one when ye are standing upright!"

Muira guffawed and flicked her eyes toward Alistair. "'Tis Alisa MacRuaidhrí, our dear friend and famed healer," she introduced them through pursed lips. "Alisa, this is the sickened Highland rat my sister dragged in. He calls himself Alistair."

Lioslaith shook her head at her sister's overprotective ways. "Alisa," she said, addressing the cheery woman, "thank ye for the visit."

Rowan scuffled down from her chair and over to Alisa, trying to peek inside the woman's basket.

"Do ye have a treat for me, auntie?"

Alisa grinned with enthusiasm at the excitable lass and crouched down to her.

"Let's see what's in the basket, shall we?" Dramatically throwing back the cloth atop the basket, Alisa pulled out a pot with a wax lid. Rowan jumped up and down, clapping her hands.

"Clover? 'Tis the clover?"

"Aye, 'tis the last of the clover honey. Put it up safe." She handed the precious treat to Rowan who took it with something akin to reverence.

Alistair stood to the side, near his bedding, enraptured by the noise of the domestic scene. After spending a fortnight in quiet recovery, the bustle of women and children overwhelmed him, and the sense of feeling out of place once again resurfaced.

Rowan, however, would not let his emotions take over her happiness. She lifted the pot up toward him, her eyes shining with pride at her prize.

"Do ye care for clover honey, Ali?"

Alistair's heart swelled at her question. Mimicking Alisa, he also crouched low to eye the beloved pot of honey.

"Aye, dear Rowan, 'tis my favorite as well. I especially prefer it on oats."

"I love honeyed oats!" the lass gushed then walked the pot gingerly to the table to set it down. She handled the honey like the treasure it was, so delicate for such a wee bairn.

Alisa and Muira returned their attentions to Alistair. Alisa lifted his shirt and pressed her ear against his chest. Alistair recoiled in surprise.

"Mistress!" he called out again. Alisa held up a finger to shush him. Alistair lifted his nervous eyes to Lioslaith, imploring. She merely shrugged, unable to hide the slight grin that pulled at her lips. She was obviously enjoying Alistair's discomfort.

"Your chest is much clearer." She dropped his shirt and looked to Muira and Lioslaith. "The lad will be fine if he does nay push himself. Do a bit more each day, and ye should be back t'yourself complete in a fortnight, mayhap?" Alisa cut her eyes to Muira who nodded in agreement.

"Clearer?" Alistair squeaked.

"Aye, when ye first arrived, your breathing was too thick, we were no' sure ye would make it through the first few days."

Alistair's face twisted up in confusion. Had he met these women before?

"While ye were ill, ye slept much," Lioslaith explained. "My sister and Alisa came and helped me care for ye, then took Rowan for a few days. We are all three healers on this part of the Isle, aye? And ye were delusional at best when ye were awake. I am no' surprised ye dinna recall."

The awareness of the efforts put forth by Lioslaith and her family crashed upon Alistair like the waves of Lochmaddy on the rocks, fierce and intimidating. Why did they do so much to save his pathetic soul?

"Weel, then," he stammered, bowing to each woman separately, "I thank ye for your care. I would no' have survived without ye."

Alisa's bright face remained open and ardent, as Muira and Lioslaith's starker expressions mirrored each other. Lioslaith's eyes softened.

"We are just glad that ye survived."

"Aye, a dead Highlander in your house would need much explanation, as ye weel ken," Muira commented blandly, and Lioslaith elbowed her sister.

"Muira!"

Muira shook her head, waving her hand in capitulation. "Ooch, fine. But 'tis well that ye recovered. We brought ye more herbs," Muira said to Lioslaith, "to replenish your supply, and Alisa made the most delicious oat cakes. I am sure Rowan will want honey with hers."

Rowan heard her name and came running to Muira, clasping herself against Muira's leg. Muira changed as she peered down at the fair child, a mix of delight and contentment shining, alighting across her face.

"Auntie, am I visiting with ye again? Mam, can I please?"

Muira and Alisa both looked to Lioslaith with hopeful eyes.

"We are preparing for the Christ's mass. We have some gathering to finish before snow flies, and Alisa has baking at the ready. Having Rowan with us would be both a pleasure and a help."

Lioslaith's cutting, crystalline eyes shifted from Alisa to Muira to Alistair. He sensed something more in the request, probably having to do with his presence.

A fool he may be, but his mind was sound, and he could not deny he was a complicating matter for the women.

"Aye, she adores visiting," Lioslaith responded. "Let me get her dressed against the cold."

Alisa placed the basket on the table near the beloved honey as Lioslaith wrapped a heavy wool tartan around Rowan's tiny form. Alisa lifted the child easily, and casting an easy glance at Muira, she giggled with the lass as they stepped out the door into the brilliant cold air.

The door slammed shut after the flurry of women left. The rare glow of the day remained but was diminished after the brightness of Lioslaith's amicable family departed. Calmed now that the clamoring had quieted, Lioslaith gestured for Alistair to sit at the stool by the fire to resume mending his tattered stockings. Alistair obeyed, but his wide eyes were gaping green pools and his open jaw remained.

"I should probably explain about my sister," Lioslaith began. "Weel, both of them. I consider Alisa my sister as much as Muira, aye?"

Alistair blinked several times, clearing his thoughts. "Nay, ye do no' have t'do any such thing. I am an interloper in your home, at best. Your affairs, your family, are your business."

Lioslaith shook her head, her shimmering blonde hair even brighter than normal, as though the visit from her sisters enlivened her somehow. Alistair found it difficult to look away.

"My sister is no' like other women," Lioslaith started, her voice resonating in the empty space of the cottage. "We were so close as bairns—"

"The resemblance is uncanny, t'be sure," Alistair commented as Lioslaith began to repair a large hole in the toe of his stocking. Watching her work, he admitted the stocking may be more thread than fabric by the time she finished. "Had I not known ye, 'twould be difficult to tell the two of ye apart. Ye could be *cariad*."

His voice heartened in reverence. Lioslaith grumbled in return, indicating what she thought of *that* idea.

"'Tis good and bad, ye ken? We weren't *cariad*, but Islanders believed as much. Many came t'us, my mam included, for herbals and the like, thinking we had ties t'the old ones. Others . . ." Lioslaith twitched her head to one side dismissively. "Ooch, they were afraid. My da and mam were shunned a bit, aye? But 'twas no' until later, when—" here she paused, flicking her icy gaze to Alistair, evaluating him. Alistair watched her choose her words. "Weel, ye ken what I am."

Lioslaith did not look at him as she spoke, and Alistair again sensed there was much more she wasn't sharing with him. He sighed, wishing he had the words to let her know she could trust him, confide in him. As it stood, he was naught more than an exile himself, hiding from his own past. Mayhap if they grew more familiar with each other . . .

Alistair shook his head at that thought, forcing it away. The lighthearted moments with Lioslaith and Rowan before her sisters arrived was not the life for which he was destined. He should leave soon, become a hanger-on for clan MacDonald, and let Lioslaith resume her life with her daughter without an extra mouth to feed.

The fire warmed his bare toes, and he felt feckless sitting on the stool while this angel mended his clothes. He reached for the sewing.

"Please, ye must allow me."

With one raised eyebrow, she presented him the needle and thread. Half of the hole was mended, and the next step should have seemed obvious, but Alistair held the needle stupidly in his hand as he regarded his sock.

"Ye just stab it in, like ye stab a man with a sword, near the hole, ye ken?"

Her voice was more patient than he anticipated, speaking to him as she would instruct Rowan. Her finger pointed at the stocking, and he obediently stabbed the needle through to the wooden knob inside the sock.

"Now, inside the sock, go t'the other side of the hole, and push the needle back up out o' the sock."

Lioslaith had moved closer to him to observe his sewing. Her hair tickled his cheek as she bent close to view his efforts. She smelled of the crisp winter air and sweet honey, and the sensation of her closeness startled him, and he dropped the valuable needle on the ground.

"Ooch, I found it," she assured him.

Lioslaith lifted the sliver of metal, and her crystalline eyes caught Alistair's as she handed over the precious tool. Alistair could not tear his eyes from her; his breath caught in his chest and the warmth emanating from her body heated him more than the fire in the hearth. All the air went out of the cottage as they held each other's gaze. Time stopped and Alistair found himself shifting his face closer to hers.

With a sudden movement, Lioslaith sat back, her once-open face now closed and reticent, her narrowed icy eyes cooling their heated gaze, and Alistair shivered in response as he cursed his audacity.

"My apologies, Lioslaith," he offered in a tight voice.

She waved off his apology, but removed herself to the small table, wrapping her tartan against a cold that the fire could not combat.

Cursing himself again, he resumed his sewing, mending his tattered stocking. God knew he would need it, as he had to leave Lioslaith's home before he over-stayed his welcome.

He feared he may have already done so.

Once his stockings resembled clothing again, Alistair took stock of his belongings. Lioslaith had placed them neatly at the foot of his bedding, wrapped in his rough outer tunic. Alistair dug into his sporran, noting that he had coin enough to survive for a fortnight or more on his own, if the MacDonalds did not take pity on his dire circumstance. His small agate-encrusted dirk was tucked in his sporran as well, meaning Lioslaith removed it from his belt for safe-keeping. His filthy leather shoes rounded out all of his worldly belongings, and again he cursed his luck. To have come from the house of a Laird and end up with naught more than scraps in the accounting of his life shamed him.

Lioslaith watched the amber-colored man from the corner of her eye as he regarded what remained of his life at the foot of the bed. His coloring reminded her of early fall — bright yellows, rich browns, warm colors in a cool air. Her heart clenched the longer she regarded him. While her sister and herself had subjected themselves to their own form of exile, it was nothing compared to what this slender young man endured. Her whole body called to him, wanted to reach out to him — the tides to his moon. She was drawn in a way she had not known since her time with Rowan's father. And watching him take stock of his meager life frightened her, but she was unsure if she feared he would see her exposed emotions or feared that he would leave and never return.

"I will depart on the morn," Alistair broke the heady silence.

Lioslaith's chest clenched and her throat swelled. She had to swallow several times before responding. "Are ye certain that ye are well enough t'travel?"

Alistair was touched at her bearing, as her concern was not misplaced. His breathing still ran ragged by the end of the day, and he tired easily. Just thinking about his illness made his chest ache, and a cough forced its way through. The journey to the MacDonald keep would be nothing short of a trial, but he needed to leave. He had grown too comfortable in this small cottage and would miss Lioslaith and her bairn, miss the comfort of family and the mask of acceptance desperately. Meeting her had been a miracle from the Lord above. Not only did she save his life, she touched his heart. But he would intrude on Lioslaith no longer. Neither she nor her daughter deserved it.

"Aye, 'tis time. I need to travel. How long, do ye think, until I reach the keep?"

"Walking? In your condition? Less than half a day, t'be sure. A couple hours if your chest does not ache too much." Lioslaith's brow furrowed at the prospect of his traveling in the cold so soon after recovering. *What if it should rain?*

"Ye should wait a few more days."

Her typical reticence did not stop her from voicing her more emotional stance. He would most likely be fine on his walk, tired at most, but she had grown accustomed to him, his company. She didn't feel as alone since he arrived, and as much as she hated to admit it, she did not want the man to depart. He turned his pine-green gaze to her, the heavy sadness in his eyes nearly bringing her to tears.

"I can nay thank ye for all ye have done for me, Lioslaith. I shall make it my life's mission to repay ye one day."

"Nay, Alistair—" she tried to protest, but he held up a hand to quiet her.

"I will impose on your hospitality nay longer," he said in his own clenched voice.

Lioslaith was at a loss. Here she was, losing someone she had grown to care about, again, someone she barely knew. Making decisions regarding her heart was not a strength she possessed, but watching him pack, she did not have a care. She took the only action she felt open to her.

Stepping lightly toward him, Lioslaith placed a hand on his back, feeling his muscles ripple under his thin shift. Alistair stiffened, stunned as to how to react. *Was she checking his breathing? Why was she touching him?*

She allowed her tiny hand to continue its delicate path across his backside under his shift and around to his muscled, concave stomach, curling her dainty curves against him.

⇒⇒⇒⇒ ⇐⇐⇐⇐

"What are ye about, Lioslaith?" Alistair's voice was hoarse, and he held himself in check. His limbs shook and his cock flexed, unbidden.

"I should think 'twere obvious?" she said in a husky tone.

Alistair found it difficult to breathe. Her hand moved lower, below his flat belly to the waist of his trews. Her nimble fingers dipped under the cloth, working through the fur at the base of his shaft. Alistair's entire body hummed, but he remained still. Body and mind warred over the present placement of Lioslaith's hand on his cock. His mind told him this was wrong, that he should not take advantage of the woman who had already done so much for him. His body, conversely, betrayed him, ignoring every thought to instead shake and throb.

Need and desire raged through him that he had never before experienced, never believed possible. His body was on fire, and he would be consumed unless he had her, touched her pale skin, twined his hands into her bright hair, thrust his cock into the core of her. Before he realized it, his lips were on hers, his tongue searching her mouth, as though hope and absolution could be found there.

Lioslaith roused him further, wrapping her hands around his head and pulling him down on to the rough bedding atop of her delicate form. The feel of his rough skin excited her in a way long absent. She pulled her skirts up, freeing her legs and allowing him access to that most sacred part of her that men had chased and killed for throughout history.

Alistair did not stop kissing her as his hands traced her soft thighs, then trailed up to her weeping center. He dared to touch the darker blonde curls guarding her entrance, brushing against her damp readiness. His fingers burned into her tingling skin, and she gasped into his lips, encouraging him to continue.

He shifted his hips onto hers as his blood pounded through his heart, his chest, his head. Clutching at the rounded firmness of her rear, he tried to pierce her as deeply as possible. She raised her hips to meet his thrusts. Alistair moved inside her, trying to be gentle, to draw it out, but his need to satisfy his cock took control, overcoming any ideas he had loving this dream-woman. Rather, he heaved for all he was worth, living for the sensation of her velvety sheath across his sensitive member.

Heat rippled under his skin, starting in his ballocks and rising through him, urging him to pound into her all the more. Lioslaith's soft cries of "More, Alistair. More!" brought him to his height. His seed spilled into her in one pulsing, wracking explosion that left his entire body limp, and he collapsed on her dainty chest. Alistair feared he might crush her, but the fear left his mind just as quickly as he lay on her, panting.

He lifted the tartan to cover them both, his long arms easily reaching around Lioslaith's delicate shoulders. Fierce wind and frozen rain kicked up over the evening, pattering of the rain soothing under the protection of the cottage. The frigid wind blew across the isle, and every draft in the croft exposed that icy blast. The fire struggled to fight the cold, but under the tartan, they could share the heat they created together.

Peace and contentment filled Alistair, and he regretted his insistence at leaving on the morn. Here, in this simple croft before a blazing fire with this angel in his arms, the last thing Alistair wanted to do was leave. Lioslaith's ethereal features caught the dance of the fire that illuminated her, and she seemed ever more a dreamlike creature. He fingered a lock of her hair and brought it to his lips. The smooth threads of her tresses tingled his lips, and he shivered at their intimacy. Alistair did not know what heaven was like, but entwined with Lioslaith, he could imagine it well. He heard Lioslaith inhale deeply as she rolled over to look at him.

His features also radiated the firelight, casting him in more dramatic tones of oranges and yellows. She reached up to toy with his sandy hair in return, trying to force every aspect of him into her memory. Once again, she made a choice to lie with a man in deference to her heart, not for financial gain, and she knew, like before, this decision would end in heartache.

They lay in silence for a while in the early evening, light from the setting sun highlighting the door and the cold wind and rain whipping up outside, holding the moment for as long as possible. Each understood that, after they left his bedding, this fantasy would be lost, and they would resume their ruined lives. Lioslaith risked speaking.

"Your hair is like the sand where it touches the sea, both dark and light," she whispered, playing with his wavy locks. "I may no' be of sound mind right now, ye ken, but I shall miss ye when ye leave. Please have a safe journey." Her voice hitched a bit, but she hid it as she cleared her throat.

It may have been a trifling sentiment; regardless, her words touched Alistair and a warm glow bloomed in his chest. For so long he had lived alone, rejected, and the prospect of anyone caring for him after all he had done was not one he could entertain. Yet here he was, holding a fairy-like woman who was admitting she cared for him in some regard. Uncertain of how to respond, he kissed the top of her golden head before she pulled away, her shimmering nude form rising from the bedding.

His moment in heaven had ended.

Lioslaith shrugged a muted forest-colored plaid around her shoulders to ward off the chill. The fire had burned down low as they lounged, and as the wind kicked up, the flames could not penetrate the room.

She poked at the fire and placed several more pieces of wood and peat into the hearth to help it blaze back to life, filling the croft with another thin layer of smoke. While Alistair watched her fluid movements, a horrified notion came upon him.

"Do I need t'pay ye?" Alistair's deep, apologetic tenor carried over the crackling of the fire. Lioslaith dropped her head down into the tartan.

"Why do ye ask me this? Did I do anything t'suggest payment?" Indignation tinged her voice.

Alistair lifted himself up on one elbow, facing the glowing sprite wrapped in plaid. She was a piece of magic, something he never imagined for himself. That she would give herself willingly, that she wanted to lie with him, seemed impossible.

"Nay, I mean no offense. Yet, I am naught but a clan-less stranger in your land, a man with nothing t'my name but some coin and a dirk. I nary have my health, and what I do have of that, I owe t'ye. 'Twould appear my indebtedness to ye grows by the day," he paused, sticking his courage to continue. "As does my care for ye," he said, his voice barely above a whisper.

Trying to meet her eyes, he rose up, the coverlet dropping to his waist. The firelight danced across his defined chest, his tawny hairs alighting him like one of their island deer at sunset. His whole person reminded her of those deer that ventured near her croft, majestic yet timid.

She bit her lip, and her voice broke slightly. "Aye, indebted ye are, but only for my healing. And ye have served well as a farmhand t'repay that debt. As for lying with ye —" She waved a dainty hand in his direction, dismissing his earnest words and poking at the hearth with a stick in her other hand.

"I will nay take coin from ye. I had the sense ye needed it more than any herb or victual I could offer otherwise."

She rose suddenly, the plaid swirling around her form like a selkie rising from the sea, and he wondered how she was of this earth. Stepping lightly back to his bedding, she sat next to him, cursing herself under her breath.

"I also did it for me. I ken what I am, and as such, I am much like ye, an exile." She paused, taking a deep breath, gathering her courage. "I dinna ken ye, Alistair, but my body has yearned for ye since I found ye. I feel myself calling out t'ye, but like ye, I am marked against my clan."

Alistair opened his mouth to speak, to tell her she did not need to unearth her secrets, that he too felt an echo for her, deep in his soul, but she placed her pale fingers against his lips to silence him. He did not protest. Lioslaith was a quiet woman, and this was the most she spoke directly to him since his lamentable arrival.

"Aye, I am a comfort woman, which is shameful enough, but I am exiled for more than that. Comfort women live in clans and villages all the time. My shameful position would be enough to keep me from my clan, after I had Rowan. Her father is nay more, so I am exiled as well."

Alistair did nay realize he held his breath until she finished her story, and he exhaled in a rush. He had many questions, especially why she didn't address the man as her husband. It spoke of deeper meaning. Instead of asking any questions, he reached around her, pulling her closer in his welcome embrace. They sat in the solitude of the cottage, two exiles trying to find comfort as the lonely winds swept across the moor.

※※※※ ※※※※

With a brief break in the sleet, Alistair refilled Lioslaith's woodpile by the hearth as Lioslaith served up oyster soup for the evening meal. A roll of thunder signaled more rain would soon follow. They did not speak about their time together that afternoon, as though speaking of it would steal the magic of the moment, and Alistair wanted it burned into his memory for all time. While she worked to clear supper, he watched her with veiled eyes. Knowing he would leave on the morn tensed his whole body.

Reporting to the MacDonalds was overdue, and depending on how he would be received, the odds of spending any more time with Lioslaith ended. As such, his brain and body fought a fierce combat he struggled to tamp down. A quiet life with Lioslaith, far from the politics and traumas of clan life on this barren isle of beauty and mystery was the dream he hadn't known he wanted. Now that he held it in the palm of his hand, he had to abandon it, abandon Lioslaith and her daughter, and resume a life of shame and uncertainty. The injustice of it all, once again, bubbled under his skin.

Lioslaith banked the fire as Alistair climbed into his pallet and tried to close his eyes, but his mind kept drifting to Lioslaith — the silkiness of her skin, the bright contrast of her hair on the dark plaid, the delicacy of her bones, so thin like a bird's that he feared he would crush her. He wondered if she would share his bed again, not to claim her body, but to hold her, one last bastion of heaven before his walk into hell.

He rolled away from the wall, his legs tangling in the fur at his feet when a knocking sound came at the door of the croft. Alistair twisted his face to Lioslaith.

"'Tis no' thunder?" he questioned, but he already knew the answer.

Lioslaith held her finger to her lips, her eyes bright in the dark of the room. Pulling the bolt, she opened the door less than a crack and poked her face out into the frigid evening air.

Alistair could hear a man's voice, and an aching heaviness settled into his chest, more painful than his sickness. Lioslaith flicked that blue, ethereal gaze to him, then slipped outside, pulling the door tightly behind her.

What little hope he had with Lioslaith crashed like the thunder rolling outside. She was a comfort woman; she belonged to many, not to him.

CHAPTER SEVEN

Meeting the MacDonalds

WHEN LIOSLAITH RETURNED LATER in the evening, Alistair feigned sleep, to spare either of them the acknowledgment of what had transpired between them, or with her paramour. Instead, he peeked one eye slyly open to watch her as she prepared for bed. Other than her flushed skin and tousled hair, her face appeared serene, as though they shared nothing significant that evening. Lioslaith turned her slender back to Alistair while she finished her task of banking the fire and shuffled her way into her own bedding.

Alistair watched all of this surreptitiously, feeling like an invader more than ever before. His body craved their earlier moment under his covers, when she was his and his alone, and he almost asked her to join him in his bedding for the night. He wanted to see her, *needed* to be with her, as much as he could before sleep overtook him, and his morning departure would be upon him. While a slight chance remained he would encounter her again — at a market, from afar on a hunt, at a feast — this was the final time for him to be so close, so intimate, with her. Though the span of the room separated them, he did not want to miss even these trivial, final images of her.

Lioslaith curled on her side, as far from Alistair as she could be in the cramped abode, trying not to weep. Having a caller this evening was terrible timing, but she should have known male visitors would visit, even in foul weather. Once word spreads in the MacDonald clan that her Rowan was visiting her peculiar aunts, men from all over the Isle visited to calm the burning in their pricks, and tonight was no exception. The lateness of Ian the Younger meant most of her visitors would arrive on the morrow, and thankfully Alistair would be gone.

Tears welled up in her eyes, but she felt a surge of relief. Whether she was relieved because of the shame of having gentlemen callers or because she didn't want to lessen her loving encounter with Alistair kept her mind wandering. Either way, not having a man in the house must be her preference, given her duty to her callers.

And she was thankful 'twas Ian the Younger who knocked, and not another one of her more forceful callers, like his father, or Christ-forbid, Dougie. The younger Ian did not mind a quick shag in the barn — most young men lacked the stamina or desire for a longer, torrid engagement. Older men were a different matter. Dougie would have expected a warm bedding in the croft itself, would *that* have nay been awkward?

Lioslaith's damp eyes dropped shut as her mind riffled over her lover's quandaries. 'Twas only after her breathing slowed and the shifting of her body stopped did Alistair allow his own eyes to close.

Dawn announced itself before Alistair was ready, but he could tarry no longer. Lioslaith's sweet breathing continued from the far side of the cottage, and he stepped nimbly around the room so as not to wake this sleeping angel. Only the top of her flaxen-blonde head poked out of the tartan coverlet. A damp chill hung in the air, and he placed several pieces of wood on the low-burning fire to warm the room 'afore Lioslaith awakened. The wood and peat popped fiercely as it caught the heat of the flames, causing Alistair to flinch back and gawk at Lioslaith's bed. Her slight form pulled more of her tresses under the tartan, then settled into sleep. Alistair's lips puckered as he blew out a breath of relief, resuming his task of leaving.

The ground was murky in the rain that wept from the dark clouds on the melancholy morning. All of the sweeping grasses and rock formations cast fearsome shadows in the hanging mist, as though the world itself was as saddened as Alistair at his departure. His feet sunk into the dank mud as he staggered away from the wee croft. His time in paradise had ended as it began, with Alistair mucking his way in the depressing rain into another great unknown. In all that he hoped the MacDonald keep would offer some reception, in his deepest heart, it would all amount to naught after the welcome and acceptance he received at the croft he was leaving behind.

As he approached a rolling, stony rise, he chanced one last look back at the tiny cottage, now barely a speck in the distance, huddled against the wet cold. He almost turned back, everything in his body begging him to return to the warmth of Lioslaith's hearth, arms, bed. Back in the Highlands, Alistair believed he was robbed of his birthright as Laird of his uncle's clan, but his furor over that loss was naught compared to the pain he felt in departing his fairy-like healer. In so short a time, she had unlocked a secret chamber in Alistair's heart, one he did not know existed, and now he had to walk away. A dizzying, intense ache flared through him as hope fled. Shaking his damp hair to clear his eyes and focus on the journey ahead, Alistair's only recompense was that the day mirrored his pain and did not mock him with sunlit beauty.

A sudden icy downpour tore him from his bleak thoughts. Pulling his tartan tighter around him to fend off the weather, Alistair picked his way over the landscape, using the stony earth as steps around the mucky trail toward the MacDonald stronghold. The stones were slick, and Alistair tired quickly trying to keep his balance as he trudged farther into MacDonald land.

He made slow progress, and it was nearly afternoon by the time he approached the village near the MacDonald keep. Crofts appeared, situated closer to each other and more numerous, tightly closed against the whipping rainfall and freezing air, as closed off as the MacDonald castle itself. A broken stone barbican marked the entry to the MacDonald keep proper. After identifying himself to the MacDonald guard at the gate, he was led across the muddy inner bailey to the main wood and iron door of the stronghold of the MacDonalds of the Isles. His kin.

A desperate hope flared deep in his chest, that his improvident travels had ended, and his new life could be found on the other side of the heavy, unwelcoming doors. Another sense, however, this one prickling the back of his neck, told him that the hope was a false one. Alistair already lost hope once today; he braced himself to lose hope again. He followed the guard into the bowels of the keep.

Dim light filtered past the rough-hewn door wedged shut against the onslaught of rain into Lioslaith squinting eyes as she awoke. The door bolt was not drawn, and a shot of dismay passed through Lioslaith as she scanned the other sleeping pallet. The red and black tartan from his bedding was gone, as was his sporran. Heat from the hearth warmed the head of her bed, and she turned her sights to the wavering flames. Alistair had fed the fire before he left so she would wake to a warm morning, and her heart ached at the thought behind the gesture.

Grabbing her own tartan coverlet off her bedding, she scrambled to the door and flung it open, hoping to catch the strange, exiled man before he traversed far into MacDonald land. Perchance she could reach him, ask him to stay with her and Rowan, make his life with her. But when she pressed her face against the wind and rain to peer into the distance, only the empty pathway appeared through the mist. She was too late.

Sagging in defeat against the doorway, she could not feel the cold and wet against her skin. She was numb to the elements as her chest pounded and grieved over the departure of the young Highlander.

Lioslaith returned to the empty cottage, the loneliness of the room penetrating with the absence of both Alistair and her daughter. And while her daughter would return in a few days, there was nary a chance that Alistair ever would. Once he found a place with the MacDonalds, he would not risk it to consort with a comfort woman. Lioslaith stared into the fire, oblivious to her damp clothing and dripping hair, blinking back tears, and waiting for her male clients who would soon arrive.

The MacDonalds were at a loss of what to do with the errant, distant relative from the Highlands. *A bit small for a Highlander*, Angus Og MacDonald thought as he assessed the young man shivering before him.

Not that Angus Og didn't know of the man's arrival. The MacRuaidhrí clan had sent a messenger over a fortnight ago, tattered missive in hand that briefly explained the reason for Alistair's exile.

Exile? The man was lucky to even be alive, had he tried that with my daughters. A father's rage built inside, not only in defense of his daughters, but for the father of the man as well. What manner of father raised a son who would stoop to such lowliness?

So, Angus Og and his seneschal, Dougie, had waited, and waited, and waited, for the man to appear at the gate, and when he did not, Angus Og and his men assumed the lad fell victim to some wayward MacRuaidhrí villains. Or the MacRuaidhrí brothers themselves — Angus Og would not put such an action past them. Only when one of his men, returning from a visit from the comfort woman, reported seeing a skinny stranger near her cottage did Angus Og put the pieces together. Either the lad learned of the woman and visited to assuage his manly needs, or he ran afoul with an unfortunate circumstance, and she and her strange sisters nursed him back to health.

Angus Og didn't care either way. He rather hoped the young lad would not show up at all. The MacRuaidhrí messenger suggested that Alistair's loyalties to the Bruce were in question, which was a grand statement coming from a representative of one of the most waffling clans on the Isle. Angus Og and most MacDonalds knew that Lachlan and Rudy MacRuaidhrí played both sides of the power game between England and Scotland, trying to make sure they landed on their feet regardless of who came out on top. As of late, however, the MacRuaidhrí's seemed to focus their support on the Scottish cause, throwing in their hats for the Bruce. As such, Angus Og took the messenger's comment about Alistair as a spy or traitor seriously. The Laird smelled something in the air, and it was more than just the coming winter.

What stood before him on this icy morning resembled more a drowned puppy than a Highland man. *What are my Highland relatives coming to?* Angus Og asked himself as he sized up the MacNally lad. Connected to the Highlands through a long-gone distant relative on his mother's side, Angus Og had not seen the mountains of that heritage. Nor did he want to. The Isles were his home, and to have his home violated by the cast-off of those relatives chapped him.

Then to add to the insult, the lad perchance aligned against the Bruce. To speak against Scotland was akin to blasphemy in MacDonald lands, and Angus Og chewed the inside of his cheek to keep himself silent as he evaluated the situation. What was he going to do with this errant, exiled, possibly traitorous lad?

In previous discussions, Dougie, his seneschal and Roderick, his oldest adviser, had not hidden their disgust at the possibility of the lad staying on their land. He lacked any skill, brought no value to the land, and could be a spy. They each had their reasons for wanting him sent away to fend for himself, to find his own way on North Uist. Roderick's reason was political, Dougie's prideful. Neither cared where the lad went, so long as he did not remain with the MacDonalds.

Angus Og was of a different mind. Scratching at his still-bright chestnut beard, he believed that keeping the lad under their thumb was the safest decision. They could not control what they could not see, and if the lad remained on MacDonald lands, Angus Og could watch him. Caution would be the better part of discretion. Roderick agreed with the Laird's logic, but still admonished the political implications of harboring a potential spy.

"Ye canna be serious, Angus Og, allowing the lad to stay. I strenuously object, again!" Dougie hissed into the Laird's ear as they marched toward the great hall. The large seneschal would not make the lad's stay a peaceful one. Angus Og bit his cheek all the more.

"And ye?" Angus Og tilted his head toward Rodrick MacDonald. "Do ye still strenuously object?" Angus Og's adviser flicked his shimmery dark eyes to Angus

Og. The older man was quite the enigma to Angus Og, and this bothered him. The Laird of the MacDonalds of the Isles prided himself on his ability to read and judge others, but his adviser puzzled him with every gesture.

"I gave ye my opinion, Laird," Rodrick said in a sage tone. Angus Og sighed and scratched at his beard again, eying the lad at the far end of the hall.

The drowned puppy of a boy snapped his head up as Angus Og hefted his weight into the main hall, flanked by his seneschal and his adviser. Alistair waited for the man at end of the hall to address him. Of the two men who escorted him, one was an older man with frighteningly black eyes, and the other was a larger man with the glinting hilt of a broadsword rising from behind his brutish, dark-blond head. Alistair surmised this would not be a conference among relatives. Instead, he sensed he was being judged by a tribunal, and from the expressions on their faces, they would not rule in his favor.

He flipped his sodden hair out of his eyes, pulling himself to his full height and brushing at his mended tartan, trying fruitlessly to impress the Laird. He struggled to keep his head level as Laird MacDonald eyed him head to foot. A moue of disgust crossed the Laird's face.

"What brings ye here, lad?"

Alistair lifted a quizzical eyebrow at the man. "Were ye no' informed of my arrival 'afore now?"

Angus Og's jaw set at the lad's arrogant response. He began to understand why the MacNally's sent the lad away.

"I ken what the missive read. I am asking ye."

Alistair wished he knew what the missive stated. *How much information did the MacDonalds have?* Alistair's stare, while weak, seemed prideful, and he shrugged one shoulder dismissively.

"My uncle, the Laird MacNally, and I had a wee disagreement over chieftain-ship and some of my actions. As a result, he decided 'twould be better if I were sent away to my relatives on this desolate island." *Better to say less, and find out more,* he thought.

"That's what ye say? A disagreement?" Angus Og nearly chewed off the inside of his mouth in a meager attempt to curb his own tongue. The lad was a pompous cuss, to be sure. MacNally had nay exaggerated that.

"Weel—" Alistair started. Angus Og raised a hand and shook his head, cutting him off.

"Quiet, ye impudent lad. Ye have the audacity to come t'my isle, my land, my people, my keep, and set your face t'mine and tell me untruths as ye look me in the eye? What manner of man are ye?"

"'Tis no' lying—" Alistair pleaded this time, only to be silenced by a "*Wheest*" sound from the old man with strange eyes.

Angus Og tipped his head slightly to the large man on his left, then back to the old man on his right, and wiped his hand across his aggravated face.

"I had a mind t'keep ye here, on my land, t'keep an eye about ye. Ye are an accused spy, and I dinna want ye t'work against the Bruce. Your uncle indicated ye tried t'do away with your own cousin in a play for power, and ye failed, and 'twas only her graces that kept ye alive. Ye have significant character flaws, and I thought I better keep ye under my watch. But ye are nay contrite enough to stay on my land. Ye would have a second chance, yet I dinna ken if ye will appreciate such good graces from me. I will no' taint my keep or my village. Go back t'the glen, wherever ye housed yourself 'afore ye came t'my home. I dinna want t'see your miserable personage again."

Alistair's gaping mouth snapped shut. He was supposed to be here. His Mac-Donald kin were supposed to welcome him, house him, give him a place in this forsaken land, and they were *rejecting him*? Who were these kin to deny him? He had left Lioslaith out of obligation to these kin, and now they were banishing him from their land — Lioslaith's land? *Would he nay learn?* Panic filled Alistair's head. Laird MacDonald had turned away with his retinue, leaving him to the guards in the hall.

"Wait!" Alistair's desperate voice echoed in the wide room. He had no words. *What was happening to him?*

Angus Og paused, glancing over his burly shoulder to the stranger shivering near the hearth.

"I will nay leave! I was sent here t'abide with my kin!"

Desperation exuded from Alistair, filling the hall as thick as smoke from the hearth. He stepped forward, grabbing at the Laird. His fingers clutched at Angus Og's tunic, yanking the burly man off balance. Angus was surprised at both the lad's gall and his strength. The weak pup did not appear to have either in him. Perchance the lad had more to him than his indignant attitude suggested.

Angus Og grabbed the lad's hand just as Dougie jumped at Alistair, rushing him to the ground. He lifted a leg, placing a well-aimed kick at the lad who lay in a crumpled heap.

"Dinna lay a hand on the Laird MacDonald!" Dougie's voice vibrated fury throughout the hall. He landed his first kick, making solid contact with Alistair's midsection. Alistair had curled up and managed to absorb most of the shock of the kick, but pain exploded through his still-aching chest.

Before Dougie could land his next kick, the older man stepped between them. He raised a halting hand at the seneschal. Alistair again felt grateful for a stranger's kind gesture.

"Cease, Dougie. I dinna think the lad meant any harm." The old man turned to Alistair, trying to figure out what manner of man the lad truly was. "Get up, lad, and follow the command of the Laird."

The old man stood over him, but did not offer any assistance to Alistair, who had to peel his sore body off the cold stones. Alistair gave a quick look down to make sure he hadn't pissed himself. *Temper yourself, Alistair,* he reprimanded his own behavior.

Shaking on unsteady legs, his midsection and chest throbbing, he managed to stand before the Laird once more. The seneschal dragged him back toward the large formal doors.

"I will tell ye once more. Leave this land, lad," Angus Og intoned.

"Where shall I go?" His voice was little more than an embarrassing squeak.

"I dinna care," Laird MacDonald told him. "Just get ye gone from my land. And if I hear of ye spying for the English, ye will find no mercy at my hand."

Angus Og MacDonald exited with his seneschal, and a guard by the doorway muscled open the heavy wooden door. No words were needed as Alistair resigned himself to exiting. Roderick kept his sharp gaze on the lad as he ambled out to the yard. The wise man became convinced that MacNally was more bark than bite, just a wayward lad who struggled to hold his tongue, naught the concern the MacDonald chieftain presumed him to be.

Alistair's head sagged and his chest ached all the more as he trudged out the door into the whipping rain. The slam of the door behind him shook him to his bones, the world again closing doors to him. *Why did I nay temper my mouth?* He thought dismally. The prospect came to him again, that if t'weren't a sin, he would consider walking directly to the sea and ending it all. But he valued his afterlife more than his current state, and he could not damn his everlasting soul in such a manner.

Unconsciously, however, he had no other options. Mayhap he could find shelter if he journeyed toward the setting sun. Mayhap he would find a boat to the east and sail himself off this island. Mayhap a large beast would make the decision for him, stomping him to his death. Ignoring the flash of memory of a fair-haired angel who had offered a moment of reprieve in his long-suffering life, he turned to the steps, hoping a better choice, any choice would present itself.

The door to Angus Og's study also slammed shut — the thick wood shaking against the timbered frame. He dropped his weight wearily into the overstuffed chair near the hearth, the lone comfort in the stark chamber. Rodrick stood in silent observation as Dougie leaned against the dense writing table, picking at his tartan. He rarely disagreed with his Laird, but in this matter of the rogue lad Alistair, Dougie was proud he stood his ground. Angus Og had not seen the right way until the last possible moment, and now Dougie would bide his time, patiently awaiting what his Laird's next words would be.

The Laird tipped his head toward his adviser but didn't bother to guess the old man's thoughts after the strange encounter with the Highland kin. Rodrick's ever enigmatic ways boiled Dougie's blood, though they were of a similar mind in the matter of this distant relative.

"So ye both were in the right. The lad canna stay," Angus Og's deep tone resonated in the room. His two men remained wordless, letting the silence stretch out as Angus' thoughts roiled inside his head. "What t'do with the lad now? We canna let him run amok on the Isle."

"Especially if the lad has ties to the English," Dougie agreed with Roderick.

Angus Og turned around to Rodrick. "What say ye?"

The older man thoughtfully stroked his graying beard pondering the MacNally. Angus Og's cheek twitched at his mannerism, certain the sage already had an idea despite his contemplative guise.

"Perchance 'twould be wise to keep an eye on the lad as he departs. Ye may have been in the right, my Laird. We dinna ken his motives. Aye, he may be naught but an exile trying to find his way in a new land. But what if he is a spy, or worse, working with the MacRuaidhrí's in their English leaning ways?" He did not add that he truly thought the lad harmless. He did not want to eat those words if he were wrong.

"The MacRuaidhrí's," Dougie scoffed, "with their waffling alliances. The lad could easily be working with them."

"They did reject him heartily," Angus Og pointed out. "And nay all o' the MacRuaidhrís are sympathizers."

"Could be they did it t'disguise their true intentions," Dougie countered.

Angus Og shrugged in response. What did they know of the MacRuaidhrí's intentions? The chieftain had enough on his shoulders, and in truth, he was at a complete loss of what to do with these fractious kin. He rubbed his head, an ache building behind the faint lines on his forehead.

"We must keep a watch on the lad. Rodrick is right in that," Angus Og decided. "At least until the lad is off our land. Dougie, can ye select a few men to aid ye in this task? If he be a spy, I shall ken."

Hiding his ire at having to follow around the ragged pup, Dougie nodded, shoving himself off the writing table and moving to the door.

Alistair stumbled as he made his way down the steps into damp grass and muck of the yard; his black and red plaid smeared with mud and horse dung.

He did not rise right away, instead letting himself wallow in the self-pity that had been building in him all day. His gaze settled on the dim sunlight of the west. Weighing what to do next, he decided to wander west until he saw the never-ending sea that held the interest and curiosity of so many. Then, he could just keep walking, slowly letting the icy waters overcome him until the horrors of this world slipped away.

'Twas a heavy consideration, one that should nay be taken lightly. And 'twas one with which Alistair struggled since his banishment from the Highlands. This time, 'twas different. He found some joy as of late — his time with Lioslaith, her daughter, her cranky sister and the wise woman — he had joy in those moments. And Lioslaith must have seen a measure of value in him. Although she considered herself unworthy to her clan, her employ as a comfort woman tainting her own self-worth, Alistair respected her opinions, especially her opinion of him. He saw her value.

But, were those values enough to stop him from taking that long walk to the end of the earth? Could he find joy like that again, after yet another rejection?

Alistair was so consumed with his misfortune he failed to notice the man who came up behind until he cleared his throat exaggeratedly. Alistair turned his head up to the noise. A good-sized man with a shock of gray and black hair and dusky white robes stood over him, offering a hairy hand in assistance. Alistair took the man's hand, and the man pulled him to a standing position.

He took a moment to evaluate Alistair, his bright green eyes surveying him up and down before he spoke.

"Follow me, lad," he said in a soft voice that underscored his staunch appearance.

The man had to be the local priest, Alistair realized, and obliged. Where else was he t'go? A church seemed as good a place as any.

Across the yard, the priest stopped at the low stone kirk, a rugged cross carved into the rock face and tilting cemetery markers to the rear the only evidence of the building's intent. The priest held a weathered door open, allowing Alistair to step inside.

The interior of the kirk was surprisingly warm, the hearth off to the side providing much needed heat. On a wooden pew near the front, Alistair sat dejectedly. The priest scooped his robes around his legs and reclined next to him, his intense green gaze never leaving Alistair's weary face.

"Aye lad, so ye are the exiled kin come here to roost, mmm?" One grayish eyebrow rose with the question, and Alistair nodded. 'Twas no denying it.

"Weel, lad, I am Father Stewart, parish priest to the locals here. A few smaller clans and villagers sometimes work their way here, but mostly, I serve the Mac-Donalds."

Introductions complete, Father Stewart raised his other eyebrow, questions filling his head. He started with the most obvious one.

"What led ye here, laddie?"

The priest's tone was as smooth as the worn, polished wood of the pew, and Alistair let all the details fly. Confession was, he knew, good for salvation, and he had much to confess to the priest.

The calamities of his past rolled off his tongue, surprising even himself with the ease that they came. He skipped nothing — detailing his attempts to thwart his cousin's marriage, his lies to his uncle and Laird, his alliance with an English sympathizing clan to garner favor for Lairdship, his misguided attempted murder of that same cousin, and his hastily-written note to the English sympathizing clan in a final attempt to bring down his cousin's new clan, all done for the cause of greed.

Alistair's voice changed when he talked of the woman who nursed him back to health — "she saved me," Alistair intoned — his feelings toward her, and how he felt unworthy of the care or the loving feelings he began to have for the woman and her child.

Nodding kindly as Alistair spoke, Father Stewart's face exhibited no disgust or judgment as he heard the impolitic tale of woe. His expression only changed when Alistair's commentary became denial.

"I'm nay a spy," he said in a sudden rush of words, realizing his story may paint him as one. He did not want the priest thinking what everyone else on the Isle seemed to believe.

"I thought no such thing," Father Steward responded with compassion.

"And now I sit here, banished, exiled, nay kin t'speak of, and I —" Alistair stopped, hesitant to speak aloud the sinful thoughts that came to mind often since he had arrived at Lochmaddy. The priest gave another nod of encouragement.

"I ha' an idea that maybe 'twould be a better world were I no' in it."

An abomination in the holy place, his statement hung in the heady air of the church.

"My son," Father Stewart began in a smooth, soft voice that commanded attention, "Many have had those same thoughts. 'Tis nay a sin t'think such things, but 'tis the gravest sin to act upon them. 'Tis the only sin that, once done, the sinner can no' ask God for forgiveness. I would ask that ye consider ye will damn your everlasting soul t'Hell should ye embark on such a cause of action, aye?"

"Aye, Father. That I ken."

"Weel," Father Stewart patted Alistair on his knee, "Ye have a good start in the right direction."

"But what of the rest, Father?" questioned Alistair. "I am certainly one of the worst sinners. God could nay forgive all I've done."

"'Tis true 'twill take much to atone for what ye have done. From what ye have told me, 'twould seem ye have already started on that path to redemption."

Alistair cast a quizzical gaze to the man of the cloth. "What path? I've nay done anything on a path t'redemption."

"Ooch, but haven't ye?" Father Stewart's bright mossy eyes alighted with mirth. "Ye came t'make good with your kin, and while that dinna go according t'plan, ye still did the right thing coming here."

Alistair shrugged off the priest's suggestion, and Father Stewart continued. "But more importantly, ye resided with Lioslaith, her commission notwithstanding, and aided her and her daughter while ye stayed with them. Do you nay believe that you've been valuable t'the woman? Ye lightened her workload as winter's face made its full appearance. Just chopping wood was a form of atonement."

"I dinna think —" Alistair shook his head. Father Steward didn't let him finish.

"Nay, 'tis, ye see? Ye worked in the cold for a woman who many consider to be of ill-repute, a woman who they would judge harshly. Ye did no' judge her, instead came t'care for her. Just as Jesus washed the woman's feet, ye chopped wood for a prostitute. Ye think Jesus would do any less?"

"Nay, but I—"

"*Haud yer wheest,*" the priest silenced him. "'Tis no' to say ye have more t'do. We canna ken what God has in store for us. Our place is no' t'ken his plans. But, ye can work toward atonement, nay judge others, find your place, and 'tis part o' your path t'redemption. Can ye do all that, laddie?"

Alistair sighed heavily. It seemed so much and so little at the same time.

"And ye must recite twenty "Our Fathers" and twenty "Hail Marys" o'course," added the priest, the warmth of his smile echoing in his voice. Alistair's lips pursed as he suppressed a smile at this final part of his penance.

"Others will judge ye, lad. Harshly at times. We are all judged by those on earth. God's plan for ye is t'no' judge others as ye have been judged. Help others when ye can, as much as ye can. And open your heart t'love. Love as God has loved ye, aye?"

Blinking back tears, Alistair nodded at the priest, thankful for a moment of understanding in his recent upheaval. An image of Lioslaith came to his mind. Could he find love? Was he deserving of it?

"I will make ye a drink to warm ye." Father Stewart rose in a fluid movement, patting Alistair's shoulder before working the hearth, ladling hot water from the wee cauldron hanging above the fire into a metal cup. The good father added dry-looking grasses to the cup, tamping them into the water with a slender stick and blowing across the rising steam. After allowing the herbs to steep, he handed the cup to Alistair.

"A wee trick I learned from the wise-woman. Did ye meet her when ye stayed with Lioslaith?

Alistair nodded as he sipped the steaming drink, letting the soothing verdant drink work through his body.

"She's a great healer. Many judge her, that entire family, e'en the MacRu-aidhrí's, as ye can well imagine. But ye need t'keep your mind on God, nay judge others. Can ye remember that, son?"

Father Stewart spoke with the intensity to impart his lesson on Alistair. Once again, Alistair nodded obediently, taking the priest's words to heart.

"Ye can sleep here for the evening, if ye like," offered the priest. "I can make up bedding in my chambers. 'Tis growing late."

Alistair considered the generous offer, and for a moment was deeply inclined to take it. But he had already inconvenienced the priest enough. And he wanted time alone to contemplate all the priest had shared with him that day.

"Thank ye, but nay. I need to start on that path ye spoke of," Alistair said honestly.

Father Stewart nodded, patting Alistair on the shoulder.

"Finish your drink at your leisure. Say fare-thee-well 'afore ye leave, and dinna be a stranger to this place. Recite your "Hail Marys" and "Our Fathers" as ye walk your path," Father Stewart chided with a touch of humor.

Alistair nodded a final time. He did as the priest requested, then wrapped his tartan around his shoulders against the outside chill. Trudging out into the MacDonald yard, he wondered what the next place on God's path would be.

CHAPTER EIGHT

What Was Lost

Icy rain turned to snow as the frozen air grew even colder. Alistair's boots sunk into nearly frozen muck along the overgrown trail leading west. The daylight that served as his only guide dimmed as night announced its slow arrival, and he looked for shelter against the evening snowfall. Fortune offered an option — a stone cairn tucked against an earthen swell would shield him from the light snowfall. He knew his chest would not survive a night sleeping out in the snow.

Alistair dug himself into the cairn, wrapping his mended plaid around his body to cover as much as he could. The wind roaring above him did not distract Alistair from his scattered thoughts. Sleep eluded him, slipping from his grasp over and over as his mind drifted to his youth in the Highlands. His young life was not much different from the present position in which he found himself.

As a lad, he believed himself to be something greater, the next William Wallace, the next great Laird of his clan, a man who commanded respect from his people, his country. Those dreams never materialized, and he oft found himself bent over a bench as his father paddled his backside. Trouble followed Alistair like a dark shadow: his attempts to liberate the pigs was met by his father's anger; using his mother's fine sewing remnants as pennants resulted in missing evening meals.

Was his current predicament any different? Nay, 'twas not, if he were truly honest. Instead of a sore backside from his father, he had a sore body (and sore pride, for certain). Instead of being locked in his chambers without supper, he was locked out of a home with no nourishment. Try as he might, he couldn't stop contemplating traveling west to the endless sea and throwing himself to the sea monsters that lived in that vast water (*were there Blue men in those never-ending waters?*).

The words of the priest today, however, echoed loudly in his head, and those words reflected the lessons of his childhood. And as his thoughts moved to that sinful solution, something niggled at the back of his head. His youthful dreams still had roots that burrowed deep and colored his present state. His home priest always sermonized about the dire burdens God places on great men. 'Twas the same lesson he received from Father Stewart today. What if 'twere his case? What if his burdens were the Good Lord's way of preparing him for greatness? Could Lioslaith still be part of God's path for him? What if he needed to atone for his sins to find the place God designed for him? Plus, the prospect of everlasting Hell didn't entice him a'tall. He could hardly stand his current hell on earth; eternal hell held no further enticement.

As Alistair lost himself in the dichotomy of his dreams and his predicament on the Isle, sleep managed to keep hold and draw him into its ethereal plane. In his fatigued stupor, tucked away from the swirling snow, Alistair fell into a hard sleep, and no more dreams came.

When the light of morning pierced his stony shelter, Alistair awoke with a start. Disoriented, he touched his aching head, trying to recall how he ended up sleeping in the stone cave. A cold drip splatted on his forehead, and faint *tinkling* sounds broke through his stupor. Wiping at his face, he raised his head to hear better. Alistair did not trust his ears in the echoing cairn, but it sounded like an axe striking the rock. Was the MacDonald clan trying to bury him?

He peered around the edge of the cairn's opening, brushing away loose snow that built at the entry. Fluffy tufts of snow shimmered where the sunlight hit, casting the day in an almost impossible brilliance. Amid the piles of snow, a cloaked figure with a small pick clawed at the stone, digging amongst the snowy rock and debris. Early morning sunlight glinted off the metal head of the pick, the glare shooting pinpricks in his eyes. When he squinted and wiggled back to his hidey-hole, his less-than-subtle movements called attention to his position. The cloaked figure pulled back and lifted the pick like a sword, a weapon at the ready.

The face under the hooded cloak assessed him, then poked inside the opening of the cairn.

"Alistair? Is that ye?" a female voice queried.

The shadowy face was back-lit, indiscernible, and Alistair's own face furrowed in response.

"Come out, ye fiendish man," the voice commanded, moving away from the cairn. "Och! Ye are like a bad ha'penny, always popping up! What are ye doin' here in the brush?" Alistair recognized the forceful voice.

Gusts of wind kicked up and harkened more snow would soon overwhelm the sunlight. Muira's hair danced around her as it caught on that winter wind, and the stark resemblance to Lioslaith startled Alistair, throwing him off balance. He pulled his stiff body from his hiding spot into her view. Muira watched him with one feathery eyebrow raised. She did not offer him any assistance, rather she seemed to enjoy watching him stumble about. Another difference from her sister.

Alistair lurched as he stood, catching himself on an icy rock. Muira remained rooted, her hands clasping a rough basket in front of her. Finally steady on his feet, he brushed dried muck from his tartan and found his voice.

"I'm no' sure why I'm here," he admitted honestly. Really, what did he have to hide from this woman?

"Did ye get yourself t'the MacDonalds? If nay, ye will no' get there on this path."

Her rogue eyebrow never wavered as she measured up the man who invaded her sisters' life. Thus far, in Muira's esteem, he did not measure well. The lad could barely stand in his own boots.

Alistair hesitated before replying. "Aye. I did find their keep and met the Laird, so much as 'twas."

Her eyebrow moved, shifting impossibly further upwards. "Och, aye? And what welcome did ye receive from that Laird?" Her mocking tone left no mistake as to her estimation of Laird MacDonald. Alistair harrumphed in agreement.

"Aye, well, let us say I was no' welcome on my kin's land." Alistair moved his shoulders in a dismissive shrug. "But the priest had a good bit o'advice, so I'm trying t'keep his words close."

A slight twitch of her cheek was the only hint of her smile. "Father Stewart," she mumbled under her breath. "And for the MacDonalds, ye were surprised? Ye thought your distant kin would read a missive from the clan that exiled ye and open their arms? Christ's blood, ye are a grand fool, aren't ye now?"

"That may well be," Alistair's ire was tempered with sadness, "but I did no' ken they would send a kinsman out to the wilds t'suffer in a strange land. What type of kin is that?"

His earnest question touched Muira, who well understood the pain of rejection.

"Well, lad, I canna fault ye in that. But I can answer. The MacDonalds. They are nay known for their mercy. I admire their loyalty to the Bruce, unlike other Lairds," her eyes rolled about, passing judgment on an unnamed clan. *The MacRuaidhrí's?* Alistair guessed.

"But the people o'the clan themselves are no' respectable, the good priest one of the few exceptions. Most MacDonalds will lie, cheat, steal, anything t'advance themselves on our desolate bit of rock. They are a lesser clan, no' respected, and they live up t'that." Muira turned and spat bubbling spittle onto a dull stone at her feet, making the sign of the evil eye with her thumb and forefinger.

"Aye, the priest was a goodly man t'me," Alistair agreed. "Is that why Lioslaith does no' live near the keep, or the village, I presume? T'keep distance from an unpleasant manner o' people?"

Muira's eyes narrowed into crystal blue lines. "Aye, we can say 'tis one reason for our self-imposed exile." She inclined her head at Alistair. "Ye ken another reason why, aye?"

"Och, aye. She told me straight away."

Muira nodded approvingly. "There are more reasons, to be sure. But ye dinna need t'ken them now. What ye need now," she said as her gaze swept over his pathetic visage, "is a bath, a meal, and a fire, in that order."

She reached her hand out to him, the first time assisting him of her own volition. It seemed Alistair managed to tear down one of her many walls, and his mood was suddenly buoyant. To question this fork in God's path was not Alistair's place.

"Come with me. Little Rowan has returned to her mam's. 'Tis only Alisa and I, and Alisa has fresh meat stew bubbling on the hearth. If ye bring in the water, we will heat it for ye t'have a wash. Then, perchance, we may have some conversation around the fire, without ye smelling o'cattle."

While he did not miss the taunting tone of her request, stew and a bath sounded like heaven to Alistair. Sighing in resignation and contrivance, he took her outstretched hand and escorted her over the rocks and icy grass to her home.

Alistair followed Muira through the worn wooden door and was greeted by the thick scent of meat. While he was able to prevent himself from drooling, his less-compliant stomach grumbled loudly enough for Muira to smirk at him.

"I've company, my Alisa!" Muira called out, and the delicate Alisa rose from her position near the hearth where she had sat stirring the aromatic stew. She liberated the basket from Muira's grip and eyed Alistair from around Muira's shoulder.

"Ye and your sister are truly cut from the same plaid, Muira! What manner of lost critter did ye bring home?" Humor sparkled in Alisa's soft brown eyes, and Alistair's insides relaxed under her crinkled gaze. Alisa had a sprightly, welcoming manner about her. For the first time since leaving MacNally land, he did nay feel like an intruder.

"Och, Alisa." Muira dropped her tartan atop a small trunk to the side of the door and strode to the fire. "This puir lad was a-hidin' in the brush, fast asleep like a fairy-man out in the cold. I could nay have the lad's freezin' to death on my hands, so I brought him home. Christ kens he could use a good supper. Who's t'say the last time the lad ate a decent meal since leaving my sister's?"

Alisa flitted around Alistair like a mother bird, seating him near the fire and graciously not wrinkling her nose at his stink. She thrust a bowl of steaming stew into his hand and unwrapped him from his tartan. For all that Muira was closed off and reticent, Alisa reminded him of his own mam. He closed his eyes to relish the moment before it passed.

After he scooped the last bit of vegetable from the stew, Alisa handed him a damp cloth. She nodded toward the bowl of warm, scented water she had placed on the table next to him, and he understood that she wanted him to wash up. Wiping the grime from his face, he began to feel almost human. Muira and Alisa faced the front of their cottage, their backs to him, offering Alistair a semblance of privacy as he finished his ministrations.

From the corner of his eye, Alistair beheld the two women, their heads bent close together, whispering. Muira reached out and clasped Alisa's hand in her own, her thumb rubbing across Alisa's fingers in a loving gesture. Alistair pulled his gaze away as his mind worked over the heavy emotion he observed between them. They touched each other as lovers. Were they more than what Alistair assumed? Was that why they were not welcome in their clans? Who were these Islanders?

The words of Father Stewart reverberated in Alistair's ears — do no' judge, love as God loves — was the priest hinting to Alistair? 'Tis this the reason why Muira gave Father Stewart a rare compliment? He could not deny the priest's lesson; Alistair was not one to judge them.

Once most of the dirt coated the water bowl and not his skin, Alisa moved behind him and draped a clean tartan around his shoulders, pulling it snug under his chin.

"Are ye better, lad? A few days in the wilds took their turn on ye, aye?" Alisa joked, and Alistair blushed to the roots of his hair. Alisa settled on a stool, and with a rough wooden comb, began to work the knots and nettles from his coppery waves. Even with the mess, her delicate fingers worked the comb with gentle ease.

"Ye would think Elle would have taken a comb to ye afore this. Muira, what's your sister thinking, leaving the lad in such a state?"

The lightness in Alisa's voice, a pleasant change to all the rough words he'd heard in the last several months, calmed him like the warm summer breezes that blow through the chilly Highland air, and he fair melted in his seat.

"I dinna ken that his hair is what she was lookin' at, Alisa!" Muira cackled in return, and Alistair's eyebrows rose at their words. This was the first time Muira's words were not tinged with ire or mockery. *And what was her implication? Did she know about the night he shared with Lioslaith?* A pang of humiliation jolted through his chest.

"Aye, the lad may be slender, but handsome enough to be sure," Alisa confirmed. Alistair wrenched away, his cheeks flaming.

"I sit here, afore ye. I can hear what ye say, aye?"

Muira continued to cackle as Alisa ran her fingers through his flowing hair, sending shivers down his back.

"We are just humoring ye, lad. It's a rare thing to see Elle interested in a man, ye ken?"

"T'would be an awkward relationship, given her, um, capacity?"

Alisa smacked the comb lightly against the side of his head.

"A woman's capacity does no' mean the lass does no' need love. She may have men in her bed, but nary one in her heart. She's in need of a man to love her for who she is." Alisa's piercing amber eyes cut to him, marking him to the bone. "And if she were to have a man, she would nay need to continue in her efforts, ye ken?" Her meaning was clear.

Was the woman trying to make a match with Lioslaith? The idea seemed preposterous — Alistair was unknown to these women and the Isle, a stranger exiled from his own land. Why would they want him as a match for Muira's close sister?

Alistair let his eyes roam around the cottage and his mind wander. Perchance the women saw something more in Lioslaith's care of him. And as a stranger to the Isle, he came to Lioslaith with no expectations or attachments — he could not judge her for her position in her clan. Mayhap his own position as an exile was a benefit, nay a detriment, part of his new path. Perchance Alisa was a woman who could see more than the average person. With everything he had learned of them thus far, he would not be surprised if she had second sight.

"I dinna ken if I am the man for her. I am a weak man. A broken exiled Highlander with nary pot or kin. What use am I to a woman? One with a child no less?"

Alisa and Muira shared a look that held deep secrets. Alistair already had a feeling about the relationship of the women seated with him, a relationship unwelcome in the clans at best. Did Alisa ken more than she said? Was there something more to Lioslaith, then? Something more than her status as a comfort woman that kept her far from the villages? But again, at this point, 'twould take so much more to shock Alistair.

Alistair's mind spun. What manner of world had he stumbled upon on North Uist? Was it truly an upside-down fairy world? He was so lost in his questions, he did not hear Alisa speak.

"There are worse things, lad," she said, sagely.

"There!" Alisa squealed with delight at the soft fullness of Alistair's hair, courtesy of her ministrations. Cleaned up, wrapped in a fine tartan, and his hair brushed free of dirt and debris, the man's handsomeness shone through, a true Highlander, to be sure. Muira came to him, eying him from toe to pate, and tilted her chin in approval. Her authoritative presence belied her tiny frame, and Alistair stood taller under her scrutiny.

"Aye, the lad will do. Lioslaith obviously saw this man under all that grime. I dinna think the lass will object now." Muira's lips parted in what resembled a smile, knocking Alistair off guard.

"Object to what?" Alistair asked but was ignored as Alisa bustled about, grabbing herbs and oils from a long shelf above the hearth.

"A small potion for the lad, and one for the lass! 'Tis all they need for a match."

A match? A potion? What was this? A witch's spell? Was Alisa truly a witch? "Wait, what?" Alistair repeated.

Muira nodded again. "Aye, Alisa. Ye ken the best way about it."

Alistair spent a surprisingly lively evening in the company of Muira and Alisa, an event he'd not believed possible. Throughout the eve, the women showered affection on each other, a behavior that both fascinated and confused him. Alisa's gentle spirit was the compliment to Muira's guarded self, softening Muira's hard shell and giving strength to Alisa. They behaved as lovers, touching each other's hair, allowing their fingers to linger in light moments, catching one another's eyes. But such things where supposedly a sin, abhorred by the church, repulsed from clans, turned away by kin.

Yet here they were, willing to sacrifice the safety and security of their clans to live isolated, banished to the far reaches of the island, relying only on their love to support them in these chilled, grassy wilds. 'Twas as the MacDonald priest told him: love as God loves, only God can judge; we have to let him. A flare of jealously lit within his chest, a flame that scorched his body and his pride. He had hoped for a love like that, one that was easy, passionate, powerful. The whole cottage filled with the love that simmered and popped between these two women. As much as their relationship should shock him, he instead craved the same for himself. *Who could want to love an exile? Lioslaith? Did her sister and Alisa want the same type of love for Lioslaith as well?*

Unsure if he should draw attention to their relationship, he bit his lip, stared into the fire, and kept his comments to himself. In the morning, the trio would walk the short distance to Lioslaith's lonely cottage, dump Alistair back on her hearth, and let nature take its course.

Even given Lioslaith's lowly position, Alistair held little hope her angelic heart would open to a landless, clan-less exile who made several lousy choices for much of his life. The worst clansman on the Isle had to be a better choice than Alistair, and other than the one afternoon together before he ventured to Clan MacDonald, Alistair had no hope of anything more from Lioslaith.

"Ye are deep in thought, lad."

Muira's voice pulled him from the hypnotic dance of the flames at the hearth. He turned his face away from the fire to the lovely blonde who so resembled her sister.

"Aye, that I am."

"Do ye want to share what has ye pensive?"

Alistair returned his gaze to the fire. "Ye think t'make a match with Lioslaith and I, for a reason I can no' comprehend. My situation, my appreciation for your sister, all these things make me desperate for a match. Lioslaith —" Alistair paused, uncertain of his next words. "How do ye ken —" he tried again.

"That she will want ye?" Alisa finished in her chirpy voice. Alistair pursed his lips in morose acknowledgment. "She likes ye, lad. Can ye no' see it?"

Muira guffawed. "He's no' like ye, Alisa. Nay all people can see the way ye can!"

The humor in Muira's voice again astounded Alistair. His cheeks twitched into a smile as she presently seemed so contrary to the person whose voice he heard when she first came to Lioslaith's home during his illness. He marveled at how she was a changed woman in her own cottage with Alisa, when she did not have to be the protective sister.

Muira's change gave Alistair a daring he didn't know he had. "I would be the most fortunate o'men t'have a woman like Lioslaith," he admitted. "If she will have me, I dinna care what has come afore. I will wed her."

Alisa cackled with joy, dancing around the room. Muira shifted closer to Alistair, patting at his face with her palm. "Now, there's a good lad."

She glowed like her sister when she smiled.

CHAPTER NINE

Courting Trouble

AFTER A SOLID NIGHT'S sleep in the comfort of Muira and Alisa's quaint home, on a soft pallet and wrapped in woolly plaid before the hearth, Alistair felt like a new man, stronger than he had in nigh a fortnight. From the warmth of his bedding, he heard the women of the house stir. Instead of rising with them, he remained hidden as he struggled to understand just how he arrived here.

Having fallen so far from the Laird apparent of his clan to an exile in the Isle and presently screwing up his courage to ask a fairy-angel to be his wife, he could barely recognize the man he had become.

Nor did he look the same. His illness and the cold of the isles took their toll on his weary body, and much of his mass was gone. Alistair was nay overly tall like his Highland brethren and felt almost scrawny. The chores around the croft had helped rebuild some of his muscle, but he still was not the strong Highlander he was back in Scotland. He hoped taking over the farm work for Lioslaith, chopping wood and working in the frigid wintry air, would continue to rebuild him. The good Lord ken he could not get much worse.

And his tattered plaid, his stained and stinking tunic and braes, his muddy boots — he did not even have the proper dress to propose to a woman. How could he come to her, looking like a skinny beggar? That was not the man he wanted to present to Lioslaith.

His skepticism about Lioslaith accepting him as a husband plagued him. It was an elusive dream, and the whole idea was nonsensical — what manner of craziness were the sisters about?

Alistair inhaled deeply, the earthy scents of heather and moss filling his nose and waking his senses. He peeked his eyes out of the tartan, only to catch Alisa standing watch over him.

"Aye, weel 'tis time ye are awake, ye lugabout! What good will such a sleeper be to Elle?" Alisa's soft doe eyes roved over his tartan-wrapped body. "Get ye up! We need to ready ye to meet your future wife!"

Muira handed Alisa a damp cloth, and Alisa ran the rag over Alistair's face and neck, catching any dirt he missed the night before. She ran her fingers through his hair, pulling out any remaining knots, and braided the sides in thin plaits that framed the sharp lines of his jaw. Handing him a mended tunic and baggy braes, she turned her back to him in a melodramatic fashion, holding her hand over her eyes and giggling as he changed into the clean clothing. Fresh attire and clean, plaited hair made quite a difference. And when Alisa finished dressing him by wrapping a MacDonald tartan of deep reds and greens around his waist and arms, he stood tall, a vision of a true Highlander. All he was missing was his claymore at his back. She stepped back to admire her handy work. She gave an obvious wink to Muira.

"Weel, the lad cleans up verra nice. Too skinny, to be sure, but I am certain your sister can fatten him up."

Muira also looked Alistair over, a grin slowly spreading over her dainty features. She tossed his boots at him, and he caught them with an "oomph" and a grimace.

"Come ye, then. We should be off. We have a bit o' a walk."

They picked their way across the cold, sweeping dying cotton grass and gray rocks on a rough trail that cut through the dense vegetation and patchy snow. Several whitish hares loped amid the bending grass, while the calls of brent geese rose from the peat bogs just to the north. This worn trail was unique to the women, he guessed, cleared specifically as the regular route between their croft and Lioslaith's, a vein between the families.

The women walked ahead of him, speaking to each other in hushed voices. When Alistair look up to address them, he noted Alisa's arm resting lightly on Muira's. Alistair was again struck by the nature of their relationship. Did their own displacement help keep dangerous rumors at bay? They could hide their relationship out here on the damp moorland. *Truly, hiding seems a good idea,* he thought. The indignation of the church would be the least of their worries. Women have burned at the stake for less.

Stepping lightly over a series of large stones that rose along a slight incline, as though nature herself built a stairway into the hill, Alistair caught sight of smoke against the gray horizon, a thread of life against the sky. His heart raced in his chest, anticipation flooding his limbs.

As they neared the croft, the slamming of a wooden door announced Rowan, whose little face brightened with glee when she saw them approach. Squealing with delight, she flew over the frosty grass, like a colorful thrush flitting about. Reaching Alistair, she threw herself onto his legs.

"Ali! Ye are back! Mam said ye had gone to the MacDonalds. That we may no' see ye again!" Her emphasis on the clan name was filled with disgust that mimicked her mother's voice.

Alistair lifted her high in the air, and she squealed again. He settled her on his hip as Muira and Alisa caught up, eliciting another excited squeak from the child. Fawning over the lass, the women led the rest of the way to Lioslaith's cottage.

Lioslaith had stepped out to check on Rowan, and Alistair's breath caught. In the frigid air, wrapped in a tartan, the wintry wind lifting her golden locks in a halo, Lioslaith looked impossibly ethereal. Her icy stare, like winter itself in her eyes, seized his heart. Alistair was afraid to reach out, afraid that if he touched her, she would disappear into the fog, nothing more than a dream. If this was the path God wanted him on, Alistair was grateful.

Rowan wiggled down from Alistair's arms and raced to her perplexed mother. "Mam! See who 'tis! Ali, with my aunties!"

"Come inside with me, will ye, Elle? I must have words with ye."

Muira stepped in front of Alistair, clasping Lioslaith's arm, guiding her inside. Lioslaith's bright eyes blinked with bewilderment as she allowed herself to be escorted away. Alisa occupied Rowan with a Toaty pinecone she pulled from the basket tucked under her arm, sneaking sly glances at Alistair. The message was clear: Muira was trying to convince her sister that a marriage to Alistair would be a benefit. Alistair strained his ears to hear any arguing between the two, but the cottage was eerily silent.

They were not long, which was surprising. Alistair had thought Lioslaith would need more convincing. Perchance the strange women had the right about Lioslaith — perchance she did have feelings for him as well. His dusky eyebrows raised to his hairline when both women stepped out o'the door, a knowing smile plastered on Muira's mouth. Lioslaith, while looking less giddy, did not appear sad. Instead, she moved to the side of the doorway and called to them to come inside.

The smell of snow was in the air as Muira left with bonnie wee Rowan in her arms and Alisa following. Bundled in several warm plaids and a deer fur cloaked around her head, only the lassie's tiny face peeked out from her wrapping, a shining smile on her pink cheeks. Lioslaith stepped back into the cottage where Alistair stood awkwardly in the center of the room, his fluffed, burnt hair almost touching the beams. She shivered as she closed the door, but not from the chill in the air.

"What silliness did my sister and her wise woman plant in your head?" Lioslaith's blue eyes burned like a cold fire.

"Why?" Panic filled Alistair's voice. "What did she tell ye?"

Lioslaith tossed her hair over her shoulder. "Nay, dinna try that wi'me. Why are ye here, Alistair? I want t'hear it from ye."

Alistair's knees grew weak at her commanding tone, so much like her sister, but he puffed his chest up anyway, trying to exude more gallantry than he felt.

"I ken your situation, what ye do for money, I mean. I ken about Rowan, and I ken men, clans. Women are judged when they bear bairns out of wedlock. Given that situation, becoming a comfort woman makes sense."

"Why are ye telling me what I already ken? Have ye lived this life for the past five winters?"

"Nay!" Alistair held up his hands in defense. "I am trying to say that ye need no' defend or explain it t'me! 'Tis just that I come to ye, knowing all that, and still asking to wed ye, regardless!"

Lioslaith squinted at Alistair, her bright brow furrowed. He could not believe he told this ethereal beauty he wanted to wed her. Who was he, an exiled, would be murderer and usurper, to have such a woman consider him? For all she was seen as a loose woman, he was so much worse.

"Wed me? Is that what my sister wants from ye? To wed the poor, abandoned Lioslaith?"

"'Tis no' their words, for certain. They fear ye shall be alone. They are happy together. 'Twould seem they want the same for ye."

Her face softened at his statement about the love between her sister and Alisa. She had seen it with her own eyes, and too, felt the bite of jealousy. Life had been so hard for her. That she could find joy, be wed, have a husband, a father for Rowan, was not a future she had thought for herself. But did she want such a future? Alistair wondered the same.

"Didn't Muira tell ye as much? Do ye want to wed? Or am I too forward? Your sisters just assumed. . ." He trailed off.

"They assume much. I am the little sister, aye?" One flaxen eyebrow raised, humor painting her features. "I ken that Muira feels the need t'watch over me. We are close sisters. Many thought us *càraid*, and we were no' well accepted for that. And with —" she paused, pulling her words back. "Then when what happened, happened, and I left the village to find my way with Rowan . . ."

Alistair remained quiet, enjoying her rare long speech. She looked at her bare stockings peeping from under her dress.

"Why do ye want t'wed me?" she asked, her voice demure.

Alistair collected his thoughts before speaking. He wanted his best words to come forth, not scare her away. In the dancing light of the fire, that fierce face she normally put on strayed away. She resembled an early red deer, light, skittish, and uncertain. She left herself vulnerable, awaiting his answer.

"I am alive because o'ye. My clan, the men of the boat, the MacRuaidhrís, my own kinsmen here, they left me for dead. Ye did no' ken me. I was no one t'ye, but ye took the risk, the time, the effort, and rescued me from the edge of hell. And ye could have banished me from your home as soon as I awoke. Ye ken what I did and who I was, but ye let me stay, regain myself, and e'en welcomed me with your daughter and sisters."

He stepped closer to her, risking the chance to take her dainty hand in his rough fingers, the nearness of her filling his senses.

"And then ye captivated me," his voice broke with huskiness. "Nay shame, nay judgment, nay fear, nay but strength that shone from the top o'your fair head to the depths of your eyes. And the love that is shared in your home with wee Rowan, that ye share with your sister and your good-sister, what they share with each other. I have no' ken love like that since I was a young lad at my mam's knee. I would be honored t'be a part o'that love again."

Unable to stop herself, Lioslaith stepped to Alistair, leaning into the comfortable warmth of his embrace. His arms enclosed her without thought or hesitation, his bristled cheek resting on her smooth, sunlight hair. With the crackling of the fire and the peaceful calm of this moment with her, Alistair could almost believe the world was a good place.

That moment, however, was fleeting. If he were to wed this woman, be a father to her beloved child, he must also be honest with her. He let the embrace linger for several sparse seconds before laying the truth of his exile bare before her.

"Lioslaith," he choked on her name.

Clasping her dainty arms in his gentle grip, he pulled her away to look her in the eyes. He wanted no lies, no untruths before them if they were to embark on this noble venture. All Alistair wanted in this new life was within his grasp, and he could, if he wanted, keep his big mouth shut — the big mouth that caused him so much grief in the Highlands — but if he did that, then their great venture would be built on a shaky foundation of deceit, and the foundation was precarious enough as it was.

Lioslaith's intense blue eyes watched him as he struggled to find the words. She of all people understood the internal dilemma he faced. Did she nay have her own secrets? Ones that she best lay bare before Alistair? Her heart fluttered viciously in her chest at the prospect of admitting her indiscretions to this handsome man who was willing not only to wed her but seemed to care for her and her daughter as well.

She placed a warm palm on Alistair's scruffy jaw, holding his large face close to hers.

"We shall both share our secrets today. And if we can forgive them and look past them, I will wed ye, then we shall nary speak o'these dark pasts again, aye?"

Alistair nodded. While the condition was spoken aloud — to look past these indiscretions — the possibility of a future hung on her words. Swallowing heavily, Alistair began to speak in a subdued tone. They sat on his bedding, still stacked neatly on his pallet across from the hearth.

"I am an exile, to be sure," he began, "and 'twas for trying to usurp my uncle, the Laird o'my clan. That alone is an offense, aye?" Lioslaith nodded, and Alistair continued. "But I did nay tell ye how far I took my quest to be chieftain. The rumors of my alliance with the English are no' unfounded. They have a spark of truth."

Alistair dropped his pained gaze from Lioslaith, whose hands had moved to hold his in his lap.

"My lassie cousin, the Laird's only bairn, was to wed a minor chieftain who was aligned with the Bruce, and I made it seem that this alliance was one of treason, that the Bruce would nay be the rightful king, that the English had a claim to Scotland's throne. It was a small charge on a truly powerless clan, but one I thought t'use to my advantage. I even employed the aid of a more powerful, English-leaning clan in this haughty endeavor. My aim was t'wed my cousin, become Laird of my clan, and let the smaller clan just rot."

He lifted his verdigris eyes to Lioslaith, pleading. "Ye see? I din nay care a whit for the other clan, for the English, or anyone else. I am no' an English spy, just a selfish, weak man who wanted t'claim something that was no' his t'have. I—" He paused and swallowed again, beads of sweat forming on his sable brow at the memory of his dreadful actions.

"I was too caught up in my own plan, I had no' care for who I may hurt. And I tried to hurt my cousin, hurt her badly, *kill* her even, t'have my way. My brain was on fire with power. The idea of it all consumed me, and I was crazed with it."

Alistair took a deep breath, unsure of how to continue. Lioslaith said nothing, but still held his hands in a soft grip— she did nay pull away in horror, so perchance the full atrocity of his actions was not the sort to shock her? He licked his thick, dry lips.

"The worst part of it is my cousin survived, and she demanded nothing in recompense. My harpy-like cousin, renowned for shrewish behavior, who I tried to kill, looked me in the eye as I was bound in a dank chamber and said she understood and forgave me. I still attempted to have her routed, sending a note t'the other clan.

"Even after I was banished, I betrayed them at every turn, but she forgave me, the least penitent man in the Highlands. She's the reason I am here today." Alistair huffed a bitter laugh at the irony of his life. "Since my uncle and her husband could no' kill me, they banished me. My uncle exiled me to some distant kin here on the Isle. The verra same kin that then rejected me and would leave me for dead."

His story was done, the weight of it that he had carried for months rising from his shoulders. Alistair had not realized how freeing 'twould be to confess every detail to her.

Lioslaith remained still, her steady gaze disorienting. She did nay flinch or pull back, which is what he had expected. Instead she leaned close him, breathing in his musky male scent.

"I am truly an exile, lass," he whispered, shame weighing in his voice. "I am nay deserving of anyone, least of all ye."

Lioslaith pressed her milky brow against Alistair's, her fingers threading through his wavy hair. His breath was hot on her face. The fire popped and crackled as they held each other.

"Ye are nay the only one with secrets," Lioslaith broke the silence.

Alistair closed his eyes against Lioslaith's words, knowing that whatever secrets she held were nothing compared to the repugnant actions of his past he was trying to forget. They kept their fingers entwined as Lioslaith sat back, holding Alistair's sad, mossy gaze with her own hooded eyes.

"Secrets eat away at us, from the inside, until we can no' handle it," she told him in her tender voice. "And I see the fruit of my secret every day, and my love for her haunts me. I did no' ken how a person can feel so much love and pain in the same breath."

Misery exuded from Lioslaith's pores. Alistair had to resist the urge to take her in his arms and silence her woeful words.

"My lovey, my Rowan, my greatest love, and deepest shame."

His heart yearned to silence her, to tell her that being a widow of a man was no shame, but her broken tone bade him nay to speak. Lioslaith's voice choked as she continued.

"I lied to ye, Alistair. That first night, when ye asked me about Rowan's birth. I told ye what I tell anyone who asks, that I was marrit and Rowan is the result. But 'tis nay true and the shame is all mine. At least ye are nay responsible for anyone's death, no matter what ye did."

Lioslaith twisted to the side, away from him and, for the first time since Alistair met her, she dropped her intense aqua gaze.

"I try no' to think on it, which is what I did with ye when I first told ye. But I do, I think on it all the time. 'Twas nay an acceptable man, 'twas a man I thought I loved. He told me we would wed, that we were handfast. On the isle, we take handfasting with a bit more authority than elsewhere, ye ken? He was a man from the village. I met him shortly after —" here she paused, as if selecting her words.

"After Muira and Alisa, um, joined? Aye, and we were no' welcome in the village. This man, I kent him to be different, that he did no' care for the gossips of the clan. He wooed me, bed me, filled me with Rowan, and left nary a fortnight after. I was naught more than a fool.

"At first, I could hide the bairn growing in my belly, aye?" She lifted her watery eyes to him, and Alistair nodded. She was not the first woman to hide an illegitimate bairn. "But soon, Alisa can see more than most? She kent it 'afore I did." Alistair's breath caught in his chest as she spoke.

"And Muira kens me better than I ken myself. They approached me, with such kindness. Had I come to her earlier, perchance Alisa could have helped me slip the bairn, but it was too late. And in truth, how could I do such a thing to an innocent bairn? I lived with them, Alisa delivered wee Rowan, and nursed the both of us back to health. 'Twas the love and care I needed after my heart was torn asunder."

To Alistair, the confession did not seem so dire. Women had bastard children all the time. He opened his mouth to inquire, but snapped his scruffy jaw shut. She had not spoken as he revealed his past to her; Alistair must show her the same respect.

After the span of a few short heartbeats, she inhaled deeply.

"The man, ye ken. He was the problem. He returned to the village and made a mockery of me. He spread gossip throughout the MacDonalds that I was a trollop. This man I believed to be handfast, who I believed love me, called me a trollop," she said in a suffocated voice. "That mockery, 'tis most likely why I became a comfort woman. I was already branded as such. What other hope is there for a fallen woman? I started to wan. I lost my milk, and poor Rowan had to nurse on goat's milk. Muira's anger was unmatched, and Alisa, who could find the best even in Edward Longshanks, harbored a hatred for the man. This anger ate away at us, and I asked Alisa t'help me. I wanted t'release this anger, and she has, um, means, aye?"

Here she clenched Alistair's hands, clinging to him for strength to speak the words she had never spoken aloud.

"I thought Alisa's means would work on me, aye? But mayhap 'twas more my intent. 'Tis what I think, and the, uh, means, did nay work on me. They worked on that man."

Lioslaith resumed her fierce stare directly at Alistair.

"The man fell to his death off the cliffs, into the sea. The clansmen say he splattered on the wet rocks like clay falling t'the earth. 'Twas no' my intent. I wanted t'forget him, what he did t'me, t'my heart, t'Rowan. I wanted a potion, a spell, to forget. But instead I pushed him off the world. 'Tis nary a person in the clan to recall him, as he had no kin. The world has truly forgotten him, t'be sure, but they have no' forgotten my crime."

Her lips pressed into a thin line. "Ye may have tried t'kill another, but ye did no'. I did. Whether ye believe in the old ways or no', I ken that I killed that man."

Like Alistair, her last words were little more than a whisper in the shadowy croft. Her words were the dense weight she carried, and now shared that weight with him. The old ways, Alistair knew, were practiced by many, especially in ancient places like the isles. North Uist was well-known for its druid fauna and standing stones. Though the Christians tried to eliminate the old religions, *Teampall na Trianaid* church was a testament to those battle-scarred, religious endeavors, the old ways never died. While Alistair did nay practice those ways, he would not discredit the practices. There were many, however, who would, who could accuse her of being a witch, her sisters of witchcraft, for doing so.

Perchance Lioslaith and Alisa did cause the death of the man. It mattered not if Alistair believed it; Lioslaith did, and she bore the guilt of that man's death, the death of Rowan's father, in her soul.

And like Lioslaith, he did not pull away. He released her hands from her grip on his fingers, so solid she left marks on his skin, and encircled her in his arms. 'Twas his attempt to pry away the guilt, sadness, and hopelessness that plagued her for so long and take it onto his shoulders. He told her all this, promising that their shared sins were now behind them.

They were both unbelievably broken, yet their broken pieces fit together to make one whole. Together, they were more than they could ever be apart.

CHAPTER TEN

What Was Found

THE AIR IN THE croft was thick with emotion when their words ended, and they sat by the fire, gathering strength from each other's embrace. Alistair wanted to soothe her, let her know that her secrets were now his, and that he would nay turn her away. He was searching for the right words when Lioslaith pressed her cool lips against his heated mouth. Her desire, an aching need to lose herself in him, flowed through her kiss. Alistair crushed her dainty form to his chest, and let the kiss consume him and burn through all the secrets they had shared, leaving their lowly past in ash.

Their first coupling was one of desperate need, of unconscious mating. Now their longing to unite as a husband and wife and sharing of their darkest secrets colored their movements. This kiss was more than everything that came before — more than their sins, more than their guilt. This kiss was the intimate promise of a future, of love and hope, for them both.

Alistair's tongue played gently against Lioslaith's, touching and retreating as if searching for a deeper part of her. She lifted his hand, pressing it to her breast so he could feel the jolting and pulsing of her heart. He lifted hers to his chest so she could feel his heart reflected hers.

She stood in front of him, pulling at the ties of her shift, allowing the shift and her woolen skirts to fall to the floor. Her fair skin radiated light, a small sun inside the dim cottage. Her hair danced around her head, almost a halo, and Alistair saw her as an angel grounded on earth. Pale and bright at the same time, she was the embodiment of his dreams and desires.

His eyes skimmed over her skin, taking in all of her, burning her into his mind. Her breasts were small and high, like early apples. The rosy nipples sprung taut against the air. Her limbs were long for such a slight woman. Shiny slivers lightly marked her belly, the only sign she had borne a child, marks of a warrior woman, he thought.

Alistair pressed his face against the satiny skin of her belly, kissing those jagged scars, and she shivered at his kisses. His hands lingered on her backside, the rounded mounds of her buttocks fitting his palm, and pulled her closer to his mouth. He trailed his tongue along the fine lines of her stomach. Working his mouth up, he kissed along her pert breasts, her nipples tightening and tingling at his touch. She arched her back, urging him to take more of her.

Lioslaith pushed him back and grasped at his tunic so he stood before her. Lifting his tunic over his head, she exposed his defined chest covered with a thin tuft of tawny hair that narrowed to a line at his breeks. She pressed the tip of her tongue to that hair, and he shivered as she teased his hair and skin. The room seemed suddenly warm, and thin droplets of sweat sprung out on his forehead. He didn't realize he was panting.

Her lips followed the line of hair to where it narrowed at his waist. Tucking her thumbs into the waist of his pants, she dragged them down his powerful legs and off his feet. He kicked them to the side, anxious to have his hands back on her body.

Trailing her fingers up his body, his skin prickled, every hair standing on end at the delicate touch of her fingertips. She placed a kiss on one side of his chest, then the other, then placed her lips on his again. Alistair gathered her in his strong arms, returning her kisses with wild abandon. His cock, hard and ready from the first kiss they shared, probed against her, seeking her hidden treasure.

His hands explored the hollows of her backside as he pulled her even closer and whispered her name over and over. Skin touching skin, they grew drunk on their kisses. The heady excitement of kissing blossomed within them, triggered by the eager work of their hands and lips.

Alistair eased her onto the bedding and worked his lips to her neck, sucking at the pulse that pounded in her neck. She inhaled at this sensation, a need for him filling her core and encouraging the damp readiness between her legs. His lips continued their journey to the delicate globes of her breasts, sucking gently at one swollen nipple then moving to give attention to the other. One of his hands stroked her belly down to the mound between her thighs where his finger found her ready dewiness. He dragged his finger lightly over her sensitive bud, and she quivered in response, sucking in air at his touch.

"Touch me again," she whispered into the dark of the cottage. He did as she asked, his fingertip teasing her most sensitive flesh.

"Now, Alistair," she begged.

'Twas all the encouragement he needed, and his body inflamed with the need to possess her. She grasped the firm roundness of his buttocks as he guided himself to her open sheath and slipped his full cock in, his brain spinning at the soft pull on his shaft. Lioslaith gasped as he entered her, raising her hips to meet his entry and caressed the muscles of his back with her hands.

That gasp roused his own passion even higher, and he increased his motion, the pulling and dragging creating a fire between their bodies. He pushed in deeper, as deep as he could go, wrapping his strong hands around her slim shoulders. Alistair wanted them to be as close as possible, one skin, one person, so the fire building would consume them both.

He tried to move slowly, to draw out the passion between them. In truth, he wanted this feeling of being with her, the headiness of their open hearts, the excitement of their bodies to continue forever. The pleasure he felt inside her was pure and explosive. Too soon, he felt himself build, his ballocks clenching in anticipation.

Moans of ecstasy escaped Lioslaith's generous lips as her whole body filled with yearning. The flames of passion and desire alighted deep within her core and between her thighs, meeting in a thundering crescendo of pleasure that rocked her and left her a quivering mass.

The feel of Lioslaith's clenching velvet sheath sent him over the edge, and his thrusting became uncontrollable. He cried out her name over and over as he came deep inside her, releasing so much pent up emotion he was nearly brought to tears. Unable to keep his shaking body above hers, he collapsed on her panting chest, nestling his face into the sweet, damp curve of her neck. They remained entwined as they recovered from the passionate fire that left them both consumed and fulfilled.

Lioslaith had many men in her bed, but never had she encountered such an intimate moment of passion as she did with Alistair. His head rested on her breast; his steamy breath warm on her skin. 'Twas so natural, here in the bedding with this man, it seemed as if there were no other people left in the world. When most men fastened their plaid and departed with her skirts still upraised, Alistair remained, touching her, holding her. Time spun away as her fingers played with the damp waves at the base of his neck.

"Are ye well?" he asked.

She kissed the top of his head, baffled. "Why do ye ask this?"

"I guess the question I want t'ask is, do ye still want to wed me? After all this, are we well-met?" He lifted his head off her breast to watch her face as she responded.

Her own gaze softened at his childlike concern. He was searching for validation, for acceptance, and she was content to gift it to him. Her fingers pulled at his hair, lifting his head up further, and she pressed a hard kiss on his firm lips. While it was an answer of sorts, she wanted him to know with certainty.

"Aye, Alistair. I think we are well-met. I still want to wed ye."

He smiled like a lad, and her heart fluttered. Opening her heart was not an easy gesture.

"And ye, do ye think we are well-met?"

She watched as he turned the question over in his head, and her eyes widened with panic.

"Since we are telling our secrets, I should share my most recent confession with the priest."

"Ye saw the priest?" her brow furrowed quizzically. Alistair wiggled his head on her chest, then rested his chin on his arm that he draped over her breasts.

"Aye, Father Stewart. He found me in the muck outside the MacDonald keep." A faint smile passed across her lips, which urged him to continue. "I was at my lowest point, even lower than when ye found me on your doorstep."

"'Tis nay possible," Lioslaith teased, and he chucked his finger under her chin.

"Nay, 'tis! And he walked me t'the kirk, seated me by the fire t'warm myself, and I gave up my confession, much as I told ye, at his gentle probing."

"The good Father is a master at the gentle probing for confession," Lioslaith agreed.

"Aye, and he spoke t'me in a way few have for many years. Instead of making me feel lowly, or chastised like a wee laddie, he told me that all of this," his eyes roved around the cottage, "was no' punishment. Nay, he said 'twas my path, God's path for me."

"And do ye believe that? That God has these vile things happen to good people? So they can find their path?" Her harsh tone expressed her disbelief in that idea.

"My mam always said we canna have the good unless we have bad. I ken that to mean God's path. I had t'go through misery, lose everything, akin to Job from the Bible. And when I arrived here, at my lowest, what I found was an angel, one that took me in, healed me, saved me, and is now agreeing t'wed me. I would no' have found such a good without the bad that chased me from Scotland."

Alistair traced the line of her cheek and jaw with his fingertip as a rosy blush stained her skin. His words of love were welcome and had been sorely lacking, she didn't know how to respond.

"And if ye were no' here with Rowan, ye would no' have found me. And ye would no' be in bed with me today."

These large ideas, so contrary to everything she had known to this point, made her mind reel in confusion, and her emotions roiled in her chest.

"I thank God for those trials, Lioslaith," he said as he shifted up, his face above hers. "They put me on God's path to ye," he finished, kissing her with such tenderness, tears welled under her eyelids.

"Then I am grateful for my trials, Alistair," she whispered, kissing him back.

Muira and Alisa's determination to create a love match would not be deterred. While they brought wee Rowan home, they returned two days later to retrieve her again. Their intention to have Alistair and Lioslaith spend time alone was embarrassingly obvious. Alisa was quick with suggestive winks and comments, laughing wildly every time she made color rise in Alistair's cheeks.

Rowan held no hesitations with the green-eyed Highlander who lived in her home. She took to Alistair as a selkie to water, with ease and grace and childish curiosity. She followed him around the snowy land, wanting to help as he collect-ed eggs or repaired the lean-to door. Rowan was his fair shadow, light instead of dark, and she never questioned his sudden presence in her life.

Alistair also held no hesitation, but it was difficult to not find the wee Rowan winsome. Her ready, impish smile and excitement won him over. And he pon-dered who he had become when she curled up on his lap to listen to Lioslaith's fascinating stories of fairies and Blue men. He didn't consider himself a likable fellow, particularly after his exile, but both Rowan and her mother found him likable enough.

Lioslaith was convinced of the moment she fell in love with the humbled stranger who stumbled into her life. After Alistair and Rowan collected the morning eggs, Lioslaith noted several hen feathers clinging to both their plaids, but the thought quickly passed. Later, when Lioslaith blew back into the house on the back of a snowy gust of wind, she saw Rowan and Alistair squatting by the fire. Their backs were to her, one small, shockingly blonde head tipping to a larger darker blond one, a pile of feathers between the two of them. Their silhouetted outline was a perfect tapestry of tranquility.

Rather than interrupting the tender scene, Lioslaith remained by the door, watching. Alistair lifted a larger, black and white Scottish-hen feather, wrapped a thin twine of fabric around the quill, then assisted Rowan to do the same.

Lioslaith noted a small pile of twine-tied feathers between them, and she wondered what they were about.

"Now," Alistair explained to Rowan's enraptured, upturned face, "we need to tie all the twine to a stick. Like this."

He held up a slender stick and nodded his head for Rowan to do the same. She clasped a stick in her tiny fingers, mimicking Alistair as best she could. With nimble fingers, he tied each twined feather to the stick. When Rowan could not tie the knot, he reached out and tied it for her. Rowan leaned in closer, resting against his lap, and Lioslaith had to bite back a smile.

In her mind, she sent up a silent prayer that Alisa and her sister were ardent in their matchmaking. Even if Lioslaith was guarding her heart and slow to let herself love the man, fair little Rowan had no such compunctions. The lassie loved this exile; her adoration for Alistair shone from her face brighter than the summer sun.

Alistair must have seen Lioslaith out of the corner of his eye, and he twisted his head toward her. His eyes softened at the sight of her watching from the door, her shimmering fair beauty stealing his breath before he could speak.

"Hello, Lioslaith," he said after a moment. "Would ye like t'join us? We are making wind-catchers."

Rowan jumped up with excitement, dragging Lioslaith to their space on the floor before the hearth. "Mummy! Look what Ali and me's done!"

"Aye, my sweet." Lioslaith squatted between the two of them, admiring their handiwork. "What's a wind catcher?"

Alistair's mossy gaze caught Rowan's bright blue one. "Do ye want to tell her?" he asked.

"They's for play, mummy! After our supper, Alistair and me will take them outside, and they will fly on the wind!"

Rowan's excitement was contagious, and Lioslaith let a rare smile escape her lips. Alistair returned it with his own easy, wide grin.

"And if ye have a cat, they will chase it. Mine did when I was a lad. Ye will join us, aye?"

Lioslaith could not turn down Alistair's earnest face. She dipped her head down, lifting one of the wind-catchers to Rowan's gaze. The concept of playing was something she lacked, and something she desperately wanted her daughter to enjoy. Her smile grew wider at her daughter's happy countenance.

"Aye. We shall play outside in the snow after we eat."

>>>>> <<<<<

Muira and Alisa found Alistair outside the cottage, which seemed likely to blow away in the screaming wind. His wavy hair danced around his head like a hazelnut kerchief, his muscles flexing with effort under the thin tunic as he swung a worn axe. The small chunk of wood splintered into slivers of gray and brown.

Alisa tipped her nose to the sky, sniffing deeply.

"Smells like snow."

"Aye," Muira agreed. "Good day for it, aye?"

"Aye." Alisa nodded, unable to halt the smile that pulled at her lips. Dimples played peek-a-boo in her cheeks as she stepped toward Alistair, calling his name.

"So ye look hale," Alisa began, slapping Alistair on his burgeoning backside. He clipped to the side like a skittish pony.

"Mistress!" he yelped. Both Alisa and Muira cackled at his reaction.

"Alistair," Muira interrupted, "ye are still here, looking healthy and well cared for —" Alisa, catching the suggestion, laughed between pursed lips. Muira cut her eyes to the woman. Clearing her throat, Alisa gestured for Muira to continue.

"Are ye ready, lad?"

A knot of confusion formed on Alistair's forehead. "Ready for what?"

Alisa giggled like a lass and a surge of apprehension swam over Alistair colder than a wave from the Minch. *What now?* he wondered.

"The handfast," Muira answered. "Ye and my sister seem to get along fine, aye, quite fine. As such, ye should handfast, then ye can be wed properly in the springtime."

"Handfast?"

"What, ye though ye would just wed the lass here in the snow?" Muira shook her head, clicking her tongue. "Not that Father Stewart would no' love that. He would surely race up here like an excited lad! Nay, handfast first. That way, if she does no' like the marriage, no harm's done. If she does take to ye, then ye can have a proper spring wedding."

Handfasting, that old Gaelic tradition, was still readily practiced in the Highlands, but not among those in chieftain positions — not in positions which he had back at Clan MacNally.

Here on North Uist, however, he was no longer a man of power, if he had ever been. He was nothing more than Alistair MacNally, exiled highlander, present outcast. Handfasting seemed a ready option, a promise that he would wed the fair Lioslaith and take Rowan as his own. Once again, the words of Father Stewart danced across his mind — this was part of God's plan for his life. And if it tempered the MacDonald men, perchance sending a message that this comfort woman had found redemption, then all the better. And while he did not fancy the thought of Lioslaith putting him aside, her bright smile and lithe form warming his bed made the decision for him. Alistair nodded and struck his axe into the nearby stump.

"So, what do we need for this handfast?" he asked.

Alisa and Muira clamored into the wee cottage, all but dragging Alistair behind them.

"Come, lass!" Muira exclaimed while retaining her air of austerity, "Let's handfast ye to the man!"

Rowan jumped up onto the bedding, clapping her tiny hands at the buzzing excitement. She may not know what she was excited about, but she cheered happily, regardless. Her cheeks took on a rosy glow, and with her tiny form, she appeared as much a fairy-like creature as her mother.

Lioslaith kept her own excitement at bay. Her cheeks flushed at the prospect of making what she shared with Alistair more official just as caution corralled the rest of her emotions.

Grabbing the rough edge of Alistair's tunic, she pulled him near the fire, keeping one eye on her good sisters.

"Are ye certain, Alistair? What we have now, 'tis nay much but does nay force ye t'do what ye may no' want."

Her crystal blue eyes remained steadfast as she spoke plainly. Ever guarded, she would nay take the past fortnight for granted.

"I am more concerned o'your potential hesitation over another handfast." A flash of a shadow passed across Lioslaith's eyes as Alistair continued. "I think after sharing our darkest secrets, then your bed, I would hope ye could see what I do want."

Alistair waggled his bushy amber eyebrows, eliciting a cautious smile from her pale rose lips. Her smile was the only answer he needed. He turned his head back toward his future good-sisters.

Alisa clapped her hands like young Rowan, and gathered up her supplies, which included a bit of heather, a strap of tartan, and a wee dirk.

Muira clasped Lioslaith's hand with hers, smiling widely at her dear sister. She took Alistair's hand and pulled them to the warmth in front of the hearth. Alisa handed her small stash of supplies to Muira, then lifted Rowan from the bedding into her arms to watch.

A thin film of sweat burst onto Alistair's forehead, tiny droplets rolling down his chestnut hairline to his short growth of beard. He had known his actions with Lioslaith would lead to marriage, but he did not anticipate a handfast, nor one so soon. He felt unprepared and truthfully, still felt undeserving as well.

His brain had little enough time to finish these thoughts before Muira held the nubby knife to Alistair's palm and cut swiftly, barely scoring the skin. A bubble of bright red sprung from the wound, and Muira turned her attention to Lioslaith's ready hand.

Alistair felt more pain at the prospect of marking Lioslaith's fair and perfect skin than he had his own. Muira, however, had no such qualms, and nicked Lioslaith in the same manner. The pearl of red stood in stark contrast to the paleness of her skin. Before the blood had a chance to well up further, Muira was pressing their hands together, twining their blood, and chanting under her breath:

"These are the hands that will love you.
These are the hands that will hold and comfort you through the years.

These are the hands that will give you support and encouragement.

These are the hands you will each work with, create with, and use to build a life together."

Then, the strip of plaid dangling from her fingertips, she wrapped them in a tight binding, knotting the plaid at the top. She continued her incantation in that same chanting voice:

"The knots of this binding are not formed by these cords but instead by your vows, the promises you make in your hearts and uphold each day through your actions. Remember, you hold in your own hands the making or breaking of this union."

Before Muira released their hands, Alisa came around them, having placed Rowan back on the bedding. Taking the bit of heather from Muira, Alisa began her own chant, in an accented old Gaelic. As she sang in her old words, she pressed the tip of the flora against their bodies — starting with their bound hands, then brushing it against their foreheads, down their cheeks, across their lips, and over their chests. Alistair had the sense he was engaged in something older, deeper, and more meaningful than a mere handfast. The warmth of the fire, the room, the occasion, heated his skin and made him sweat all the more.

When he could finally raise his eyes and regard Lioslaith, he expected her to be as flushed and damp as he. Alistair was sorely mistaken. If anything, she looked more relaxed, more soothed by the chanting than she had when he first entered the cottage. Her nearly white hair hung in wispy locks down her back, the heat of the room gracing her cheeks with smudges of pink. If serenity were embodied, 'twould be Lioslaith.

Once Muira's chanting ended, Alistair and Lioslaith stood in each other's gaze, their hands joined by cloth and blood that joined their lives as well. They were drawn out of their reverie when the women and Rowan cheered and clapped, and Alisa threw dried petals of buttery-yellow trefoil and dusky-purple butterwort over their heads in celebration.

Christ's mass was less than a month away, and spring would arrive with its relentless rainfall. Three months, perhaps four, to show Lioslaith that, contrary to his arrival on the Isle, he was a man of his word, a man she could trust, a man she could wed in a kirk come springtime. She had already gifted him so much, and

Alistair promised himself, amid the smiles and celebratory chatter, that he would prove to Lioslaith he was the husband she needed and desired.

Christina rode into the MacRuaidhrí bailey, not bothering to wait for the stable hand to gather the reins before slipping off her mare. Wet snow stuck to her walnut hair and dark plaid, and she shook herself off, stamping her feet against the stone floor of the great hall. From the doorway, she could see her witless brothers laughing drunkenly with several other clansmen.

A moue of discontent flitted across her strong features. She inwardly cursed the world that set her brothers higher than herself; between them they didn't have a brain to share. Over the course of her life, her father lamented she had been born a lass, not a future Laird. The MacRuaidhrí's were the most powerful clan on North Uist, and the chieftain legacy passed instead to her brothers who all but shared the title, and her father died in dismay that his chieftainship was left to a pair of drunken sots. Drunken, *English-sympathizing* sots, no less.

Lachlan noticed Christina standing by the door and raised his tankard to her.

"Sister! To what do we owe this miserable visit? Can ye nay take your judgmental mood elsewhere?"

She stormed over to her unruly brother, knocking the drink out of his hand.

"Says the man who can no' hold whiskey, so he drinks common English ale. Did your spies bring ye this?"

Lachlan grunted as he bent over his belly to retrieve his mug. Rudy let a silent chuckle shake his own large frame. He turned his hazel gaze to his sister.

"What storm blew ye in, Cat? Are ye here t'report on our actions t'your man?"

Christina snorted at Rudy's casual reference. She pressed her fingers to her eyes, collecting herself.

"Nay, Rudy, nothing such as that. I am here to see if ye have followed up on the strange lad who passed through here. 'Twas suggested he was an English spy, something ye could understand well, aye?"

While they wanted to protest, both brothers pursed their lips but said nothing. They despised the air of righteous indignation their sister wore like a cloak and often found it easier just to hold their tongues with her.

"So ye have no'? Do ye even ken where the lad resides?"

"Since ye think us on the side of the English anyways, why do ye think we would tell ye?"

Cleaning her throat, Christina reigned in her tone, hoping her brothers might see some sense.

"I ken ye are trying to play both sides, hoping to land on your feet and fill your coffers regardless of who succeeds. If ye were just clansmen, I would no' care. But ye are Laird of this clan, and the Scottish need ye more than the English. I will ask ye again to swear your alliance t'the proper cause."

When her brothers remained silent, sipping their ale, she sighed heavily, changing her tactics. "Do ye ken the whereabouts of the exiled lad?"

Lachlan eyed his older brother who shrugged his heavy shoulders. Neither cared for the life of one strange lad, English associations or not. Lachlan told Christina as much.

"I have heard that the lad ventured toward the MacDonalds. They rejected him soundly, o'course, but he found a place with t'comfort woman, of all people. Village gossips daresay he lives with the woman."

"Aye, I've been told he's with the comfort woman on the boundary land south." Christina's brow knitted in deep lines as she spoke. Why could her brothers not just speak plainly like real men?

"Ye've 'been told'?" Rudy asked with one eyebrow raised high. "From our erstwhile sister?" When Christina did not respond, he continued. "Gossip tells that the comfort woman is doing a lot less comforting as of late."

Lachlan leaned over to slap Rudy on the side of his furry head. "Ye would ken, aye, brother?"

Rudy punched his brother's shoulder in retribution. "Nay, no' as well as ye. I have my own women here. What need have I o'the comfort woman?"

"She rarely comes this far north," Lachlan continued. "Mainly she is under the banner of the MacDonalds, but there has been grumbling about the woman and the strange man who now resides with her. I think that is where we will find yon lad."

Rudy cut his slovenly eyes to his sister. "Ye see, Cat, ye have naught t'fear. What English spy will take up with a remote Scottish comfort woman? What secrets will he take t'the English, other than how t'please a man?"

At that, her brothers burst into peals of laughter that echoed to the rafters of the great hall. Grateful to confirm her brothers were at least trying to keep pace with the events on their Isle, Christina placed her hand on Rudy's dark head.

"Thank ye, brothers. We can appreciate that at least one man fewer supports the English cause on these isles."

Lachlan sobered enough to respond to Christina's less-than-subtle barb at their loyalty.

"We are not the traitorous monsters ye think us to be, Cat. Any good hunter must ken his terrain, aye?" His hazel eyes flashed with more knowledge than he spoke aloud.

Christina looked down her nose at her drunken brother, allowing his surprising insightful words find a place in her head. Mayhap her witless brothers were not as witless as they appeared.

"Help me keep an eye on our dear sister, aye?" she requested, accepting Lachlan's peace offering.

Her brothers nodded their chestnut heads in unison. Tapping each brother's scruffy hair in affection, Cat exited the warmth of the heady chamber to the fierce, wet cold of the bailey yard. Two clansmen appeared with her sturdy mare, and she mounted easily, riding in the deep rosy rays of the setting sun.

She had great hope that her brothers were honest in their explanations to her, especially Lachlan's final words. But she also had learned that English sympathizers could not be trusted, and she was not certain she would trust her brothers all that much, yet.

The salty scent of the Minch and its inlet fjards battled with the smell of snow on the air. Christina inhaled the mingling scents to try and clear her head as she rode off into the night. The return ride to her own small keep was short and uneventful. Though the stone structure was nothing more than a remnant of one of her father's outbuildings, it provided Christina a comfortable place away from her brothers. Her father, in his infinite wisdom, ensured her security regardless of any actions or behaviors of Rudy or Lachlan. With a small garden, a sound barn, and a sturdy hearth, her stronghold provided all she needed just a stone's throw southwest from the main keep of the MacRuaidhrí clan. The proximity to the stronghold helped her maintain a close eye on her brothers' activities.

And it was a place where she could have companionship with little interference. Said companion rose from his seat by the hearth when she entered the modest hall. Robbie was not much taller than she was, and his scruffy brown beard and hair, shot with rich copper tones, were a welcome sight. It was his eyes, though, his soft, doe eyes, always full of compassion and a ferocity that lit her on fire and emboldened her heart.

Robbie turned those tender eyes to her as he helped Christina remove her heavy outer tartan, shaking the snow from the fabric.

"Did they ken? Or was their ignorance greater than their ability t'drink?"

The twinkle in Robbie's eyes at the jest wasn't lost on Christina. Her cheeks pulled into a wide smile.

"Aye, ye were in the right. They have followed the exile's journey. While they joked about his attachment to the comfort woman, they did no' appear overly interested in the lad," she told him.

The admission almost chapped her hide, but perchance it was the start of a show of fidelity to the rightful king of Scotland. If they didn't want to engage with the supposed English-sympathizing lad, mayhap it spoke of their decision to finally support the Scottish cause. Christina wanted to believe that. More than anything, she wanted to know her brothers, as the leaders of the powerful MacRuaidhrí clan, could be trusted. But she could not quite bring herself to believe it fully.

"Weel, 'tis promising," Robbie replied, kissing her forehead.

"'Tis my brothers," she said through pursed lips. "I would nay trust it until I see their loyalty with mine own eyes."

Robbie took her hand, leading her toward their shared bedchamber.

"When Scotland needs them, they will be there. I have faith in that."

"Ye always did have more faith than anyone," she sighed, following her lover to the warmth of their bed.

CHAPTER ELEVEN

When Trouble Knocks at the Door

HAMISH MACDONALD SMACKED THE back of Dougie's fair head as he passed by, excitement bristling every hair on his body.

"Where are ye off to, ye lack-wit?" Dougie asked. The lad was too early and too restless to be heading out to collect the black-faced sheep from the fields. The lad had other plans, Dougie guessed. Hamish grabbed at his manhood through his rugged tartan, shaking himself toward his kinsman.

"T'find a warm release, old man," Hamish taunted.

Only a year younger than Dougie, Hamish mocked the older clansman whenever the opportunity presented. Dougie shrugged off the taunt, a slick smile spreading across his face.

"What of your wife, laddie? The Laird will be none too pleased if he finds ye are slinking off to the comfort woman."

"She's ill again, and a man has needs. Dinna tell the ol' man, aye?" Hamish begged conspiratorially.

While Dougie didn't approve, he couldn't begrudge the young man a woman's comforts. "Just dinna take too long. The sheep will no' find themselves back in their pens without ye."

"I'll take longer than ye could," Hamish shot back, his broad smile never wavering. He strutted past the gate to the north.

When he arrived at the comfort woman's croft, he hoped her daughter was off visiting so he could warm himself by the hearth. The barn was fine, especially in the summer, but the biting wind of winter made for a cold romp in the lean-to.

Rapping at her door, he stamped his feet as he waited, trying to get feeling back into his toes. The sharp wind only grew colder as it blew over the land from the Western sea. *Why is she taking so long?*

Assuming her delay meant her daughter was still in the croft, Hamish resigned himself to a quick lay in the freezing barn. When the door finally sprung open, a distracted and disheveled comfort woman greeted him.

He gave Lioslaith a wide grin as he ran his hand over his unkempt auburn hair, trying to tamp it down. Then, pressing his hand against the door, Hamish leaned into the heat that emanated from her tiny croft. The sun was dying, as was any warmth that came with it.

"Is your lass inside? Or do I need to freeze my ballocks off in the barn today?" he asked in his suggestive tone. Lioslaith's panicked eyes darted around the moorland.

"Hamish, I was no' expecting anyone this eve. I would have thought the cold air to keep all by their hearths. Or with more local women."

"I was willing to risk the cold for ye. What good Scotsman would no'? Now, come along, woman. I have a cock and coin for ye."

Hamish grasped her hand, pulling her away from the door. Lioslaith flicked her head back toward her croft and wrestled her wrist out of his rough hand.

"I can no' be with ye this eve, Hamish. I, um, am otherwise occupied." Lies fell easily from Lioslaith's lips, but she was not completely untruthful. Alistair *was* occupying her time.

"Do ye have another man? 'Tis fine! I'll wait."

Lioslaith shook her head, her eyes frantic. Placing her dainty palm on his thick chest, she gave the large Scot a gentle push from her door.

"Nay, 'tis no' another, like that. I just can no' see anyone this eve. Please, Hamish, ye will have to return another time."

But the shadow that came over Hamish's eyes told her he would not leave easily. All the hope she built inside her head waned as the man's anger flared.

"Is it your daughter? Then come out to the lean-to. I will no' return another time. I have a need, and ye, comfort woman, must remedy it."

Hamish grabbed at her hand again, but Lioslaith was tiny and lithe, and pulled back into the cottage easily. Only when she moved to fasten the door did Hamish pull his full frame into the doorway, shoving the door aside.

The unexpected quaint scene of Lioslaith's lass at the table for supper, a strange man standing by the child's side, roiled Hamish's frustration all the more. His eyes knit as he peered inside the cottage.

"Who is this, Lioslaith? Does this stranger no' ken your position? Ye just should've come out t'the barn."

He leapt at her suddenly, arms outstretched. Lioslaith ducked and shoved his arm to the side as Alistair shouted at him and jumped into the fray, pushing Hamish off balance and out the door. The thick man fell heavily into the frozen dirt. Alistair stepped into the doorway, back lit like the devil himself stood before Hamish.

"Lioslaith is no' your comfort woman anymore. Find your ruttings elsewhere."

Alistair slammed the door, wedging it tight in the frame, and secured it with the heavy wooden bolt. They waited on bated breath for Hamish's response. It was not long in coming.

"Ye bitch!" Hamish's muted voice hollered from the other side the door. "Ye are naught more than a whore! That is all ye shall e'er be, man at your hearth or nay! And I will come back!"

Fortunately, Hamish left after his braying insults. Lioslaith ran to Rowan, whose cerulean eyes were as large as saucers. Ever the curious child, she was the first to speak.

"Mama! Who was that loud man?"

"He was only a man looking for something that is no' longer here," Alistair answered for her. He left his post by the door and placed a protective arm around Rowan and her fair mother.

"He said a bad thing, mama! Will his mam punish him for behaving 'propriate?"

Rowan's mature mispronunciation caused a small smile to pass from Alistair to Lioslaith and lightened the mood after Hamish's shocking interruption. Lioslaith's shoulders relaxed into her daughter, and she found it difficult to stifle a giggle.

"I dare say his mam should, lassie. We should no' tolerate inappropriate behavior from anyone."

"Ye would lash me if I behaved 'propriate!" Rowan's small voice chimed. Alistair covered his head with his hand, hiding his laughter. Would the child not let this pass?

"Aye, I would," Lioslaith agreed, resettling the child in her place at the table, biting back her own grin. "Perchance his mam will do the same when that man gets home. Now," she pushed Rowan's bowl closer to her, "finish your supper."

Alistair followed suit, resuming his seat at the table. Watching Rowan take a too-large bite of her stew, he let out a relieved breath. If the bairn's mouth was full, she couldn't ask any more awkward questions.

Lioslaith as well began to eat, a blush staining her cheeks. Whether from her daughter's questions or the man's aggravations, Alistair did not ken. What he did ken was this would make for an interesting conversation later this evening. What would the village men do when an outlet for their lust was no' available? They had not considered that as fully as they should. Surely other women in the villages can fill the position. Would there truly be an outcry over the loss of one comfort woman?

Hamish raced back to the MacDonald keep as quickly as his stocky legs could carry him. His anger did not cool in the frigid night air, but fanned, flaring harder so he seemed to emit steam from every exposed piece of skin. His reddened face burst in on Dougie, who was finishing his own supper in the main hall and flirted with the kitchen maid he hoped would join him later in his chambers.

The smile on Dougie's face only widened when he saw Hamish enter, but the taunting barb he wanted to deliver fell silent as the angered Hamish approached. The man resembled an ornery Highland bull, and Dougie pushed the buxom kitchen maid aside to receive his kinsman.

"What ails ye, man?" Dougie asked. Hamish's chest heaved several times before he answered.

"Yon comfort woman. Something's amiss. She would no' service me, no' e'en in the barn! Her daughter was there, but with a strange man."

Hamish spat out the final word. Dougie's sandy brow darkened.

"What man?" Dougie asked.

"I dinna ken! Some skinny, brown-haired fool who behaved like he lived there!"

Dougie sat back hard in his seat, pressing his thumbs against his eyes. He had thought the exiled kinsman wandered off to the west coast of North Uist, hopefully to fall into his own demise in the rough waters of the western sea. He had seen the lad head west and reported his movements to the Laird. That the cretin circled back, found himself sanctuary at the comfort woman's home, Dougie's comfort woman no less, inflamed his own anger. This exile was becoming more trouble than he was worth.

Rising in one fluid movement, Dougie rested a hand on Hamish's shoulder. At first, Dougie considered taking this information to Angus Og, but to what end? Angus Og's present position was if the exiled MacNally was out of his sight, he need not pay the exile any mind. And if they did ken his whereabouts, then the Laird would let him remain to "keep an eye on the lad" as he said — a chore Dougie did not want to take on. The exile was out of sight but was still in MacDonald territory. Suddenly, the MacNally lad was a problem for him again.

Dougie's mind raced with implications. Was the exile in hiding, trying to spy? If so, for whom? The MacRuaidhrís? Was this a play for power from the larger northerly clan? The English? Was the war with the English pigs about the cross the Minch? And what were his intentions with the comfort woman? *Why was the lad still here?*

Instead of running to his Laird, Dougie decided to investigate the exile on his own. 'Twould be better to bring answers to his Laird rather than another problem. Grabbing the back of Hamish's tunic, he dragged the man from the hall to pick his brain and create a plan to bring the exile back in check.

After several days of contemplation, Dougie had decided to confront his chieftain with the information Hamish provided, and with the banished MacNally. Hamish may have felt put out at the comfort woman's rejection, but Dougie needed to focus on the larger concern at hand. The day prior, he hiked up near the comfort woman's lonely croft to see the banished kinsman with his own eyes. Contempt simmered like a smoky peat fire at the exile's audacity to remain on MacDonald land after the Laird had sent him away.

Dougie assumed the exiled bastard had planned to make his way back to the would-be traitors, the MacRuaidhrís; let them embrace a possible English spy as one of their own. The MacDonalds did not waver in their loyalty to the Bruce and wouldn't suffer a traitor on their lands. The MacRuaidhrís, on the other hand . . . Dougie shook his head. What loyalties that clan had, only God Himself would ken.

But if the exiled lad hadn't found shelter with the MacRuaidhrís but reposed on MacDonald land, Dougie could not let that stand. He didn't want to think Hamish was right — that the lad was living with the comfort woman, but Hamish was no liar.

The misty morning air held the remnants of the frigid night, and Dougie shivered from his hiding place behind the low brush. He wrapped his tartan across his arms and chest against the wind blowing across the dead grasses. Dense smoke from the cottage blended with the gray morning skies, and Dougie hoped the exile would be man enough to tend the goats and hens tightly tucked into the sagging lean-to.

Fortune smiled on Dougie, and he didn't have to wait long. The slender Highlander stepped out the door as the day began to brighten, a worn wooden pail clutched tightly in his left hand. His hair was still a pasty mess on his head, and the lad looked as though he could use a few more good meals. His color, though, had improved since Dougie last saw the sallow lad a fortnight ago, so whatever plagued the MacNally most assuredly deserted him.

Shock at the vision of the very man whom Angus Og had banished from MacDonald land shook Dougie to his core. What audacity did this man have to refuse an order from his Laird? What manner of man hid in a woman's house? What?

Dougie's thoughts came to a grinding halt when Lioslaith herself, unmistakable with her shimmering fair hair and pale skin, followed the lad outside, pulling her own heathery tartan around herself. The MacNally man turned to her, and she stepped into his embrace. Dougie's eyes narrowed to slits as the exile wrapped his own tartan around her, drawing her near.

Why was the comfort woman letting the man stay in her cottage? Why was she embracing this man whom her Laird banished?

His eyes could not believe it when they kissed outside the rotting barn door, then held hands as he escorted her inside. Whatever was going on, it was more than a customer for a comfort woman, of that Dougie was certain. Nothing else mattered. Hamish was not ejected from her doorstep because she was occupied; he was ejected because the exile was living with her like they were man and wife. Dougie wanted to assault the man here and now, drag him bound to the Laird. But on his own, given his prior relations with the woman, there was a chance the man may not come as agreeably as Dougie would like. Better to have an accomplice when he came to arrest the lad. He could then bring the exile before Angus Og for the crime of treason against the Laird.

Dougie, no longer cold now that the fire of rage exploded inside him, slipped beyond the brush on stealth toes. Without a glance back at the croft, he made for the MacDonald keep as swiftly as his feet could carry him.

"Hamish!" Dougie yelled before even reaching the outer yard. "Hamish, get ye on a horse! We are to nab a traitor!"

Hamish's face lit up with expectation. Reiving people was nearly as fun as reiving cattle. Without a question to Dougie, he raced for the stable, calling for the stable lad to saddle their horses. With urgency, the lad worked as quickly as he could, and once the saddles were secured into place, Hamish and Dougie rode out before the noon time meal, the devil on their heels.

Several Scottish hens pecked at the sparse grass of the croft when they rode up, sending the hens flurrying away in a flurry of black and white feathers. Dougie dismounted before the horse completely stopped, throwing the reins at the hook on the barn. Hamish followed suit and reached the cottage door as Dougie pounded, the wooden door creaking in its frame.

Voices inside silenced at the unexpected intrusion. The door opened a slit, just enough for Dougie to make out the crystalline eyes of the comfort woman.

"Come, now, Lioslaith. Turn 'im over," Dougie demanded in a growl. Lioslaith's bored expression did not change.

"I dinna ken what ye mean, Dougie."

Rubbing his hand over his sweaty brow, Dougie tried to speak rationally. "Ye ken the man is an exile and a traitor. Angus Og banished him from MacDonald land, ye ken? He should no' be here, yet I find him in your home? *Assisting* ye in the barn?"

Dougie let the implication of his words hang in the air. The comfort woman's expression did not alter. *She wears a face of stone, that one,* Dougie thought.

"Ye are no' welcome here. There is none here that should no' be."

The wording rang strangely to Dougie, but he was not to be denied. Raising a fist, he beat on the door, thrusting it open.

The scraggly Highlander stood in the center of the room, his own fists clenched. Dougie laughed at the lad's fighting stance as Hamish joined him in the doorway.

"Ye may try to take me on, laddie, but ye would no' best both Hamish and I."

Dougie reached out a long arm and grasped Alistair by the back of his neck. Lioslaith roared at Dougie, kicking at his legs.

"Ye leave him be, Dougie MacDonald! The man is naught to ye!"

Dougie flashed his own icy glare at Lioslaith, who managed to remain stoic in his threatening presence.

"Aye, and who is he t'ye, Lioslaith? Eh? Mayhap that is the question we should ask."

She knew that fighting the two men was fruitless. Better to let them take Alistair back to the Laird, where he would once again be released. He had done no wrong. Lioslaith's pursed her lips at Dougie and stepped away, waving her hand dismissively.

"Fine. Take him to Angus Og. He will see the error of your ways. 'Tis no' what ye think, Dougie."

The large blond man gave one final glance at Lioslaith before dragging the confused Alistair out the door. Lioslaith mouthed "Dinna worry," to him. She waited only until they mounted their horses and reared around before racing to Muira's croft.

⟫⟫⟫ ⟪⟪⟪

"Muira!" Lioslaith's voiced carried on the wind. Muira opened the door well before Lioslaith crested the knoll by the cottage.

"Christ's blood, Elle! What brings ye screaming like a banshee?"

Lioslaith gulped the air, trying to form words and breath at the same time. She bent, resting her hand on her skirts.

"They 'ave 'im! Muira, they took Alistair!"

"Who?" Muira asked as Alisa stepped into the doorway.

"Aye, who took him, Elle?" Alisa asked.

"Dougie MacDonald. I did no' ken as much, but Angus Og had banished him from MacDonald land."

Muira paled at this news. She was the one who had brought the lad back to her house, like a lost puppy, and then foisted him upon Lioslaith in hopes they would make a match. The fact that he was ordered to leave MacDonald land was never raised. *Why did the lad say nothing?* While a moue of anger burned under Muira's skin, she wanted to give the lad the benefit of doubt — fear, most likely. Fear of rejection, a fear with which Muira and Alisa were familiar.

Alisa smirked at Muira and Lioslaith, knowing the impotent power the Mac-Donalds wielded, or believed they did, in North Uist. Only one clan held power on this copse of rocks, and 'twas not the MacDonalds.

"Come, Elle, sit and warm yourself by the fire," she directed in her calming voice. "Say hello to your dear Rowan, and I will ride for MacRuaidhrí's. My clan will defend 'im and claim our position on the borders of the two lands and his association with me puts Alistair under MacRuaidhrí protection. I will have a missive sent as soon as I arrive."

Lioslaith obeyed mindlessly. Relieved to have the support of her sisters, she reclined by the fire. Rowan climbed on her lap to nestle into her mother's arms. Alisa wasted no time in gathering a heavy plaid about her shoulders. She raced out the door, urging their aging palfrey into the fastest pace the poor animal could manage.

Alistair was, for the second time in his life, thrown ankles over backside across the rump of a horse. The ride back to MacDonald land, while thankfully short, was also a jouncing trip that made Alistair want to vomit up his supper.

The large blond warrior didn't bring him to the chieftain right away. Instead, he dragged Alistair by his tunic down a set of deep stone steps to the cells below the keep. Giving Alistair a forceful shove, the blond monster slammed the thick door shut. Alistair stumbled as he entered, catching himself on a low bench that apparently served as both a bed and table. The hinged metal shutter in the door swung open, and the blond's bulbous nose poked through.

"Ye will remain here until the Laird can figure what to do with ye. Ye should learn to follow directions, ye fool."

The shutter then slammed shut with a small click, locking it in place. Alistair glanced around the narrow stone dungeon. While it was much less accommodating than the prison that was the upper chambers of his uncle's keep, at least

Alistair knew where he stood. Death was often the punishment for a treasonous act. Was his presence on MacDonald land considered such a heinous act that he might hang for it?

Wiping his limp hair off his face, he sat heavily onto the bench, clasping his head between his hands. The irony of these events was not lost on him. He had been banished for a second time and contemplated his own demise. Then the strange women decided he was a love match for Lioslaith, and he formed a strange bond with her and found a sense of peace and contentment with life he'd not experienced since he was a young lad.

Now, having found her and a place for himself in the world, he was facing the same demise he had considered when he first came to the isle. What manner of world was this, what God would taunt him by placing the seed of death in his mind, just to stave it away with the companionship of a beautiful woman, then let that seed come to fruit? Was God truly that unkind?

Alistair fell back on the bench and draped his arm over his eyes. The sun was rapidly setting amid the cloudy mist of winter, but even the weak light penetrating the slitted window far above his head pained him. His head throbbed, and once again he wondered why Lioslaith and her sister didn't let him expire out in the elements when they found him.

Several hours passed before the sound of thumping feet on the dirt floor echoed, and the cell door flung open. The barrel-chested Laird Angus Og stepped into the cell with aplomb, flanked by the annoying blond, an elderly man, and two other kinsmen with swords drawn. While hardly an army, Alistair was not inclined to try and fight them, regardless. Much of his fight fled from him before he was plucked off the ass end of the horse.

And if they expected him to rise out of respect to the Laird, they were mistaken. These supposed kin abandoned him to the elements. Alistair owed them no loyalty, especially for doing naught more than living with a woman on the borderlands. Sensing a larger issue at play, Alistair did his best to play dumb. Fortunately, Angus Og was a talker.

"I thought I told ye t'get off MacDonald land. We have no need of exiled English spies."

When Alistair didn't respond, the chieftain continued. "Even if ye are kin, I can no' trust a man aligned with the English. And if I can no' trust ye, ye are nay welcome."

The large man moved closer to Alistair, the older man staying close. "Why are ye still on my land, lad?"

At this question, Alistair lifted his head, giving the Laird and his men a fierce green glare.

"Even if I say the truth, ye will no' believe me. Why should I say anything?"

A smart response to be sure, but Alistair was so bone weary of these accusations and politicking. Once he lost his chance to be Laird of the MacNally clan, he no longer cared. He was never truly an English ally; he was Highland born and bred. To be rejected by all he knew and cast off to another clan that also rejected him left him jaded. The only alliance he had was to Lioslaith and her kin.

"Oh, ho, ho, look at this!" Angus Og mocked, his large belly jiggling as he laughed. "Ye should try to speak on your own behalf, lad. There is nary another who will speak for ye."

Alistair resumed his petulant silence. Angus Og sighed as the older, graying man waved the Laird away.

"Leave us," the older man told him, his voice surprisingly virile.

Alistair kept the bored expression on his face as he watched the entourage march out the low cell door. Only the older man remained.

"I am called Rodrick MacDonald. Do ye ken who I am?" The man's hearty voice softened as he spoke.

Alistair shook his head at the question. The man sat on the bench next to him, his old knees creaking with the movement.

"I am the Laird's adviser, as I was for his father," Rodrick continued. "I have spent the better part of the last month trying to understand your position here on the Isle. We only received a brief missive about why ye were exiled, and what happened in the Highlands is rather unimportant. What is more important is your behavior here on Uist."

The old adviser shifted, trying to find a comfortable spot on the bench. Waiting for the man to settle his old bones provided Alistair a moment to read Rodrick. Why was the man having a private conference with a supposed traitor?

"And while ye did nay leave the land, ye did at least make it t'the borderlands. I would have preferred ye t'stay nearer so we could watch ye but having ye gone served just as well. But we worry. Ye were near the MacRuaidhrís, who may no' be the most loyal t'the Scottish cause, and we dinna ken your loyalties. Do ye see our problem?"

The old adviser's bushy gray-white eyebrows pulled together as he tried to read Alistair, who didn't respond. Rodrick rested a bony hand on Alistair's back.

"I think ye have a good heart, lad. I can read people, aye? Ye were so thin when ye came here, gossips said ye had fallen ill, and the comfort woman and her strange sisters nursed ye back t'health. I wanted t'be certain, but I did nay ken ye are a worry. And ye didn't really leave, so I must surmise ye are no' trying t'hide something. I would think ye would live with the MacRuaidhrís if ye were truly a spy. Ye are just a lost lad. Is my estimation correct?"

Alistair didn't speak, only hung his damp, bronzed head between his hands. He didn't know what to make of this old man who spoke without guile. Silence was the better part of valor at this moment, so he continued to keep his mouth shut.

"Aye, lad. Ye are in a tight spot, that is true. I will speak t'the Laird. I dinna believe that I will change his mind, but ye deserve a chance. He wanted t'keep ye close anyway. And if ye are with the comfort woman, well, I think we can keep an eye on ye from there."

"I think 'tis God's plan for me," Alistair finally spoke, keeping his head held in his palms. He had a rush inside his chest that told him to trust this man. "Father Stewart, he says that God is forgiving, and if we atone, we can find God's path for us. I'm trying t'find that path."

Roderick's expression remained still and serious, taking in the lad's words. There was more to the lad, Roderick surmised, than the lost exile who had turned up months ago.

He shifted to leave, then returned his eyes to Alistair, giving him a warning. "And be wary of Dougie. He has power, as the Laird's seneschal. He's fiercely protective of the clan, and he does no' appear t'like ye overmuch."

Alistair nodded at the sage advice. Rodrick patted the lad between his thin shoulders, rose stiffly, and closed the squeaky cell door as he left.

CHAPTER TWELVE

Family Reunions

Laird Rudy MacRuaidhrí spat on the ground as he cantered into the outer yard of the MacDonald keep. He tugged his plaid tighter around his neck to keep out the biting cold and gazed at the stone bulwark in front of them. Truly, he hated his present situation, leading a band of men across the rocky landscape of North Uist, inland from the sea, heading south to the MacDonalds.

That the MacDonalds wanted to usurp the MacRuaidhrí's position of power on the island was not a secret, and Rudy despised any interaction with that lesser clan. The MacDonalds had come to believe that their alignment with the Bruce gave them a preferred position on the Isle, and that attitude chapped Rudy's skin. He despised engaging with the MacDonalds. Yet, here he was, riding in the middle of the night to Castle MacDonald, in defense of some banished outsider at the behest of his sister.

Christina had ridden like the devil once she received the message. She did not know why the MacDonalds would bother with a lowly man just trying to find his place on their island, and who found it on their borderlands. She expected it was naught more than a way for the MacDonalds to throw their weight around, and Christina knew that assumption was the best way to get her brothers involved. Like most men, Lachlan and Rudy wanted to show all the other clans on the island who was the most powerful. And they had a soft spot for their sister and all her commanding ways, even if they didn't show their affection.

And it worked. Lachlan won the draw to remain warm at the MacRuaidhrí keep, taunting Rudy as the Chieftain of the clan grumbled and gave out the call. They estimated a small band would suffice, and Lachlan advised to start with honey, and only turn to a warring hand if niceties failed. Rudy departed with the only four men he could find so late in the evening. Hot-headed young men not yet into their cups, they were eager to answer their Laird's call, if only for something as minor as a ride to the neighboring clan. They grabbed their broadswords and sobered up on the ride south.

Rudy hailed the MacDonald clansman as he rode in. Slipping off the horse, he handed the reins to a young man and marched to the large iron and wood doors of the main hall. Without announcement, he burst through, followed by his men, and bellowed for Laird Angus Og.

"Angus, ye meddling fool! What are ye about?"

The MacDonald chieftain rose haltingly from his cushioned chair by the fire, surrounded by several other clansmen caught by surprise. They jumped from their seats and reached for swords and curled their hands into fists, ready for a fight.

"Rudy," Angus Og bit out, trying to hide the shock on his face. "T'what do I owe this pleasure?"

"I have it on good authority ye have a captive. Some worthless lad without a home?"

A smug grin spread across Angus Og's face before he lifted his tankard of ale to his lips. He took a deep swig before answering.

"What business is it yours if I have the lad in my cells? Do ye need him t'help ye spy for the English?"

The tension in the hall crackled like fire between the two chieftains. Rudy stepped forward and slapped Angus Og with a hearty thump on his shoulders.

What he wanted to do was plant his hammer-like fist in the man's arrogant face, but a pat on the back would have to suffice.

"I would ask that ye release the lad. We do nay need any issue with the Highlands. We want them on our side with the Bruce! The lad is no' a spy. We would ken, aye?" Rudy winked at Angus Og. "And he was nay on your land, fully. He's on the border land, where we can both watch him. And I hear tell that he may be trying to bring respectability t'one of your women. I dinna think that is a traitorous offense."

Laird MacDonald guffawed at the MacRuaidhrí's words. "Ye dinna ken the men in my clan. The woman, she is a favorite, aye?"

At this, both men laughed as the other kinsmen visibly relaxed and entertained their own smiles. Suddenly the talk changed from traitor and spies to whores, a much more titillating topic. Dirks and swords returned to their hiding places, fists relaxed, and more ale was consumed.

"Ah, well," Rudy shrugged, "I am certain another will soon fill her place. 'Tis important t'some in my clan that this woman find respectability, ye ken? And we can no' waste our efforts on something as trivial as who's living with a comfort woman." Rudy winked at Angus Og.

Angus Og nodded knowingly, recalling his earlier conversation with Roderick concerning the lad. "My adviser is of a like mind with ye. We have too much conflict on our small isle, the old man thinks. He would like us t'have some peace as we work toward the independence of Scotland."

"'Tis an agreeable position, t'be sure," Rudy replied diplomatically. "Will ye see that the lad is released on the morn? The fool should find his way back t'the woman's cottage."

Laird MacDonald sighed again, but acquiesced, bobbing his half-drunk head to Rudy. "Aye. But we will send him off with a warning. I dinna need strife on my land, ye ken?" Angus Og lifted his head and peered down his bulbous nose at the other Laird. "Would it do me any good to ask if ye would confirm the lad is no' a spy for the English?"

Rudy cut his dark eyes to the man but did not respond to Angus Og's final words. Laird MacDonald sighed at the MacRuaidhrí's enigmatic mannerisms.

Angus doubted he would ever fully trust the wily brothers of the powerful clan to the north.

"Will ye stay for a drink 'afore ye leave?" the Laird asked Rudy.

The MacRuaidhrí had already turned to leave, but the appeal of a strong drink before a warm fire won out over a cold ride home. The smile returned to Rudy's woolly cheeks.

"I am no' one to turn down such hospitality," he answered, moving to a chair near the hearth.

Angus Og joined him, resettling in his cushioned chair. Perchance a strong drink with the Laird would loosen the man's tongue while building some much-needed solidarity with the MacRuaidhrí. He lifted his cup to Rudy.

"*Slainte.*"

Time passed slowly for Alistair in the confining cell. Clouds obscured what little moonlight could permeate the narrow-barred window, but the cold air had no limitations. Icy wind blew in and dank cold seeped through the weather-worn stones. Water droplets formed on the walls, forming patches of thin frost, chilling the cell all the more and reminding Alistair of his wet voyage across the Minch. As he did then, he wrapped his entire body, including his head, in his wool tartan to ward off the ever-present cold.

Sleep eluded him. Even after his body stopped shivering, his mind would nay settle, skipping from image to image of the past months. At first he tried to understand how his captivity could be part of God's plan. When he gave up, he let his mind wander. The image that returned to his mind the most, however, was that of the lithe, fairy-like angel who rescued him. Her wispy hair brushing against his chest, her delicate skin, so soft to his touch — reminders of Lioslaith kept him awake as they calmed his racing heart. He kept those thoughts close as the night wore on.

The night was well past gloaming before Alistair finally rested his weary mind. He expected to be awakened with the rising sun and was surprised to see the weak sunlight brightening the cell when his eyes finally opened. Frost rimmed the edges of the stones and window slits and crusted the edges of his tartan. Keeping the woolen wrap pulled around his shoulders, he shuffled off the bench and pressed his ear to the door, anxious to hear the approaching steps of his final judgment. *How much sway would the old adviser have with the Laird? Would the angry blond giant hold the same sway?*

Resettling on the bench, Alistair picked at the remains of his previous evening meal, the meat dry and cold, the bread mealy. The icy water in the metal cup, though, was refreshing, and he gulped it quickly, spilling it down his chin. At that same moment, the shifting bar on his cell door announced his time had come.

"Good morn, ye scrappy lad," boomed the Laird's voice as he entered. This time he came alone, his large girth filling most of the doorway. And this time, Alistair rose to face the man directly.

"Good morn to ye, Laird." Alistair tried to keep his voice from shaking. After his previous encounter with the man, Alistair sensed that maintaining a strong front would make an impression. He was not wrong.

"Well, lad, ye canna seem t'keep yourself out o'trouble, aye?"

Alistair remained silent, only tipping his head in response. The heavyset laird settled his weight onto the worn bedding, much like Roderick the day before.

"What is it with ye, lad? How do ye invite trouble so?" Angus Og clicked his tongue. "Mayhap 'tis no' all of your own accord. Ye were dumped on my shores, nary a coin t'your name, taken in by a woman of ill-repute, rejected by your only kin on the Isle, and ye managed t'strike the ire of one of my closest men. Mayhap ye are the sort who trouble seems to follow."

The Laird paused, scratching at his beard, keeping his gaze on the man next to him. Angus Og felt pity for the man. After listing his recent troubles, 'twas easy to have sympathy for the lad, even with all his faults. And he could see the man was trying to atone, if in his own strange way.

Clearing this throat, Angus Og continued. "But ye seem to have found a bit of a home with the comfort woman, even if my men dinna like it. My adviser does no' think ye are a concern, and I trust him unfailingly. The MacRuaidhrís vouch that ye are nay a spy, or much of anything, 'twould appear. And the fact your presence in my keep opened a conversation with the MacRuaidhrís, that goes a long way with me." The Laird clapped his hand on Alistair's back, rocking him forward with its force.

"So, lad, after conference with my most trusted advisers, and with the MacRuaidhrís themselves, I have decided to, once again, let ye leave. Some of my men may no' like this decision, losing a favorite this way. But go back t'your bonnie lass. Ye are both trying to make yourselves on this cold rock in the sea. I will no' begrudge ye, or your woman, that opportunity."

The Laird hefted his weight off the bedding with a loud protest from his knees and stepped to the door. He stopped before exiting.

"Ye may no' think yourself fortunate, lad, but in many ways, ye are. Try to count your blessings 'afore ye sleep next to your woman tonight. Men have been killed for less than what ye have done."

"Thank ye," Alistair finally found his voice.

The Laird's attitude was a welcome change compared to his first visit, and a sense of surprise and hope welled up in Alistair's chest. His kinsman didn't seem the monstrous chieftain Alistair thought him to be. The weight of the man's words was not lost. Perchance Alistair had to land on this remote isle to find what he had been searching for all along. The more time Alistair spent with the MacDonalds, the more he believed Father Stewart's wise words.

Angus Og tipped his head and departed, leaving the door open behind him. Alistair, who didn't want to spend any more time in the dank, cramped cell, followed.

Alistair once again trudged north through frozen grasses and blowing winds to Lioslaith's croft. His release from the MacDonald's, his conversation with the sage old man, all were steps on this path of redemption, he believed. That he could be with a woman like Lioslaith still astounded him, the idea of this being part of God's plan surely must be a mistake. But God was perfect, the church taught, and he desperately clung to that belief.

As he crested the small hill leading to Lioslaith's croft, a flapping in the grass pulled his attention from his heavenly thoughts. Easing through the moorland turf, he came across a smallish-owl, gray and brown and panicking, struggling in the grass. One wing did not move with the rest of the animal. *Broken, poor wee thing,* Alistair thought, and made to resume his journey. The owl flapped again, making a cooing sound as it did so. Alistair paused.

The owl reminded him of himself, struggling alone on this isle. Realizing it may not be the most prudent decision, Alistair unwrapped a long portion of his tartan and squatted close to the now-frantic bird.

"*Wheest, wheest,*" Alistair cooed, flicking his arms around the flapping animal before it could scramble away or hurt itself more. Once ensconced in the woolly fabric, the owl stopped struggling, probably appreciating the warmth the tartan provided.

Shifting the bird's weight into the crook of his arm, Alistair shivered against the cold, and as the thin snow began to fall, he climbed his way home.

Rowan must have been watching from the doorway, for her screeching call "Alistair!" echoed across the dale. Her tiny form soon followed, a luminous figure amid the fog. She crashed into Alistair's legs, the force of her hug rocking him on the backs of his heels. He laughed and pulled her up into his left arm.

"Careful wee one! I have a gift for ye and your mother!"

"A gift?" Her eyes alighted with joy.

"Weel, a type of gift. It needs some care, ye ken?" he asked as he placed the lass down near the barn and escorted her inside. "Go get your mam," he instructed, and Rowan raced off to deliver her important message.

Lioslaith soon entered the lean-to with Rowan, her golden aura brightening the dim interior with her very presence. Alistair shook his head, embarrassed with how enamored he was with this woman. Turning his attention to the animal still wrapped in his plaid, he called Rowan to come close to the low bench. She leaned over the tartan, her eager hands gripping at the wooden seat, and Lioslaith stood behind her, her eyebrows high on her forehead.

"What have ye brought home, Alistair?"

The question was a benign one, but larger questions hovered just behind it, wanting to know what happened with the MacDonalds. Alistair raised one eyebrow in return, heightening the drama of the unknown gift.

He slowly unwrapped the bird, its tiny gray face and large eyes cautiously wiggling out from the tartan. It whipped its head back and forth, trying to take in its current location. Alistair stroked the top of its head with a gentle finger, and the owl blinked in one long motion.

Rowan emitted a quiet squeal, clapping her baby-like hands with excitement. She held out one tiny finger over the owl's head, waiting for her turn to pet the owl. Alistair held it still while she rubbed her fingertip lightly over the bird's feathery down, and it blinked again. It opened its sharply hooked beak in a silent *whoo*, trying to speak. *Maybe he's hungry?* Alistair wondered.

Lioslaith leaned in to have a better look at the little owl, curiosity painting her features. "How did ye get 'im, Alistair?"

"I think its injured," he said, exposing the limp wing to Lioslaith. "Do ye have healing skills to mend an owl's wing?"

She shrugged offhandedly, biting her lip. "'Tis nay the first time I have rescued a bird. Muira and I saved and nursed many when we were lasses. Hold him tightly, please."

Alistair did as directed while she pressed her fingers lightly against the wing. The poor bird quivered and tried to escape her ministrations.

"We can bind the wing t'the bird for a time, and it should heal if we care for him here in the barn. Mayhap he will stay, become our own barn owl."

"Rowan and I will feed him, care for him." He smiled at the lassie and wrapped the owl's wings within the tartan again. "Owls are supposed to be guardians, even warriors. I believe we could use a guardian for our place."

Alistair passed a sheepish smile to Lioslaith, who returned it with her own pale lips. He was not wrong, that she knew for certain. Perchance this owl was a sign that now life would go right for them. She collected a wood-slatted box from behind the bench and placed a handful of fresh peat along the bottom. With a tender grip, she lifted the fluffy bit of owl into the box. It flapped about in a panic for several heartbeats before settling into a corner, eying its captors with those deep, amber eyes. Lioslaith cooed at it while it settled, then placed the box on the bench.

"Let us go inside. We will find a wee bit of food for the laddie, a small dish of water, and Alistair can tell us what happened while he was away."

Lioslaith's icy gaze regarded him pointedly, and then returned to the cottage, ready to hear all about Alistair's adventures.

After caring for the newest member of their family, Lioslaith prepared the evening meal of broth and brown bread. Alistair regaled them with comical recitations of his forced voyage to the MacDonald stronghold, some of it invented, and both Rowan and Lioslaith laughed uncontrollably. His impersonation of the pompous MacDonald Laird was near perfect, and Lioslaith could not recall the last time she had laughed so heartily — probably not since she was a wee lass, sharing a bed with Muira. She hadn't believed she could feel such happiness again in her lifetime.

Rowan begged for more Blue men stories and drifted off to sleep to her mother's soothing voice. Tucking the coverlet around her shoulders, Lioslaith caressed her daughter's clear brow, then joined Alistair on a low stool near the hearth. She clasped his hand and turned her lucent eyes to his. Now that story time was over, he took a deep breath and confided in Lioslaith everything he left out at supper.

Lioslaith was notably surprised at the reception he received, both from the sage adviser and from the Laird himself. Dougie over-reacted — even a blind man could see he harbored ill-will toward Alistair — and since Lioslaith no longer served as his comfort woman, toward Lioslaith as well. Foreboding shrouded Lioslaith. Though the MacDonalds released him with naught more than a "go with God," she feared that Dougie would not let them alone and spoke as much to Alistair.

"Nay, bright one," he told her, kissing Lioslaith's forehead, keeping her close. "My standing with the MacDonalds seems much improved, and he even thanked me, of a sort, for encouraging discourse with the MacRuaidhrís, though how I did that, I dinna ken."

He kissed her forehead again. "My hope is that our concerns with the Mac-Donalds are at an end. Hopefully, we will be left in peace for the rest of our days."

CHAPTER THIRTEEN

What Happens When We Take Matters into Our Own Hands

DOUGIE DID NOT WANT to upset the present, tentative alliance between the MacDonalds and the MacRuaidhrís. Angus Og had spent too much time and effort trying to bring the MacRuaidhrís to commit to the side of the Bruce, and it seemed, after their last evening with the Laird MacRuaidhrí, such a meeting of the minds was finally at hand for the isle. With a harsh admonishment, Angus Og cautioned him against further action against the MacNally lad. Dougie had too much respect for his own Laird to disobey and upend the tentative alliance now.

But the ratty exile was still on his island. Still on MacDonald lands, though on the far reaches. Still with the comfort woman, and the MacNally lad's presence rankled Dougie to his core. As seneschal, he knew he was correct — the lad should not remain on MacDonald lands, kin or no. And his own Laird was permitting this interloper to stay within their borderlands! To what end would that serve?

The large blond Scot was uncertain if 'twas the lad's history as a Highlander, as the mainland Scots dumped their refuse on Dougie's shores, the lad's position as a supposed English spy, which was even worse, or the fact that he was told to leave their land but remained and ensnared himself with the comfort woman and witches at the clan borders. Truly, Dougie did not know which offense was most egregious.

The worst was the loss of the comfort woman, he admitted to himself. Thawing his raw, reddened hands by the fire, he lamented the loss of an eager, warm woman after a cold day of work. On days like this, where the snow touched the waves and the inland rivulets seeped into icy muck that clung to the boots, freezing everything below the knee, a man needed to sink into the warmth of a welcoming sheath, to lose himself as she heated him to his root.

That's what a man needed, and the outcast Highlander, the scrawny pup that he was, robbed Dougie, and the entire MacDonald clan, of convenience.

Hamish had followed Dougie in from the stables, noting the man's quietude, so unlike his normal, jovial self. The gray-gold hay of the stables clung to his hair, getting lost in the thick swath of Dougie's hair and beard, and clung in contrast to his heavy, deep red tunic. Dougie took no notice of these trappings, lost in his thoughts by the stone hearth of the great hall.

Better to remain silent, Hamish thought as he slipped onto another bench to warm his own hands before searching some repast to calm his hunger. His stomach clenched and growled in response, and Hamish turned his head to the kitchens, wondering if Mistress Maddy had any supper prepared. Surely some dried haddock at least?

"Get ye some food, ye annoying bear of a man," Dougie's voice was flat in the large hall. Hamish had the good sense to blush at being caught thinking of food.

"I think I will, ye *dobber*. I'll bring some for ye as well, and then mayhap ye can tell me what has ye as moody as a crone."

Expecting a response to the insult, Hamish pursed his lips and shrugged dismissively when it did not come and headed to the kitchens on a quest for sustenance.

Mistress Maddy met him at the doorway to the kitchens with a wooden platter full of dried fish, oats, a wedge of cheese, and a sliced, grainy late apple.

"Here, ye loudmouth!" she teased with a smile on her plump cheeks. "Take this for ye and the mountain over there, and I will bring out ale."

Mistress Maddy had flicked her head in Dougie's direction, and Hamish had to bite his lip to hold back a laugh. The large man, hunkered over so dismally, did resemble a mountain. Hamish smacked the platter down on the bench next to him.

"Here, eat. Mayhap ye will feel better with some food in your wame."

Dougie complied, selecting a dried haddock and slipped it between the bristly blond hair hiding his mouth. He chewed absently as he continued to stare at the fire.

"What do ye think of this Highland pup who's settled himself into our land?" he wondered aloud.

Hamish finished chewing before responding, taking the time to measure out his words as best he could.

"He's naught more than a flea on the land, Dougie. Nay worth much at all. So, what if the scrawny lad lives at the border with a woman of ill-repute. What is he t'ye?"

"That is the problem, Hamish. A flea. In that ye are right. And fleas have a way of populating, of irritating those around them. That is what this pup is t'me, Hamish. I dinna want him irritating me or my clan." His light blue eyes searched the fire before he spoke again. "Who is this lad t'just show up, a possible spy, t'find footing in our land, and because the MacRuaidhrí's say so, we have t'accept it?"

Dougie tilted his broad face to Hamish, his eyes burning with more heat than the fire. "I canna accept this lad. Ties t'the MacRuaidhrí's or no. Roderick's recommendation or no. Angus Og's decision or no. What does it show if the Highlanders can run ramshod over our island?"

Stretching his long legs before the fire, Dougie stood, dwarfing everything around him.

"'Tis an insult t'me, my clan, and my Laird to allow him t'stay. Come, Hamish. Finish your meal. We are going t'convince the lad that 'tis past time for him t'depart."

"'Tis winter, Dougie. Nearing Christ's Mass. Where would he go? Surely not back across the Minch. Nary a boat travels in winter."

"I dinna care. He can go south t'the southern isles or live on a rock in the middle of the sea. As long as he is far away from our lands. We shall convince him of the sagacity of our demands." Dougie stormed out into the yard, expecting Hamish to follow.

Hamish, familiar with Dougie's disposition and obsession with the comfort woman, gulped down the last swallow of his ale and, against his sound judgment, joined Dougie outside.

***

They rode across the snow-crusted grass north to the comfort woman's croft. Hamish searched his brain for any words that could speak sense to his kinsman, but none came to his mouth. A fool's errand, to be sure. The comfort woman would turn Dougie away, just as she had Hamish, now that she was trying to become a woman of repute. And the lad has the permission of the Laird to stay — he would not move along at Dougie's say-so. Not without a fight, Hamish knew.

A bark of laughter bubbled up in Hamish. The idea was comical. A woman of ill-repute living with an exiled man. How could either of them think they could just live as man and wife? While the idea stuck Hamish as humorous, they had the right to live their lives. Hamish was certain Dougie would see the idiocy of this trip and return home, mayhap with his pride hurt a bit, but with a better understanding of just how insignificant these remote kinsmen were. Fleas, truly.

Dougie, on the other hand, rode with a vengeance that burned beneath his skin like a fiery snake, well-hidden from Hamish and the others. Even though Dougie knew why he disliked this exiled highlander, he didn't know why the man made him crazed and infuriated. All he knew was he wanted the man gone — whether by choice or by violence, Dougie did not care.

Lioslaith's croft stood like a lonely bastion against the pale winter sky. Dougie knew the comfort woman's sister and that vile witch her sister lived with (*and wasn't that a crime against God in itself? How did these people remain on Mac-*

Donald land? Ship them off to sea and let the water take them, was Dougie's belief) were nay in the cottage, as their pathetic excuse of a horse was nay in the yard.

Tying their steeds to the barn, Dougie stormed up to the door, banging his hammer-like fist against the wood until it threatened to splinter. The door swung open, and the Highland pup stood there in naught but a shift and a dark plaid, his sandy brown hair stark against his pale skin.

The first thought that registered with Dougie was the man did nay look as scrawny as he had when he first visited the MacDonald keep. He had watched the lad amble into the yard and followed him as he exited the keep. Dougie had observed the wretch's rejection from the Laird, and his sad walk on spindly legs out of the hall.

The man before him now was not that same scrawny pup. Keeping up the chores for Lioslaith had rebuilt the muscle lost to illness, and the lad looked more like a Highlander than he had a month ago. While still more slender than most of the MacDonald men, Dougie and Hamish included, the lad would put up a fight this day. Dougie's heavy beard pulled into a hidden smile at the thought. He was not afraid of a fight.

"Aye?" Alistair asked.

He was not surprised to see the men at the door but had hoped most of the MacDonalds who had frequented Lioslaith were informed she no longer served in the position of a comfort woman. Alistair shook his head. Dougie was the type of man who didn't like to be told nay.

Dougie gave no pause. He slammed that hammer fist into Alistair's unsuspecting face, reeling him backwards into the croft.

An explosion of pain wracked Alistair's head as he stumbled backwards. Trying to regain his balance and his vision while one hand held his swelling, bloody cheek, Alistair took no time to react. This time, Dougie would not drop him at the foot of the Laird — the man had other intentions, ones that did not include Alistair living out his life with Lioslaith.

Alistair knew it would be a losing battle to fight the giant of a man with fists. Instead of lifting his own hands, Alistair lowered his bloody head and rushed forward, clasping the larger man around the waist and managing to fling him onto his back like a turtle on its shell.

Alistair could hear Lioslaith shriek in protest, and he hoped she and Rowan were far back in the cottage. Scrambling to avoid Dougie's swinging fists, Alistair wrapped his hands around Dougie's heavy beard and log-like neck, trying to keep him under control.

His hands were ripped away when another man grabbed Alistair's arms, pulling him through the doorway. Dougie choked and coughed, catching his breath as another round of hammer fists worked at Alistair's head. From his lowered position on the ground, he could barely shift and weave, and several of the punches seemed to knock his senses loose. From his crouched position, he moved to tackle the russet-haired man as well.

A sudden thudding sound, followed by a grunt, made Alistair look up. The onslaught of fists had stopped. In front of him, Lioslaith stood, feet apart and the metal fire-poker upraised in her hands, Scotland's smallest warrior, and the russet man in a crumpled pile before her. The expression on her face told Alistair that she also knew this fight would not end well for Alistair.

Dougie sat up, his hair standing on end at the sight of his downed kinsman.

"What have ye done?" he choked out. "I'll kill ye—"

Lioslaith cut him off, swinging the poker. "Nay! Ye will leave my home 'afore I do the same t'ye!"

Dougie moved to gather up the prone Hamish, but Lioslaith brandished fire-poked like a sword. Alistair rose and stood next to his wee warrior, adding his own presence to her stance.

"Leave him be. We will treat his wound and return him once he is recovered." Her command left no room for argument.

Dougie squeezed through the doorway to his horse, eying them as though they were the devils on earth, mounted his horse, and rode off. Alistair noted with a smile that the man continued to rub at his neck.

The wry thought of Dougie was quickly replaced with dread over their present predicament. Lioslaith had placed Rowan on the floor behind the table to shield her from the brawl at the door. The dear bairn had obediently played with her cloth toy and didn't move from her space until Lioslaith checked on her. She gave the child a small bannock and told Rowan to keep playing in her spot under the table, then Lioslaith returned to where Alistair stood near the senseless young man.

"Come, we must put the man on the bed," she said and gestured toward Alistair's old sickbed.

He was able to lift the MacDonald man to the pallet, placing a wad of tartan under his injured head. The wound gaped, the skin peeling back, and bled like a flood.

"Will ye ride t'my sister's and bring Alisa back with ye? I will need her herbs."

Lioslaith cautiously placed a cloth against the man's head as she asked, and Alistair was outside before she finished her request. He quickly moved the russet-haired man's horse into the barn, then ran as though their lives depended on it, and perchance it did. He ran until his chest threated to burst. And as the sun set beyond the cloudy sky, Alistair arrived at the end of the path, racing for the door.

Alisa and Muira jumped in unison at the pounding at the door. Alistair's voice carried through, and Muira flung the door open.

"What ails, ye, lad, t'come screaming t'my home?"

"Alisa, Lioslaith needs ye now," Alistair's words poured out in a rush. "There was a, um, a fight? A man is bleeding, senseless, and Lioslaith said t'bring your herbs."

Alisa did nay respond but immediately went to gathering what she would need, placing jars and skeins in her basket. Muira gathered their heavy wraps.

"I will go with ye, to help and in case more men return."

Her gaze was determined, that same crystal blue intensity manifested in Lioslaith. She strode out to their lean-to and prepared her horse.

It only took a few steps from the house for Dougie to regain his full senses after the events that unfolded with the comfort woman and her exile. The horse ambled forward in the darkening sky of gloaming while Dougie rubbed his hand against his face. *Had the pup managed to knock him to the ground? Nearly strangle him? What of Hamish?* Fury at his own actions roiled inside his belly. 'Twas Dougie's own fault — he underestimated the scrawny pup, who was evidently not as scrawny has he had been a month ago. Or Lioslaith, who ken the lass could wield a weapon so? Dougie's pride was as bruised as his neck. Then Hamish —!

Spurring his horse onward, Dougie raced toward the MacDonald keep. He did not know if his good kinsman yet lived and wanted to return with reinforcements as soon as possible. The wicked whore packed a wallop with her fire poker. While Hamish had a hard enough head, to be sure, all that blood did not bode well for the man. The woman did not know what she had done. Dougie would have his vengeance for the injuries to himself and Hamish, and if Hamish died, well. . .

The Good Book dictated an eye for an eye and a tooth for a tooth. Dougie would see the witchy comfort woman, and her whole family if necessary, burned at the stake for such atrocities.

Wasting no time once he entered the MacDonald yard, Dougie threw the reins at the stable boy and raced inside the keep, bellowing for Angus Og. Hamish was the Laird's own good-son, and his injury would not sit well with Angus. Not that the Laird cared for the man overmuch. Dougie knew few men cared for their daughter's husbands, but Hamish himself was a good warrior and strong worker, and that alone gave him value in Angus Og's eyes.

"Angus! Ye must come! We need kinsmen to ride to the comfort woman's croft and arrest her!"

Roderick, unnoticed in the corner of the room, raised a downy white questioning eyebrow at Dougie's barrage of words. Dougie was nothing if not overly dramatic, Roderick knew.

Angus rubbed his thick fingers against his forehead. *Again, with the comfort woman? And probably that MacNally lad?* Angus Og was truly weary of dealing with this strange man who appeared unbidden on his shore, settled himself on his land, and sowed discord with his men. He had tried to let the lad be, but here he was, again in the middle of discord. He was also tiring of Dougie's obsession with the lad and the comfort woman. A sharp snap of pain unfurled behind Angus Og's heavy brow, a sign of a headache surely to come on the heels of that pain.

Dougie, taking the silence of his Laird as an encouragement to continue, approached the wide table at the far end of the study.

"The MacNally lad attacked me and the woman attacked Hamish, knocking him senseless!"

Not the full truth, Angus Og surmised, but the mention of his good-son made the pounding in his head louder. *The mongrel, sleeping with a whore instead of his wife!* Was Angus Og's first judgmental thought. Some men had no character. Then, right after, *What happened to his good-son?*

"Where's Hamish now?" inquired Angus, noting the obvious absence of his good-son.

"Still with the comfort woman!" Exasperation tinged the edges of Dougie's voice.

"Ye left my good-son in the hands of those who attacked him?" Angus asked. *Ooch, this headache will only get worse this eve.*

"They threatened t'do the same to me if I did no' leave! She's a witch, that one, I am certain of it!" Dougie banged his hand on the table, causing Angus to flinch.

"Well, she is a healer, so perhaps —" Roderick tried to contribute, calling from the shadows, but Dougie cut him a fiery glare.

"Ye must *haud yer wheest!* 'Tis your fault that Hamish is senseless, perchance dying, in some run-down hut! If ye had nay let the lad go, Hamish would be here with us now!"

"My fault?" Roderick began to rise, his old bones creaking with the effort, but he was not about to permit this hothead to speak to him without respect. Angus Og, seeing Roderick's efforts, held up a hand, giving him pause.

"Dougie, why did ye go t'the comfort woman's? Isn't the MacNally lad her man now?"

"Why do ye think, my Laird?" At least Dougie kept his respectful tone when it truly mattered. "To find comfort, aye, and t'run off the MacNally. He may be naught but an exiled rat, yet we still dinna ken his intentions. He has treated ye disrespectfully, disobeyed a direct order — he can no' be trusted. Ye may no' see that, my Laird, but living with kinsmen of ill repute on the borderlands of another clan disloyal to the Bruce? 'Tis all too much of a coincidence, my Laird. As your seneschal, I would feel better if the lad was dealt with."

Angus held his pounding head in his hands, trying to pretend one of his most trusted officers did not just go behind his back, confront someone he was told to ignore, and then get his own good-son injured or killed in the process. In truth, he began to question the seneschal's sanity.

Cutting his amber gaze to Roderick, the Laird searched for help, advice, anything to solve this impasse. Roderick shrugged. So much for the sage advice from the old man. Angus Og returned his attention to the impassioned young man before him. And though he did not see Alistair MacNally as a problem per se, especially after discussions with both Roderick and the parish priest, chaos seemed to have followed the lad all the way to the isle. That could not be denied. And to have someone attack his good-son? Well, that did need to be dealt with, as Dougie said.

"I can see your point. And 'twas the woman who attacked Hamish?" Angus Og needed confirmation.

Even in the throbbing fog of his brain, the presence of the comfort woman and her sisters, for lack of a better word, did not sit well with Angus Og and never had. Not only was Lioslaith MacDonald a woman of ill-repute and a stain on the MacDonald name, her sister and the MacRuaidhrí woman she lived with were reputed to be witches. A trio of abominations against God, Angus Og had always believed. However, as long as they lived on the margins of their land, the borders of the MacRuaidhrí's, then Angus thought they could be left well enough alone.

The last few months, though, had shown him differently.

Lioslaith was washing Hamish's hair when they returned, his wet russet locks almost black in the dim firelight. The water in the pail was low, but Lioslaith didn't slow her ministrations to the unconscious man. Panic rose steadily in her chest, fluttering like a rogue butterfly. She managed to tamp it down as she focused on the man, but it was still there.

How had everything gone so wrong? Just as she was finding happiness with Alistair, for the first time in years, and now this? Lioslaith looked over at her dear Rowan, the blessed child still playing in the corner by the table, keeping to herself.

The bairn was so good, so dear, Lioslaith feared upsetting the tranquil balance of the girl's life.

Lioslaith was so like Rowan as a young girl. She had many dreams, when still playing with Muira on the rocky grasses, that she would find a husband, have a family, raise children. She dreamed of the life as a wife of an island Scot. Now she was nothing more than a fallen woman frightened for her daughter. What manner of life was that for the wee bairn?

In the midst of her self-pity, Alistair entered with both Muira and Alisa. Muira's face was dour with concern. Surely, Alistair explained what happened, but Lioslaith feared the fretful thoughts that Muira would turn over in her mind. As the older sister, she took on the mantle of watching over little Lioslaith — even as adults, she was looking over her, protecting her, and now Rowan. Muira took on too much, Lioslaith believed, and she did not want the trials of her life to intrude on Muira more than they already had.

Bracing herself for a confrontation, Lioslaith explained to Muira that this time, *she* would take all the blame for the near-dead man in her bed. Rowan would live with her sister, and Alistair could strike out on his own, find his way without her. Muira just clicked her tongue and waved off her words, taking charge of the situation again.

Lioslaith regarded the bleeding man on the bedding. The MacDonalds would want retribution for this offense. She hung her head, resting back on her heels as Alisa assumed Hamish's care.

The only sound in the room was the light chatter between Muira and Rowan. Alisa spread out several herbs, mixing them with a bit of water to make a poultice to lay upon the man's head. She pushed his tartan to the side and laid her ear on his chest, listening to his breathing. The man's chest rose and fell in a steady cadence, his breathing deep. Alisa didn't fear for his health, but if he didn't wake . . .

Tipping the water pail to collect the remaining water with the cloth, Alisa raised imploring eyes to Lioslaith.

"Do ye have another bucket of water?"

Lioslaith shook her head. Alistair stepped forward, clasping the bucket.

"Give me a second bucket, too. I will collect water from the stream while ye care for him."

Lioslaith grabbed the second bucket off the hearth, and her icy gaze spoke of her concern just as loudly as her words.

"Hurry back, Alistair."

He kissed the top of her head. "I will, my brilliant love."

A small smile tugged at the side of her nervous lips, and he returned it as he marched out into the cold evening. He had never spoke the word "love" to her before, and even in the midst of catastrophe, her heart fluttered at the endearment.

Snow swirled in the air as Alistair picked his way over the frozen rocks to the stream. The brackish water barely flowed, and the banks of the stream were coated in a thin sheet of ice. Balancing himself between the mucky grasses and a slick rock, he dipped the buckets into the freely running water. Picking his way up the bank, he made slow progress as he headed back to Lioslaith's cottage.

It wasn't until the small croft came into clear view that he saw the horses collected before the house. Every nerve in Alistair's body alighted with dread.

He stepped behind some low brush, watching the horrific events unfold from his darkened hiding space behind the brush. A chord deep inside screamed at him to intervene, to step forward and take accountability with Lioslaith and her sisters. He hated himself for his cowardice.

At the same time, perhaps his cowardly ways would work in their benefit. Surely, he would be of no use if he too was arrested, dragged off and thrown, yet again, in the MacDonald dungeons. Prudence won out, and he remained rooted in his vantage point.

The noise of their activity carried on the frosty night air, making this contemptible situation even worse. Lioslaith's hair shone like its own bright moon as she was herded outside with Muira and Alisa. From this distance, the only way to tell the difference between the two sisters was their height, with Muira standing scarcely a thumb's length taller than her sister.

Why were they taking Muira? Or Alisa? His brain puzzled as he watched all three, hands bound in bristling rope, led to the collection of horses. The giant, blonde MacDonald man's booming voice directed his men as they corralled the women. Another man approached the horses, the limp figure of Hamish draped over his shoulder. He placed the figure over the saddle of a steed and climbed onto the saddle himself. Then, mounting his horse in one swift movement, the blond MacDonald man rode off, his parade of kinsmen, Lioslaith, and her sisters right behind.

Alistair waited, his breath small, white puffs in the cold, watching his woman, his hope for the future, the only people, it seemed, who gave him a second chance, be herded off like crass criminals. He could not permit this clan to take away his new chance at life, this woman who not only brought him back from the brink of death but helped him find his heart at the same time.

Only then did he realize he didn't see Rowan with the women. Where was the lassie?

With a bucket in each hand, he scrambled to the croft, keeping his eyes on the trail the MacDonald took back to the keep. He barged through he door, searching for Rowan.

"Aye, lassie. They are gone," he called out in a soft tone. "Where are ye, within?"

A sly movement caught his eye, and he saw her pale head peek up from behind her mother's bedding. His whole body quivered with blessed relief at the sight of her tiny form.

"I hid," she whispered in her little voice. Alistair reached across the bedding to pluck her from the narrow space between the pallet and the wall.

"Aye, ye did, little lass," he replied. He sat her on the bedding next to him. "But now I need ye t'do a bit more. I have t'find your mother. Can ye stay here, stay hidden if ye hear anything amiss? I will return shortly."

"Are ye going t'get mam?" she asked, her innocent blue eyes tugging at his heart.

"Aye," he answered with surety. He made a promise to himself with his promise to Rowan. "I will see that your mam returns. But t'do that, I need ye t'be a good lassie, stay in the house, stay hidden. Aye?"

The child nodded her fair head, and Alistair leaned over to kiss the top of it, just as he had done to her mother. These precious women in his life, these gifts that he had been granted, he was not about to let anyone take that from him. He had lost far too much.

He grabbed his heavy, forested tartan off the hook by the door, and with one last look back at wee Rowan atop the bedding, he secured the door and went off after his heart.

'Twas not a far distance to the MacDonald keep, Lioslaith knew, but to cover the distance in winter, with the icy wind blowing at her, stepping over the frozen earth, the walk was longer and harder than she ever recalled. Behind her, Muira remained stoic. Lioslaith's ire peaked again when she thought of her sister stepping forward, claiming to be Lioslaith, claiming to have knocked the MacDonald man senseless.

And Lioslaith knew why she did it. 'Twas how they got into mischief as children. They could pass as *leathon* sisters, and oft did so to avoid trouble or confuse kinsmen. Now, Muira used it to hide Lioslaith and her actions, taking that mantle upon herself as she always did, protecting little Lioslaith. Uncertain as to who was who, the MacDonald men took them both, defeating Muira's noble intentions.

Poor Alisa, however, was also caught up in the chaos. Once the MacDonald's saw Hamish, with Alisa tending his gaping wound covered in a mysterious poultice, 'twas all they needed to claim witchcraft and sweep away all the women, Alisa included. Lioslaith could hear Alisa struggling as they marched, and Lioslaith's heart went out to the woman who had done nothing more than befriend Lioslaith, love Muira, and help her raise Rowan. Alisa would nary survive an accusation of witchcraft, not again. So many rumors already circled about her consorting with the devil, all the clan needed was one more excuse to try and have her hanged. Lioslaith shuddered at the thought. Was that the fate for all of them?

Lioslaith hung her head lower as she walked, both against the wind and in shame. 'Twould seem she brought naught but disgrace to her sister and Alisa. Then to stumble upon Alistair and with him came a light into her life when she thought there would not be one again. Now she would certainly lose Alistair as well.

And Rowan? What would happen to her bairn? Any scandal with Lioslaith would reflect poorly on her. And who would raise the lass, with her gone?

She felt she may swoon under the weight of these worries, until a tug pulled at the rope from behind. Lioslaith looked over her shoulder at her sister. Muira's silvery-blue eyes sparkled brighter than the stars, and she gave Lioslaith a gentle bow of her head — her way of letting Lioslaith know that everything would end up as it should, a movement Lioslaith was intimately familiar with. But this time, Lioslaith feared, everything would not end up as it should.

As soon as they arrived at the foreboding stronghold, Dougie led the horses to the rear of the keep, all but dragging the women into the dank lower cells. Frost crept along the stone and the iron bars, furry white against the dark rock. Lioslaith pressed a finger against the stone as they walked, watching the white fuzz drop away, freezing her fingertip. Her heart was just as icy toward these men of her clan.

The narrow cell was barely large enough for one man, let alone three women, and they were cramped in the cell. 'Twas better that way, Lioslaith realized, watching the snow blow in through the window. They would stay warmer if they huddled together.

Dougie and the rest of the men were silent the entire time, slamming the door as they departed.

Dougie left his men in the main hall and scouted out Angus Og to inform him of the events of the night. He found the Laird slouched in his chambers, brooding by the fire. His heavy scarlet robe reflected the flames dancing in the hearth. Looking almost reposed in prayer, with his hands folded atop his large belly, Angus Og acknowledged Dougie's entrance. Dougie closed the door quietly.

"My Laird," Dougie kept his robust voice just above a whisper. "We have the women in the cells below."

Angus Og slurped a drunken swig from a mug of spiced mead, then wiped his beard with one sleeve.

"Hamish had some strange balm slathered on his head, and a few of the men suspect witchcraft. What, with their past . . ."

Angus Og raised his arm, waving off the suggestion. "Do ye think such a thing, Dougie?" He sounded as tired as he looked.

Dougie leaned his long frame against the door. "I dinna ken, Laird. But I think it bears consideration."

Angus Og lifted a scraggly eyebrow at his seneschal. "Consideration," he repeated. "Aye, consideration. On the morrow, I will send for Father Stewart, and most likely a priest from Trinity Temple t'assist him. Perchance they can figure out what we must do."

The thought of a Trinity priest sent a chill down Dougie's backside. He had heard stories about witch hunts, but sending for a high-ranking priest from Trinity? Those priests oft made up their minds for a guilty verdict before even seeing the woman in question. Would that same thing happen here? Should they not resign themselves to the local priest?

"See if Rodrick is awake, aye?"

"Nay, I dinna ken that he is. The man's door was secured when I came here."

"Mmm," Angus Og responded, gulping at his mead.

"Do ye think sending for a Trinity priest is the right thing t'do?"

Did he want to be responsible for the death of three women? Dougie's previous convictions against the comfort woman, her sisters, and the exile, flew from his head when he imagined the havoc a Trinity priest could wreak. As much as he hated to admit a mistake, perchance his zealotry regarding the exile had gone too far.

"I will speak to Roderick, but I think ye are correct. It bears merit. Given their history."

Angus Og's head began to sag under the weight of the mead, and Dougie exited on silent feet. He could hope the old Laird would sleep hard and not recall the conversation, thus keeping the Trinity priests on the western shores.

CHAPTER FOURTEEN

Dangerous Accusations

THE NIGHT PASSED COLD and long for Lioslaith. Curled up tightly against Muira, Lioslaith shivered with her sister and Alisa under the single length of plaid Muira had the good sense to grab as they were hustled out of the croft. Muira always seemed to have such good sense, and where did it lead her? Lioslaith despised that her older sister felt the need to keep Lioslaith as her charge, looking out for her all of her life. Now, at the height of this madness, Muira was swept up because of her strong resemblance to Lioslaith and her utmost obligation to protect her.

"Why do ye think they called us witches?" Alisa asked. "They ken I use herbs and poultices for healing. I am a healer, nay a witch! This they well ken."

"Think ye they care?" Muira responded in her wry tone. "The MacDonalds have always disliked us, only suffering us because of Lioslaith's placating vocation and your connection t'the MacRuaidhrís. Which, I may add," her voice became, if possible, even drier, "has nay helped keep that relationship a sound one, aye?"

"The animosity between the MacDonalds and MacRuaidhrís has gone on long before we were involved," Lioslaith pointed out. "But I ken your point. The MacDonalds will use any excuse to keep their odds with MacRuaidhrís."

"Do ye think they will help us?" Muira questioned to Alisa, who twisted her lips up in response.

"I dinna ken. If my sister has any say, then aye, we can count on an army descending on the MacDonalds. But if she does no' ken what has trespassed here this eve . . ." Alisa let the words hang in the air, causing the women to shiver for a reason other than the cold.

"If we can somehow show that all this is Dougie's manipulation, that his own pride in thinking ye belong t'him," Muira told Lioslaith, "then we can perchance prevent any further accusation of witchery."

"I dinna ken how they could think 'twas witchcraft," Alisa interrupted. "As a healer, I must pray to God, I recited the Gospel names, as the priest would. Father Stewart even taught me some of the prayers I recite! If the russet man were awake, surely he would attest to that . . ."

"We have to hope the man wakes. And I am certain that Dougie heard ye recite the Gospel names as well," Muira said. "We were both close enough t'hear ye. I dinna ken what is in the man's head, Elle," Muira shifted her frosty gaze to Lioslaith, "but the man is obsessed with ye, 'twould seem. He does no' care what Alisa recited."

"We will ken on the morrow what will happen. Perchance Hamish will come t'his senses and open his eyes," Lioslaith hoped out loud. "Or Dougie will."

<hr/>

A strange crunching sound drifted in through the frosty window. Their faces turned in unison to the sound and mirrored the same shock at the dark-haired face that peered in.

"Alistair!" Lioslaith exclaimed, throwing back the tartan and risking the cold to scamper to the window. "What are ye doing here? Is wee Rowan well?"

"Aye, she is fine. I have her at the croft and told her I would come rescue ye."

THE EXILE OF THE GLEN

Lioslaith's moonlight hair glistened as she shook her head. "Nay, Alistair. They would just as soon throw ye in here with us. Dougie has a fierce vengeance against ye."

"Aye, that I kent already," Alistair agreed, his breath blowing in gentle, white puffs. "But I ken get ye out of the cell, take ye —"

"Where?" Lioslaith asked, Muira and Alisa nodding at her question. "The isle is a small rock in the middle of the sea. They would surely find us and hang us without recourse. And ye, and perchance my wee Rowan." The depth of her pain shone in her icy tears.

"My family will care for Rowan," Alisa promised with surety in her sweet voice. Lioslaith pursed her lips.

"I can no' risk ye or anyone else." Her eyes flicked to her sister, and Alistair caught her meaning.

"That is all the more reason I should go t'them. I can take the blame! Christ's blood, Lioslaith! They hate me enough as 'tis! Then ye and your sisters can leaved this dungeon, live in peace —"

"Is that what ye would call this, Alistair? Peace? Being outcast by my own kin? Fearing for my dear Rowan? For my sisters? At least with ye . . ."

"With me, what?"

"I thought I had a chance," her voice broke. "I could shed my ill reputation, provide a real life for my daughter, mayhap have more bairns." She dropped her chin to her chest, embarrassed at the depth of her emotion. "But this night has shown me that can no' happen. I will do all I can t'save my sisters and my daughter, Alistair. Please understand that."

Alistair's dark green eyes pleaded with Lioslaith, shimmering from his darkened silhouette, trying to tell her all he could not find the words for. To tell her that he finally found his home, the life he wanted with her, and though he may not say otherwise, he would never allow her to suffer for the absurd behavior of others.

"Alistair!" Alisa called to him, her dainty brown head barely peeping out from the tartan. He shifted his intense gaze from Lioslaith to Alisa. "Go to the MacRuaidhrís. Tell them what has happened. They will see ye and assist ye if ye mention my name."

Nodding once in response, he turned his attention back to Lioslaith, reaching his hand through the frozen bars. Standing on her toes, Lioslaith was able to capture his cold hand in hers. He spoke to her, keeping his voice low against the icy wind.

"I love ye, Lioslaith. I will find a way out of this for ye, whatever it takes."

Even amid the freezing cold, a rush of warmth flooded Lioslaith at his words. Long had it been since her heart was open, and this stranger stumbled into her home and her heart in one fell swoop. She squeezed his fingers.

"And I, ye, Alistair. Be safe."

"Ye and your sisters as well. And here." He unwrapped his own heavy plaid from his shoulders, dropping it through the window. "I will be warm enough without the extra plaid, but I fear for your health if ye dinna have it."

Lioslaith wanted to protest, especially since he had been near death only a short time ago, but her shivering conquered her protests. Grateful for the extra wrap, she pulled the tartan, still warm from his body, through the window.

"I will come for ye, soon, Lioslaith," he promised, then turned and ran off, afraid that if he stayed long, he would never leave, and they would find his frozen body stuck to the rock in the morn.

Silence descended in the cell at Alistair's departure. Sleep slowly overcame the three women huddling together under the tartans against the aching cold of the night.

⇻⇻⇉ ⫷⫷⫷⫶

Alistair raced back to Lioslaith's croft, hoping he was not too late, his chest aching and his heart beating out of his ribs. He prayed that the lass stayed hidden. He could not imagine the MacDonalds would return to take dear Rowan, but when an accusation of witchcraft was thrown about, people, islanders in particular, could lose all their senses. The sins of the mother could be inflicted upon the daughter.

Then he had to figure out who would aid him in rescuing Lioslaith and her sisters. He was a nobody on this island, less than a nobody, an assumed spy no less. The odds of anyone listening to his request ran against him. Even Alisa's claim to the MacRuaidhrís seemed a slim option. Most likely, he would end up in a dirt-hole prison, just like Lioslaith. What good would he be to anyone then?

As he ran through the clearing, Alistair noted a thin film of light around the rough wood door and slowed his pace. A noble steed, tied to the lean-to, plucked at the slender grasses sticking up from the patchy snow. Someone was already in the house with the girl, and Alistair's chest clenched with panic. Was it the MacDonalds? Did they beat him here? Was it one of Lioslaith's men, looking for *comfort*?

Creeping close to the cottage, he grasped the axe from the chopping block near the lean-to. A snuffling from the goats spooked him, and he shook his head, refocusing his attention on the door. It was not fully latched, and Alistair was able to push the door ajar enough to glance around inside, his axe at the ready.

Warmth and quiet welcomed him, and low, feminine voices carried from near the hearth. He opened the door farther, peering around the edge to see who chatted at the hearth. A richly dressed, light haired woman sat on the low stool by the fire, Rowan on the bedding near her. The bairn's voice was soft, amicable, not frightened in the least. Keeping the axe by his side, Alistair stepped into the room.

Rowan's eyes lit up like a bright summer sky. The elegant woman, on the other hand, whirled up in a burst, a knife glinting in her hand. Uncertain of the woman's intent, Alistair dropped the axe to the floor in time to catch Rowan as she flung herself against his leg.

"Ali, ye've returned! I tole the lady here that ye would be back, but where is mam? Did she nay come wi' ye?" The sprightly lass chattered non-stop. Alistair lifted her up and tousled her hair, never taking his vigilant glare from the woman and her fighting stance.

"And who is the lady?" Alistair put the question to Rowan in a kindly voice but waited for the woman to answer.

"I am Christina MacRuaidhrí. Does that name mean anything to ye?"

Alistair inclined his head with caution. Of course, he recalled his short time at the MacRuaidhrí keep, and Alisa's command to seek out the clan. Christina pursed her lips and stepped forward, stabbing the knife into the satchel around her waist.

"Ye ken Muira?"

This time Alistair bobbed his head. "Aye, Lioslaith's sister."

"Her woman, Alisa, is my bastard sister. Och, do I detest that word. She is my lifelong friend and confidant. The best person I have kent in my life. I had heard some of the MacDonald grumblings. I came here to find them to see if she needed help."

"Ye heard?" Confusion spread over his eyes. How could she have heard anything?

"I have my ways," she said cryptically, waiting for Alistair to answer.

"Aye, that she does -- need help. Lioslaith was taken wi' Muira and Alisa. They are imprisoned in a dark hole, to be tried as witches by the MacDonalds."

All the color in Christina's face drained away, leaving her pale and stumbling. She clutched the edge of the table. "All of them? Alisa, too? How did the lass remain?"

Alistair turned to Rowan. "She hid, when her mam was removed."

He set the wisp of a girl down, and she scrambled over the bedding she shared with her mother, tucking herself deep in the side against the wall. She threw a tartan over her head and all but disappeared.

Christina turned her attention from the lass to Alistair. "So, the feckin' Mac-Donalds have all three of them? Did ye hear their claim against them?"

"Nay, but I did see them in their cell. I was outside, and the back of the keep is loosely guarded at best. Lioslaith says they were accused o'witchcraft, but I am certain they levied more against Muira and Alisa. I believe Lioslaith got caught up, as the MacDonalds could nay tell the two sisters apart."

Christina sighed heavily at the implication. "Muira and Alisa do dabble with herbs, and incantations, to be sure," Christina admitted with a sigh, "but they were most likely accused due to something that happened years ago, and 'acause of their, um, relationship with one another, ye ken?"

Alistair slowly nodded again. "A lover relationship, aye?"

Christina's eyes widened at his guess, then she slumped down on the stool, bowing her head in confirmation. When she raised it to look at Alistair, he could see the fear stamped across her features as she blinked back tears that threatened to fall.

"Alisa was always different. I ken that. So pretty as a lass, but nary a care for the lads. Always close t'me or off in the scrub or inlets, searching for plants or wee animals. She wanted t'be a Druid apprentice, ye ken? Then she met Muira, who was so like Alisa, like two shells of the same clam — they matched. Together, they made one whole. They found a croft on the border of MacRuaidhrí land, where they could live together and still be close t'Muira's sister. Help her with the lass, aye?" Alistair continued to nod in understanding.

"Alisa's relationship with me, as her sister, she had some protection. But on MacDonald land, one misstep . . ." Christina let the innuendo hang in the air.

Witches were either hanged right away if they confessed, Alistair knew, or drowned by trial if they did not. In the trial, the priests would bind their hands and feet and toss them in the loch. If she floated to the top, she breathed life-giving air but died as a witch. If she sunk, she would drown, but at least she wasn't a witch. And this was only if the priests did not confirm their suspicions before arriving, in which case they all could be tortured before burning at the stake. A fearsome chill passed over Alistair as he considered the options.

He rubbed his hand over his damp hair, not wanting to make matters worse, but he needed to be honest with this woman.

"I fear I may no' have helped the situation, as Lioslaith has recently, um, halted her encounters with the men."

Christina rolled her eyes. "Aye, that I also ken. Och, that would anger some MacDonalds, t'be sure. Then add to that they did nay care for two women living together, the MacDonalds. And Lioslaith's and Alisa's history with the clan — the MacDonalds would find any excuse to bring them low. 'Tis a false claim of witchcraft."

Christina's light brown eyes caught Alistair's, burdened with sadness.

"Alisa said if they come for her, t'make sure Lioslaith and the lass were safe. But Lioslaith is no' safe, and I will no' permit my beloved sister to die at the hands of insipid monsters."

"Alisa said if I could get word t'the MacRuaidhrís, they would help. That would be ye, I presume. What is to be done?" Alistair asked in a subdued voice, noting that Rowan left her hiding spot.

Her tousled fair head popped up from her bedding, her eyes wide with the interest only small children can have when eavesdropping inappropriately on the conversations of adults.

Christina clutched her head in her hands. "Aye, they shall. I have an idea, but I dinna ken if 'twill work." She shrugged, talking as if to herself. "Weel, it should. And ye will need to do something to help."

Alistair held out his hand as Rowan scrambled off the bed toward him, tucking herself into his arms. His heart quickened at the thought of any danger coming to her. When the word "witchcraft" was thrown about, the fevered craze could overtake even the most rational of people, turning them into a frenzied mob. Child or no, anyone could fall victim to a witch-hunt. The thought of Lioslaith in that dirt pit prison was enough to make his chest ache; the prospect of wee Rowan joining her? Alistair near swooned like a girl. Of course, he would do anything for Lioslaith and Rowan.

Rowan cuddled her head into the curve of Alistair's neck, slipping a pale, dirty thumb into her mouth, then just as quickly pulled it out.

"Ali," she asked in her still-baby voice, "Mama's coming home with ye soon?"

"Aye, my sweet," he lied easily, patting her fine hair in a comforting manner. She relaxed into his chest all the more, her thumb taking residence again between her lips.

Christina's gaze never departed from the pair, her whiskey brown eyes fiery and intense, a plan taking form behind them. Alistair's own eyes flicked at the woman who was now standing in the center of the cottage he called home. This strange world that had been forced upon him, the cold winds that swept over stony glens and were tinged with sea salt; the fairy-like Lioslaith who had opened her home, her arms, and her heart to him; this ethereal child he cradled in his arms, this was all his home, his life now.

That petty revenge could rob him of the purest happiness he had found in his life consumed him with impotent rage that he hid from the woman and the child. At the risk to his own life, he would invade the MacDonald keep alone and carry Lioslaith out on his back, but what of her sister? Of Alisa? What would stop retribution against this tiny lass that was the daughter of his heart?

He would take any risk, consider any option to save his new family.

"What's your idea?" he asked. Christina smiled.

Christina reached her hands out for Rowan as Alistair shifted her in his grasp. Cuddling the lass close, Christina dipped her face into the child's hair, inhaling the baby-sweet scent only young children exude.

"Ye will have to trust me, as I must trust in ye. We are family now, ye ken? Through my sister and Lioslaith's, and, if I dinna miss my mark, ye would to all in your power t'save it?"

Alistair had not realized his heart's desire showed so freely upon his features, and he closed his face, narrowing his eyes, trying to hide this seemingly unmanly affect. Christina waved it off.

"'Tis of no accord. But what I am saying is, I can take Rowan t'my family. They will guard her with their very lives, as she is of MacRuaidhrí blood, if weakly."

Relief flooded Alistair's face, the fine lines of stress and fear lessening visibly. Christina's face softened a bit in response.

"Aye, 'tis a fine plan. Better than leaving the child here where she's exposed."

Christina nodded and continued. "I will send the MacRuaidhrí kinsmen to the MacDonald stronghold on the morn. Though they will nay admit it, they adore Alisa as much as I do. They will keep Angus Og and his men occupied and hopefully away from any priests. And I ken someone, one who is almost more powerful than the pope here on the isle. I can bring this man t'the MacDonald stronghold, and we will have our family returned t'us. But I must ride t'the MacRuaidhrí's first, and 'tis late. Then we have to ride back here. We need time."

Alistair barely heard the rest of her words. Was there a Monsignor or Bishop close by? Mayhap at the Trinity Temple he heard spoken of in reverent tones? Or did she mean her brother, the Laird MacRuaidhrí? Did he have the power to command a priest?

"Och," Christina tapped her hand against his chest. "Are ye listening?"

Alistair's hazy green eyes shifted back to Christina, who was probably thinking him dense and regretting having to come to him for aid.

"Aye, aye, I'm listening. Do ye mean for me t'ride t'this man? Or—" His face scrunched up in confusion about the role he must play in her machinations.

"Nay, I would no' ask ye t'do such. I need ye t'ride back to the MacDonalds, request a conference with Laird Angus Og."

Alistair nearly clutched his chest like an old crone. Go back to the Laird himself? What in God's name was the crazed woman thinking?

"They will throw me in the pit with them! I dinna ken the Laird likes me overmuch. His seneschal nay a'tall! What good would it do?" Panic rose as he spoke.

Christina clicked her tongue at him, like he was a child. "Nay, I dinna think they will do that. If you request a formal audience, especially as the nephew of a Highland Laird, a kinsman, then I expect the MacDonalds will show ye some respect. They let ye free the last time, aye?"

Alistair scoffed. "Aye, say that happens as ye claim. What should I do then? Beg for mercy? I can no' think of how that would be received."

Christina shook her head, hugging Rowan close, placing a fair hand over the lassie's ear. "Dinna be a fool," she hissed at him. "If ye come in lieu of a Laird, ye must behave as one. Argue their case — Lioslaith's at least. Explain she has a family, a child, that she attends the kirk regularly—"

"But she does no' —" Alistair started to say.

"'Tis of no consequence! They dinna ken! Tell them she says her prayers, that she is a godly woman, whatever ye need to say t'argue her case! And if ye can do the same for Muira and Alisa, then do so! Just keep talking! Do no' shut up for anything. The longer ye can argue, the more time ye buy the MacRuaidhrís and me t'get back with the person who can assist us. Pray that we can arrive 'afore the priest from Trinity, should they send for him. If we can do that, I promise ye, we can save Lioslaith, her sister, and mine."

Alistair's brain struggled to keep up with the conniving woman. Keep talking? After being told to shut up by his family as of late, he welcomed the opportunity. But save Alisa? Alistair had to bite back his response to that. If they believed her to be a witch, well, then she was a witch. From what Alistair had seen in his time here on the island, he could not deny that. No one, save the pope, could stop *that* trial.

And who was this powerful man that Christina believed could intervene? Surely not the pope, as he was much farther than a day's ride from the Outer Hebrides, for certain. Alistair rubbed his face with his hands. The woman's plan appeared foolish. How could they succeed?

"Fine, ye have me convinced," Alistair lied to her. "Since ye seem to have a strategy, when do ye suggest I depart for the MacDonalds?"

Looking satisfied with his response, she worked her way around the room, gathering a few items Rowan might need while she was away, speaking with her back to him.

"Nay later than early morn, ye ken? The MacDonalds need the day t'have the priests come in and evaluate. That should no' happen until the afternoon or tomorrow, if fortune abides with us. The ride will no' take ye too long."

Alistair cleared his throat to interrupt politely. "I dinna have a horse."

"Oh." That one detail was lost on Christina, who waved it away. "Well, then ye should leave at daybreak, perchance afore sunrise, for that walk, ye ken?"

CHAPTER FIFTEEN

Finding God's Plan

CHRISTINA DID NOT STAY the night and left rather abruptly with Rowan wrapped against the cold. Her mare was swift, and she assured Alistair that Rowan would be securely bedded in the MacRuaidhrí stronghold before the moon peaked in the nighttime sky. At Rowan's behest, Alistair promised to check on the owl in the barn, then placed one more kiss on Rowan's delicate head, so much like her mother's, and watched them ride off into the swirling snow.

He hated leaving Lioslaith in the dungeons for the eve, but Christina's option seemed the best one. As for his own night, Alistair slept only in patchy naps, waking often to worry about Lioslaith and consider what he could possibly say to the MacDonald Laird in her defense. In the deep recesses of night's blackness, Alistair recalled the words of the kindly priest who offered him absolution from his sins in exchange for penance. God's path, it appeared to Alistair, was blatantly clear, and perchance his opportunity to live his moment of atonement — save Lioslaith and her sisters as she saved him — was at hand.

Alistair woke with dread in his chest as the sun crested the horizon. In his most feeble attempt to make an impression, Alistair donned his scarlet and forest plaid gifted from Muira and Alisa and his leather belt and sporran — the only remaining finery left to his name. With the thick tartan wrapped snuggly about him, Alistair felt presentable enough to command a conference with the Laird. Perchance there was something to Christina's assertions that he could stand as a kinsman and demand respect, exile though he was. Not for the first time, Alistair sent up a silent prayer the MacRuaidhrí woman's strategy would work.

The only piece that was missing from his Highland regalia was his broadsword, stripped from him by the MacKenzies when they dragged him back to his uncle back in the Highlands, giving to James MacNally all the horrid details of Alistair's actions. Since Alistair didn't feel himself worthy to bear a sword yet anyway, it was probably for the best he lacked that marker of home and honor.

Sticking his small dirk into his belt as a replacement weapon, Alistair left the warmth of the cottage early, when the sun's light was barely a pink line through the frosty clouds. His legs ached from his misadventures the day before over the frozen, rocky landscape. He pushed the pain aside, feeling weak for even putting thought to it when his dear Lioslaith lay asleep in the cold cells of the MacDonald keep, her future uncertain.

The frigid air helped him keep a brisk pace as he ventured to the MacDonald keep in the early morning. He could only hope that he arrived at the keep before the Laird sent a messenger to the priests at Trinity Temple. Lioslaith and her sisters could not be subjected to the harsh dictates and delusions of grandeur that accompanied high ranking priests or worse, a bishop. Better to deal with such ludicrous accusations at a local level, to be sure. He had heard tell it ended so much better that way. Father Stewart appeared to be an intelligent, thoughtful priest, which would benefit the women. He could be a token of reason in a field of fearful MacDonalds.

Before reaching the entry guideposts of the yard, Alistair clipped to the rear of the keep, avoiding the half-sleeping guards. 'Twas early enough that many of the MacDonald men seemed still asleep, or even in their cups, the drinking of the previous evening lasting far into the early hours of morn. He prayed that Lioslaith and her sisters had been safe throughout the night.

A MacDonald man stumbled around the low brush near the base of the stone keep, and Alistair pressed himself against the icy stones to avoid being seen. That man appeared to be nursing the remnants of drink from the night before, as he held his head with one hand while relieving himself into the snow with the other. Alistair held his breath in his hiding spot until the man finished, and the crunching steps on the snow told him the man had walked away.

Alistair moved to the barred window where sunrise granted him a brighter view of the women in their cell than he had the evening before. Huddled together, they shivered against the cold. He leaned his face as far into the cell as the bars would permit.

"Lioslaith!" He tried to keep his voice low enough so only the women would hear him. Lioslaith's blonde head popped out of the coverings, her sister's right after.

"Alistair!"

She didn't want hope to rise in her chest — she kent what she and her sisters were up against. But to see the man here, a beacon of hope, a small bubble of faith started to form. Lioslaith scrambled from the bedding over to the window and clasped his outstretched hand.

"What do ye ken?" she inquired.

"Weel, Alisa was nay wrong about her sister. She was in your cottage last night when I arrived."

Hearing her name, Alisa's sparrow-like head appeared from under the tartans. "Aye, she already heard?"

"Of a sort. She was coming t'visit ye?" Alistair dismissed the thought with a wave. "She says she kens how t'save ye, especially if we can work 'afore any priests arrive. The local priests will be more malleable, ye ken?"

All three women nodded. "Father Stewart is a good man, a goodly priest. And I ken Christina would have a plan. She's a powerful woman here on the isle." Pride overtook Alisa's voice as she spoke of her sister.

"Do ye ken who she speaks of? She claims t'ken someone powerful enough t'intervene."

Alisa shrugged but looked away, hiding her amber eyes. "I dinna ken for certain, so I would no' want to wager a guess."

Alistair had an idea that she did indeed know. The woman didn't lie well, but he let it slide as more pressing matters were at hand. The mysterious hero would make his appearance soon enough. Dipping his shaking hand into his sporran, Alistair pulled out a small, wrapped bundle.

"Here," he reached through the bars. "I dinna ken when ye will eat this day, or if ye ate yester eve. 'Tis only some bannocks."

Lioslaith accepted the biscuits gratefully, passing them over to Muira. She turned her nervous, crystal gaze back to Alistair.

"What are ye t'do now?"

"I am under strict orders by one powerful sister t'distract the MacDonald. Either prevent him from sending for the priests or to slow any intended actions the MacDonalds would take 'afore they arrive. I do no' ken what good 'twill do. The last few times I have tried to speak t'the Laird, he has done naught but send me away."

"Well, ye look fine in your clothing this morn, better than your earlier visits, most likely. Perchance he will entertain a longer audience with ye."

Alistair's cheeks, already pink from the cold, colored all the more at her compliment, and he gave Lioslaith a wink.

"Time for me t'try and talk my way t'the MacDonald Laird, *again*," he joked.

He leaned in through the bars, pressed a quick kiss onto her goose-pimpled hand, and marched off on his mission.

Rounding the front of the keep, Alistair saw the few men who were able to stand guard had slowly come to life, wiping the grains of sleep from their eyes and pissing away the night's ale. And they were on edge with the rumors of supposed witches being held in the keep. Alistair's arrival only increased their edginess. He held up his hands as he walked toward the long doors for the front hall, indicating he was of no danger to anyone.

A slender, young MacDonald man, puffing for all he was worth, advanced on Alistair, intercepting him before he reached the steps to the entryway.

"State your business, stranger." Alistair did not miss the inflection on the word "stranger." While the guard may not recall him, they were all wary this morn. Alistair certainly did not recognize the young MacDonald from his previous visits.

"I'm a distant kinsman, requesting an audience with your Laird."

Before he finished his statement, another kinsman, this one in a stained tunic and smelling of day-old fish approached, his hand on his sword.

"I ken who ye are, exile. What would the Laird want with ye?"

Annoyance rose in Alistair, and he wanted to respond with his usually abrasive manner but bit his tongue to keep himself in check. Acting pretentious would not give him the audience he needed this day. And he could not risk the Laird kicking him out on his backside again. Alistair hadn't come this far only to ruin all that he had managed to reap on the isle.

"Please, sir, 'tis in regard to Lioslaith and her sisters." His tone wavered when he said her name.

The MacDonald man spat on the ground, a gooey lump near Alistair's worn leather boot. "Aye, the witches, ye mean."

"Nay, I —" Alistair bit his lip, reigning in his bearing. "Please, announce my audience t'your Laird."

Keeping his hand on his sword, the MacDonald man looked Alistair up and down, then turned abruptly, leading Alistair toward the main doors of the keep. Alistair rolled his eyes heavenward, thanking God above that he was making progress in seeing the chieftain of the clan.

A rush of snow ushered Alistair through the doorway. The MacDonald closed the doors securely, then gestured to the exact same bench Alistair encountered on his first visit to the stronghold. Shaking his head at the absurdity of this situation, he perched on the edge of the bench as the mangy MacDonald disappeared into the recesses of the keep.

The house help had risen earlier, the raging fire in the hearth attesting to their steadfast attendance to the necessaries. Alistair moved closer to the fire to warm himself when Angus Og entered loudly and full of irritation.

"Really, lad. I'd naught expected to see ye in my hall yet again. I thought I'd made that clear. Ye are nay wanted here." His stout face wore a mask of frustration.

Alistair rose quickly, holding up his hands. "Please Laird MacDonald. A moment —"

"'Tis about the witches below?" Angus Og was nothing if not astute.

Alistair could see the old sage, Roderick, surveying the scene from the shadows beyond the hall, the blond seneschal poised directly in front of him. Alistair hoped the wisdom of the sage would carry the day. Surely, the old sage was not afeared of healers? Dougie, on the other hand, well, Alistair was certain the man would be a problem.

"Aye, but Laird, I feel 'tis presumptuous to call them witches —"

"What would ye call a woman who attacks men and uses strange potions on their injuries? Hamish still has no' regained his senses! Ye are fortunate ye are no' sharin' a cell with the women!"

"Nay, I—" Alistair began.

"What, ye did no' do it?" Dougie interrupted, stepping into the main hall next to his Laird. "Look at ye, leaving the women with the guilt of your actions! What manner of man are ye?" Dougie's fair features tinted with a flushed pink. He was spitting as his voice rose with his anger. His hand began to pull his sword from the scabbard.

"Dougie, that's quite enough." Roderick's calming voice carried over Dougie's vengeful crescendo. Angus Og stepped closer to Alistair.

"Why are ye here, lad? What do ye hope t'accomplish?"

"I would ask that ye err on the side of caution. Ye ken that Lioslaith is no' any witch, nay her sister. I would ask that ye reconsider these accusations of witchcraft 'afore ye send for a priest from Trinity."

"Are ye in any position t'judge a witch?" Angus Og queried. "I think nay. Ye are bewitched by her. I dinna believe ye are fit t'speak on her behalf."

Angus Og flicked his head toward Dougie, who nodded and retreated into the keep. He kept his gaze on Alistair as his seneschal departed.

"We shall first conference with the parish priest, find his opinion on judging the witches. They have killed a man 'afore today, and now my good-son lays in deep repose up in his chambers. I dinna think they will find a sympathetic audience here. But if our priest feels strongly enough, we will send a missive to the legates at Trinity."

Alistair pulled himself up to his full height. When he first arrived at the keep, he was recovering from illness, thin and sallow. This day, in stark contrast, his cheeks held the fullness of health, and regular meals and working at Lioslaith's croft had rebuilt his muscles. He more resembled the strong Highlander he had been in Scotland, before his fated trip across the Minch. He inhaled deeply, allowing his broad chest to expand, taking up more space and exerting his presence in this hall. He would not be shamed or turned away this time. Not when Lioslaith's life may depend on it.

"My Laird MacDonald," Alistair began, keeping his voice tempered, respectful. "I would ask —" But he was unable finish the thought.

Dougie appeared at the rear of the hall, the three women in tow behind him.

"Lioslaith!" Alistair called out, but Angus Og stepped between, blocking him. As they entered, Alistair noted both Dougie's smug expression, and Alisa leaning in toward Roderick. The old man stepped away to the steps leading to the upper chambers, and Alistair's heart sank as the most level-headed of all the MacDonalds left the hall.

Dougie threw the binds that held the women's hands to the rushes in front of the Laird, and Lioslaith fell to her knees with his action. Alistair raced forward to help her regain her feet, but Dougie unsheathed his sword, halting him where he stood.

"We have many crimes that we would levy against these women," Angus Og's voice was ominous, harrowing, and sent a shiver down Alistair's spine.

He wiped his hands across his MacDonald plaid. *How was he to do this?* Alistair thought dismally. *Who would listen to a disgraced exile aligned with supposed witches, no matter his finery?*

"We can begin with the potions of Lioslaith and Alisa," Angus Og continued, and he inclined his head at Dougie. The seneschal again departed, this time out the main doorway to the yard.

Alisa rolled her eyes, and Alistair marveled at how well she maintained her disposition. Anger, meanwhile, flared behind Muira's eyes, an impotent rage at the treatment of her sister and her lover. Fear was the only emotion Lioslaith exhibited — it shrouded her in a fog of despair. It pained Alistair to the depth of his soul to see her fear and have no recourse of how to help her. *Keep talking*, was all he could think.

"They are known to use such potions to heal the sick. But if that 'twere all, then we would no' be here today. Nay, her use of such potions has potentially entrapped my men. Ye see how Dougie, how the ill-fated Hamish, are with her? Yet ye want t'lie with her still, take her as your woman, even though she is used as such? A woman of ill-repute?"

Alistair mumbled under his breath. Angus Og cut his deep, intense gaze to him.

"What say ye?" The sneer in his voice was unmistakable.

"I said, she is no' just my woman. We are t'be wed. We are handfast."

The small crowd in the hall fell silent at the implication of Alistair's words. He hoped that playing on the man's emotions, showing repute for his dear Lioslaith, would speak some sense into these senseless accusations.

Angus Og barked out a laugh. "Ye think she has no' witched ye as well? Do ye think that ye could have a real marriage t'a woman such as this? One who gives herself t'any man for recompense?" Angus Og shook his head pityingly, clicking his tongue. "Oh, dear lad, your health may have returned, but nay your good sense."

A rumble of laughter from several other MacDonald men in the hall echoed in Alistair's ears. His own claims of endearment for Lioslaith had no effect, and Alistair's heart sank, if possible, even lower. 'Twould appear that Angus Og had made up his mind already.

Before the Laird could continue, a rustling at the doorway drew their attention, and Dougie entered, practically dragging the village priest behind him.

Father Stewart must have just awoken, for his vestments were twisted, damp at the bottom where the robe dragged through the snow. Flecks of mud stained the white, from the yard most likely, Alistair figured. The priest lacked a stole, making him seem almost naked, and the bewildered man's hair stood on end, as if he just rolled from his bed.

A moue of pity sparked through Alistair, replaced quickly with dismay, knowing Father Stewart's dictates could mean the worst for all three, Lioslaith in particular.

Only, he didn't believe that would happen. He turned his begging eyes to the priest, praying the man would have more sense than those collected in the hall. Out of respect, Alistair bowed his head briefly toward him and was brushed aside by the Laird.

"Father Stewart!" Angus Og's voice boomed once again, fairly dragging the priest off his feet to present him in front of Lioslaith and her sisters. "We need your counsel on a very serious matter!"

The priest hobbled over to Lioslaith, helping her rise from the rushes to stand with her sister.

"What transpires here, Angus?" he asked, confusion and alarm casting a shadow over his face.

"Only an accusation of witchcraft, Father Stewart!" the Laird announced with aplomb.

Alistair cut his hooded eyes to Dougie, who nodded in agreement with the Laird's proclamation. *Revenge is a frightening motivator*, Alistair kent that firsthand. His own vengeance landed him on this remote rock. He knew too well the lengths a man would go to in order to find vengeance when he believes himself wronged.

"What? These good women? I hardly think —" the priest started, but Angus would not permit him to finish.

"Ye ken what they have done years ago. If not the taller one, then the darker woman and Lioslaith. Ye ken Lioslaith's position here in the clan, one of horrid repute, and the illicit relationship between her sister and the witch? Priest, ye ken that the Bible says a woman will no' lay with another!"

"Well, in truth the Bible says —" Father Stewart started to say.

Angus Og interrupted, prompted by Dougie and desperate to show his power, and layered more accusations upon Lioslaith.

"And just last eve, my good Father, Lioslaith herself led my men t'her croft, using the witchy powers of her fairer sex, then when my man was at his weakest, she slew him! She lay a potion on his injury and chanted a curse. He lays dying now, up in my chambers!"

"He's no' dying —" Alisa began. Angus Og did not let her finish but silenced her with a backhand to the face. The loud smacking sound was deafening, drawing all to silence. Father Stewart recovered from his shock first.

"Laird MacDonald, there is nay cause for violence to these women!" the priest called out.

Angus Og raised his hand again, this time near Lioslaith, and without thinking, Alistair moved forward, forcing himself between the Laird and the women attending to Alisa's wounded cheek. To place his hand on the Laird again would surely cause more discord, but Alistair cared little for his own hide. He could not, would not, let this bear of a chieftain lay a hand on his woman. Planting his feet, he shoved Angus Og away from Lioslaith.

Dougie also reacted without thought, leaping at Alistair as he drew his sword.

A moment of panic passed through Alistair's chest as he grasped at the only weapon on his person — the small silver and agate crusted dirk smuggled from the Highlands. Here he was, bringing a knife to a sword fight, and Alistair had no doubt who would lose in the end. He felt like the wee David against the much larger Goliath.

Over the protests of the priest and the bound women, Dougie brought the sword down over his head. With a quick shift of his feet, Alistair moved under Dougie's arm, his only hope to stop the arm before the nicked broadsword came down on his head. He clasped the man's thick forearm, flicking his knife across the exposed skin in a long, bloody scrape.

Dougie squealed like a piglet and grabbed at his bloody arm. Keeping his grip on his sword, Dougie twisted to the side, the sharp blade following Alistair as he scrambled backwards. As Dougie thrashed it toward Alistair, the tip caught the tartan around Alistair's waist, cutting the fabric from him. Had he been one step closer . . .

Alistair had no time to recover as Dougie spun again, so agile for such an immense man, and hammered his sword down on the other side, nearly catching

Alistair's arm. Remaining low to the ground, Alistair tried to use the distance to his advantage when he heard a shout to his left. Risking a quick look, he watched as the priest slid a tattered sword across the stone to Alistair's hand. Without hesitation, he clasped the sword with a desperate grip and rolled himself around and upright, holding the sword in both hands before him. Finally, after months on this forsaken island, he became the Highlander he knew himself to be.

Though still shorter than the giant blond Scot with the bloodied arm, Alistair allowed a sense of strength and purpose to envelop him. He drew first blood, held his own with the giant, and if the hulking islander defeated him, at least Alistair fought for a noble cause.

"Are ye going t'come at me, ye dunderheid?" Alistair taunted. He hoped that rage would rout the man, making his fighting reckless and unfocused. Alistair knew how to fight dirty, and he would put that discredited trait to use. He would need every advantage.

Most of the crowd had withdrawn to the edges of the hall, allowing Alistair and Dougie room to maneuver as they fought. Only the priest, Lioslaith and her sisters, and the hefty Laird MacDonald stood closer to the fighting men.

"Ye think ye are a match t'me, wee laddie? Let a man teach ye how to fight!"

Dougie exploded toward Alistair as he spoke, hacking and thrashing with a speed that seemed impossible, and a heavy hand that vibrated within Alistair's bones with each strike against his sword. Tiring quickly, Alistair feared the truth of the man's words. Dougie stood half a head taller and had spent the last few months healthy, hale, and sharpening his skills, whereas Alistair only recently recovered from near death.

But Alistair didn't care. He would fight this monster that haunted his Lioslaith. If this ended up as the path God chose for him, so be it.

All these thoughts whipped through his mind as Dougie continued to pound at Alistair's sword. Fat drops of blood splattered as he moved, and Alistair didn't realize how much blood the man had lost until he noted Dougie's efforts softening. As he raised his sword in another barrage, Dougie's foot slipped in the blood pooling at his feet. He lost his precarious balance, falling hard on the blood-specked stones behind him. A collective gasp echoed in the hall.

God's path, indeed, Alistair said to himself, his anger rising uncontrollably. Other than random bruising, he had nary a wound marking his skin. As he stepped to the downed giant, he kicked the man's sword away, raising his own broadsword for what would be a decimating blow.

In his stance over Dougie, the broadsword upraised, Lioslaith saw him as the Highlander he was raised to be. Strong and formidable, with tawny hair and a powerful chest, he was the very image of the Highland warrior. *Her* Highlander. Her breath caught, and she held up her hand to halt him. "Alistair!" she called out in that soft yet commanding voice.

Pausing with his arms in the air, he took several deep breaths, allowing Lioslaith's voice to permeate his blood-thirsty fog. He dropped his sword to his side, and relief flooded Dougie's agonized face. Alistair spun around to where Lioslaith stood as she lifted a graceful hand to his cheek.

"'Tis no' worth it," she whispered, her alabaster skin and tousled flaxen hair manifesting her angelic nature. Surely, she would save his life again, now. "Please, trust me. 'Tis no' worth your soul, your life for his."

She pressed her forehead to his, her lips close as she spoke. She inhaled the heat of his panting breath, trying to take the heat from battle from him as well. Her words, her touch, calmed him, driving the desperate need for blood and retribution from him, and he threw the sword from his hand. It dropped to the floor with a clatter, and chatter among the gathered throng grew louder.

Alistair placed his hand on her cheeks, kissing her deeply, the kiss of a man saved by the woman he loved. In addition to the chattering of the crowd, several jeers erupted from the men assembled. Lioslaith's blush painted her cheeks a rosy shade of pink, and she pulled away from Alistair, her attention on the wounded man.

"Alisa!" she called over her shoulder, and they scrambled to Dougie, rope dragging. He glared at Lioslaith, but discretion won out, and he presented his wound to her. He was not about to lose a fighting arm over a minor skirmish.

Father Stewart knelt next to her, a bowl of water and a swath of crumbled flora in his hand. He mixed the two into a paste and plastered it on Dougie's arm.

"'Tis nay more than a scratch," Lioslaith told him, "but better t'halt any pus that could come. Aye?" Her flaxen eyebrow raised in a gentle curve, and the disgruntled man nodded.

Muira had ripped a long strip of fabric from her shift, and Alisa wrapped the wound tightly. Better to hope that the wound heals easily; he would certainly make witchcraft accusations again if the arm decayed and began to smell.

Satisfied with the bindings, Father Stewart rose and held a hand to Dougie, helping him off the floor. The man stood with a grunt but remained stable on his feet. Dougie was forced to agree — the wound, though it bled excessively, was naught more than a scratch.

Angus Og pushed forward and directed the crowd's attention back on Lioslaith and her sisters.

"Ye may have helped my man here, but what of my good-son dying in my chambers! Ye must be held accountable for those actions!"

"My good priest," Lioslaith implored to Father Stewart. "I assure you that the man, Hamish, is no' dying! Please," she grasped his hand in a desperate motion. "I did strike the man, that I do no' deny. But I did it out of defense, for the man and his kin, the large Dougie there, did try t'inflict themselves on my person and attacked my good husband."

"Husband?" A single eyebrow rose on the kind priest's forehead.

"Aye," Lioslaith said, "my husband. But once I saw the damage t'the man's head and Dougie rode off, we placed Hamish on my bedding, and I attended him, my Laird!" Her voice rose as she swirled to face Angus Og.

"The potion, as ye suggest, was a healing poultice that I also used on your leg when ye had the infection. The priest acquired it from my good-sister Alisa. And the curse? My Laird, your men heard me chanting the gospel names, just as I learned from the priest himself." Lioslaith returned her pleading gaze to Father Stewart.

"Aye, she is correct on both counts, Angus Og," the priest confirmed.

"Father, I think that the woman is trying t'mesmerize us!" Angus Og would not halt in his accusations. "We need to conduct a full trial —" Angus Og tried to say, and Father Stewart blanched, when a ruckus in the yard drew their attention to the door.

Dougie, recovered from his flesh wound, clasped his sword and rushed the rough wooden doors, throwing them open to the scene outside.

Outside, The MacRuaidhrís had arrived in full force, like a Highland charge, Lachlan riding at the front. Their conversations with Christina and the implications of letting the MacDonald clan hold a powerful sway over their sister rang in their heads, and they agreed to leave at sunrise with a command of men to retrieve Alisa, and if they were fortunate, Muira and Lioslaith as well.

The galloping of their horses made the ground itself quake, and the MacDonald men in the yard drew their swords to fend off the invaders. Lachlan noted their stance as he and his men approached, and he hated their smug appearance, that they were somehow grander, more loyal to the Scottish cause, and thus could tread where they weren't welcome. The MacRuaidhrí clan was the larger, more powerful clan and 'twas time to put the MacDonalds in their place. Enough supposition that Rudy and Lachlan MacRuaidhrí were English sympathizers. The world would soon know what side the MacRuaidhrí clan was on.

Lachlan leapt off his horse, followed by several other of his kinsmen as they neared the MacDonald keep, his broadsword clutched tightly in his powerful right hand. His tartan billowed out behind him, like the flapping of a dark crimson sail, directing his men to rally to the cause. While something as banal as women accused of witchcraft may seem a foolish reason to invade, Lachlan and Rudy viewed it as the proverbial straw that broke the donkey's back.

As Lachlan's sword met the dull metal of a MacDonald weapon, he felt all the petty squabbles of the past build up. Angus Og, when their clans had drunk together after the discussions regarding the exile, made it appear that all such squabbles were behind them. Taking his half-sister and accusing her of witchcraft was not a way to show solidarity. Lachlan would take his vexations out on any MacDonald in his path, cutting a bloody swath, if need be, to Laird Angus Og MacDonald himself.

Dougie released his own broadsword from its sheath, sending his battle cry up to the heavens. Though his arm ached, the witch bandaged it well, and he needed to redeem himself from the beating he took from the sorry excuse for a Highlander. *Time to teach these meddling MacRuaidhrís a lesson they will no' forget,* Dougie thought as he raced into the fray. Rage and humiliation fueled his movements. Frozen mud churned with the wet snow, creating a mucky landscape of battle. *Over witches? Why are they here? Armed? Invading?* Dougie could nay wrap his mind around the MacRuaidhrí presence.

Alistair followed Dougie, rushing to the door to witness the fracas himself. Seeing the fierce fighting, Alistair had a moment of conundrum. *Should I enter the fray? Take on Dougie for my woman's honor? Or race inside and tend to her directly?* Alistair had learned his lessons the hard way, and instead of entering a battle that did not seem to be his own, he returned to the hall.

Angus Og and most of the MacDonald men, including the priest, had rushed to the yard in defense of their keep. Only one young MacDonald man remained in the hall, keeping a wary eye on the women. Alistair supposed the man thought them truly witches and feared what curses they would place on him alone. Alisa noted the young MacDonald's reticence and started toward the lad, hissing as she did so. The young man yelped and retreated near the fire. Alisa cackled at the lad's expense, and Alistair could almost see why the woman was accused of witchcraft.

Alistair moved close to Lioslaith, pulling at the bristly rope binding her delicate hands. The bonds had worn away her skin, leaving patchy abrasions along her wrists. Alistair nearly leapt out into the yard again, waiting to strike down Dougie and the Laird for such atrocities against her. Against his wife.

"Are ye well? Did they hurt ye a'tall?" Alistair hugged Lioslaith close but addressed Muira and Alisa as well.

"'Tis quite a pinch we find ourselves in, Alistair," Muira commented in her stoic voice. Alisa just cackled again.

"I told ye that all ye needed t'do was let the MacRuaidhrís ken. I may be a bastard, but I am sure ye heard from Christina that I am a beloved bastard?" Her eyes twinkled like stars on a clear night.

Alistair shrugged one shoulder. "Aye. She indicated as such." He tipped his head toward the open doorway, where sounds of the battle carried through the hall. "But I did no' see your good sister yet. Or this supposed man who is supposed t'put all accusations of witchcraft t'rest?"

Alisa took a deep breath, willing herself not to laugh again. "Ahh, laddie. She will be here soon, her powerful man with her. Have ye nay doubt."

Confusion twisted Alistair's features, that she could be so certain when he had seen naught to support her claim. Blood and fretful accusations were all Alistair had seen this day, and he didn't presume one singular man could allay the fears running rampant in the hall, or the conflict outside.

Muira's lips pressed together, but Alisa caught her crystal gaze and winked at her. Alisa knew something important, that much was evident.

"So, do I knock the yon MacDonald lad t'the ground and escape with ye?" Said MacDonald lad flinched at the prospect of being assaulted, and Alistair shook his head at the lad. "Is that the plan from here?" Alistair directed his question to the enigmatic Alisa.

"Nay, we can abide here. I think ye will want t'watch what happens."

That sly smile never left the woman's lips. And in moments like this, surety of Alisa's powers as a witch filled Alistair completely, for at that exact time, the clashing and grunting of the outside battle died down.

Dougie was giving Lachlan's sword a pounding, one eye was coated in blood, casting the combat in a red glow. The invasion puzzled Dougie, who struggled to put the question from his mind until Lachlan himself was laid low by Dougie's own blade. For an infamous drunkard, however, the leader of Clan MacRuaidhrí was a stronger warrior than Dougie anticipated, and he had to shift his attack accordingly. The man didn't fight like a drunk, but like a raging Viking, intent on taking his bounty. Dougie felt fortune was on his side, as he was several inches taller and several years younger than the soft man, contrary to what the fight between the two might reveal.

Thrusting toward the man's belly, Dougie allowed his sword to parry to the man's side. This maneuver allowed Dougie's arm to get close enough to crack the MacRuaidhrí across the face with an unyielding elbow. The MacRuaidhrí reeled backward, trying to prevent himself from falling into the freezing muck of the yard.

As he lifted his sword to take advantage of Lachlan's weakened position, a glint on the horizon caught his eye. He dipped his sword while maintaining his fighting stance and watched as two riders cantered in. One rider was a woman, her long, burnished hair flowing behind her like a sail. The other was a brown-haired man of a particular stature.

"Oh, my Lord in Heaven," was all Dougie said before Lachlan's clobbering fist made contact with Dougie's' bearded jaw, sending the man sprawling into the mud.

Several MacDonald men saw Dougie's reaction and also slowed their fighting, training their eyes on the riders' approach from the north. The fighting slowed, as the MacRuaidhrí men were instructed not to kill but to contain. Several men, mostly MacDonalds, lay in the muck, bloody, but shivering and alive. The MacRuaidhrís wanted all the MacDonald clan to see what would happen next.

Father Stewart, who had been racing amongst the downed men, tending to their wounds, rose from his squatting position in the muddy grass. His eyes followed the same line of sight at the approaching pair on horseback.

CHAPTER SIXTEEN

On Meeting a King

ANGUS OG HEFTED HIS bulk down the steps, his face contorted with confusion at the approaching riders and his clan's response to them. He pressed himself forward, trying to see who would cause the fighting in the yard to grind to a halt.

One rider was obviously a woman, her unbound, brown hair blowing about her. Her regal position and deep green velvet cape announced she was a woman of import. Her companion, however, stayed the actions of everyone in the bailey. His strong frame sat straight and confident on his horse, his broad shoulders filling the rusty-colored woolen bliaut, his arms muscular and thick. The man's own long, walnut hair swirled in the wind under his similarly rusty-hued cap and trailed down his cheeks into a light beard. For Scottish clans, there was no mistaking the man of that coloring and stature.

The clansmen pulled themselves up, swords at their sides, entranced by the arrival of the riders. As the man rode into the yard, men fell to their knees, bowing their heads in reverence.

None thought they would ever meet the King of Scotland, yet here he was, Robert the Bruce, 6th Earl of Annandale and the rightful king, riding into the MacDonald keep. Their loyalty, many in the clan believed, was graced by his presence.

After the King passed by Rudy MacRuaidhrí, the Laird bowed his head briefly, then re-mounted his horse and rode up behind the Bruce, showing his fealty to the King and thus the Scottish cause. Christina's smile touched her hazel green eyes, and her heart leapt at the final confirmation of her brothers' support of Robert the Bruce. She reached out and clasped Robert's hand, delighted that his faithfulness in her brothers was rewarded.

Angus Og's hand clutched his chest, as though his heart would burst. The King of Scotland, missing for months, had lodged himself on North Uist all this time, under the banner of the MacRuaidhrís no less. 'Twas no wonder they saw themselves as superior. And now the King himself was at his own stronghold, at the door of his hall, and Angus Og was in awe and lost all his words. The verbose Laird of Clan MacDonald was speechless.

"May we enter your hall, good Laird MacDonald?" The Bruce's voice was strong yet reassuring, the type of voice that made people want to respond to him. If anyone in MacDonald lands could be considered a witch, it would be the Bruce.

Angus Og redoubled. "Aye, my King. Aye!" he exclaimed, bobbing his head and stepping aside so the King could enter.

Robert dismounted in one sleek movement, then held his hand out to assist Christina from her own steed. The two entered the hall in a royal fashion, arms entwined and unflappable expressions on their faces.

Alistair, Lioslaith, and Muira all swept back, bowing low to the couple. Alistair's heart pounded erratically in his chest, full of panic and upheaval. He was a supposed English spy, and now he was in the presence of the King of Scotland. What fate would befall him?

Alisa, however, had no compunctions and rushed to Christina like a child, throwing herself into Christina's open arms. They hugged for a long moment under the gaze of all those who had collected in the hall.

"I ken ye would come. I told these fools t'nay worry." Alisa flicked her head toward Muira and Lioslaith, and a glint of humor sparkled in Christina's eyes.

"Aye, ye are the clever one. Ye ken we would never let any grief come t'ye."

Alisa then turned to the King and threw herself into his arms as well. Robert lifted her light form off the ground, hugging her in a bear-like embrace.

"Hello, little one. What trouble have ye stumbled into today?" Robert the Bruce inquired in a teasing tone.

"Ooch, Robbie. 'Tis a bit more trouble as of late. I have t'keep ye busy, aye?" Alisa bantered back, and they both chuckled. Robert patted her head, then turned to address the crowd in the hall. Everyone from the yard squeezed into the chamber, all wanting a look at the beloved King.

Father Stewart was one of the first to regain his senses, stumbling in awe at the revered man who stood before him, the man who ranked just under God in his worldly hierarchy.

"My King!" he exclaimed, his voice panting and nervous. "T'what do we owe the honor of this unprecedented visit?"

The Bruce's handsome face regarded the men and women in the hall, looking over the scene before him. The collective reverence could be measured with cups, filled to the brim.

"I have it on good authority," here he tipped his aristocratic head to his regal woman, Christina, then to Alistair, who reeled back in unmitigated shock, "that some kindly women, one in particular who is a beloved relation t'my companion and the MacRuaidhrí clan, are accused of witchcraft? Is that the truth I am hearing?"

Father Stewart drew himself up, puffing out his chest in defense of the women. "Aye, milord. Ye have heard correctly. These women, Lioslaith and Alisa, are healers for many in our clans, and Lioslaith's sister, Muira, appears t'have gotten caught up in this unfounded persecution."

"Do ye ken these women, Father?" The King asked in his calming voice that spun out like velvet. The crowd fairly swooned as he spoke.

"Aye, we have worked our healing skills together. The 'curses' they are charged with are nay more than prayers t'our own God, Jesus Christ. The poultices are the same herbs I use. They are good women, nay witches."

Robert gave the priest a measured look, then winked at Christina. "And what of the accusation that two of the women live together, much like a man and wife?"

The suggestion sucked the air out of the chamber, drawing a collective gasp from many in attendance. A wry smile tugged at Father Stewart's lips.

"I dinna ken what goes on behind closed doors. What I do ken is these women, all of them, love each other. And God is love. Where love presides, so does God."

The King only smiled and nodded his head at the priest's enlightened response. Muira and Lioslaith sank against each other, knowing that the call for a witch trial would not happen this day. And after the striking personage of the Bruce making his opinion known, 'twould most likely not happen in the future. Alistair, recovering from his own wonder at the King right here with him in the hall, stepped to Lioslaith, clutching her in a desperate and relieved embrace.

"But she kilt a man!" a voice from the rear called out. King Robert raised his eyes to see who spoke.

"Two! She kilt a man years ago as well!" another voice piped up.

"What, this man?" Roderick retorted as he helped Hamish descend the narrow stone stairwell.

"Hamish!" Laird MacDonald bellowed, hurrying to the pale-faced young man's side as quickly as his girth could take him. "What, are ye well, my good-son?"

"Aye," Hamish grunted. "Naught more than a whack on my head." He touched the still-tender spot on the back of his skull where the hair was matted with blood and dried salve.

"So ye did assault my good-son!" Angus Og tried to keep the accusatory tone in his voice, to no avail. Hamish waved a limp hand in his direction.

"Not that 'twasn't well deserved," he admitted with a grimace. "We invaded her home, attacked her man who defended her. We brought this on ourselves."

"Aye, weel, then perchance ye deserved the knock to the head, ye fool," Angus Og tight voice replied. He didn't forget that the man was sleeping with the comfort woman while married to his daughter, a conversation he would have with the lad once he recovered.

Hamish turned his sober gaze to Lioslaith. "And I am verra sorry for it."

Lioslaith dipped her eyes in return. "Aye, and I ye for knocking ye as hard as I did."

"This lass knocked this man's head off?" Robert the Bruce looked the broad man up and down, his light brown eyes unable to hide his mirth at the prospect of such an encounter. "She must wield a fine weapon, eh?" Hamish had the good sense to blush.

"And ye are obviously no' dead," The Bruce deadpanned, and a small titter erupted in the hall. Hamish shook his head, then grabbed at his hair, grimacing again.

"So, nary a dead clansman, and the priest does no' support a claim of witchcraft here." The Bruce's proclamation, second only to that of God himself, sealed their fate. Any claim of witchcraft would go no further.

The King lifted his eyes to the room again. "And where is this exile I have heard so much about?"

⤜⤜⤜⤜ ⤛⤛⤛⤛

Alistair stilled, rooted in his spot, clinging to Lioslaith as if again she could save him from yet another uncertain fate. An exiled Highlander with supposed ties to clans that supported the English, and now he was in the presence of the Scottish King? Alistair's heart sank to his toes, and it took all the courage, all the honor, all the self-respect he could muster to raise his eyes and meet the intense gaze of the King of Scotland, Sir Robert the Bruce. He lifted his hand like an errant schoolboy.

"Aye, milord. I am here."

The Bruce's eyes riveted onto Alistair's shorter form. Alistair felt more than saw the command from the King to approach, and the crowd in the hall parted like Moses' Red Sea, craning their necks to watch the banished Highlander-spy greet the King who held his fate in those royal hands. Alistair fell to his knees at the King's feet, head bowed, praying that the path God chose for him would not come to a sudden, bloody end on the rough stone floor in the MacDonald great hall.

That same mirthful look never left the King's face as he watched Alistair genuflect. Rather than draw the encounter out longer than necessary, the Bruce laid his hand on Alistair's shoulder in a surprisingly comforting gesture.

"Rise, lad," the King dictated, and Alistair did not hesitate. He stood quickly, keeping his eyes averted.

"Look at me, lad," the King said in a quiet voice. "I hear ye have quite a story, from how ye left the Highlands and ended on our shores." The Bruce's statement was less of a question and more of an observation, and there was no denying it. Alistair nodded.

"Aye, milord."

"And there are many, these good MacDonalds included, who believe ye t'be less than loyal t'the Scottish cause. What say ye t'that?"

Alistair swallowed; a large gulping swallow he was certain could be heard throughout the hall. His face burned with a mix of fear and shame, and his knees shook like a child's.

"I am no' spy, milord. I admit," he raised his eyes to regard the King directly, and the King granted him a respectful nod in return, "I did engage wi' the Ross clan, but never wi' the English. And I only did that out of a misguided quest for power. I had a fevered idea in my head that I should be the next Laird of my clan, and I believed aligning with the Ross clan t'help me in that endeavor."

He paused, taking a deep breath, the confession he had given in private to the priest and in a secret vow to Lioslaith now spoken aloud for all to hear. He dreaded how badly it sounded — his confessions did paint him as a traitor and a spy.

"But the very person I tried t'hurt in this misguided quest granted me mercy, banishing me rather than stretching my neck. After several misadventures once I arrived at Lochmaddy, the efforts of the fair Lioslaith and the sage words of Father Stewart provided me with things I never had 'afore. A chance for penance, for forgiveness, for absolution. T'ken the path that God has chosen for me."

Alistair flicked his eyes heavenward, as his next words were both enlightening and haughty. "And 'twould seem God's plan was for me t'meet ye, King Robert the Bruce."

His mind reeled at this realization — that all of the missteps, his failed plans, the lessons he learned on this rock at the edge of civilization — were all part of God's plan to meet the King of Scotland. God's vision was certainly more astute and far-reaching than Alistair could have ever imagined.

"Weel, I can agree with ye on that, Alistair MacNally," the King told him. "And do ye ken what your path here has accomplished?" The Bruce's burnished eyebrows rose high on his clear forehead.

"Nay," Alistair admitted with a breath that was almost a chuckle. What his tumultuous actions on the isle could have done was more than he was able to consider. What larger purpose did a low man like him serve? "I canna think of a single thing I may have accomplished, unless it was t'cause strife in the MacDonald clan. 'Twould seem I was successful at that."

At this, the King roared with laughter, his wide smile splitting his face, and many of the MacRuaidhrís joined him. Angus Og also allowed his rotund belly a snicker as well, understanding the point the King was going to make.

"Laddie, ye did more than that. Take a look around this room, will ye?" The King stretched his arm out, gesturing around the hall, from the MacDonalds to the MacRuaidhrís, all collected in one chamber, all together under the banner of the Bruce.

"Ye brought the clans of this island together. Ye helped the clans come under my banner, show their support for the rightful King of Scotland, and bring us all united for the cause of Scotland." The Bruce paused and flicked his eyes toward Lachlan and Rudy MacRuaidhrí, who inclined their heads in agreement. The pact was sealed, and the Bruce was heartily assured of his position as the King of Scotland.

He then placed his heavy palm on Alistair's scrubby cheek and continued, "That, my lad, is what I have been trying t'do for the past six months. *This*," he removed his hand and poked Alistair in the chest, "is what ye have done."

The men in the hall erupted in cheers, a mix of "Huzzah" and "To the King" and "For Scotland!" at Robert's words. Alistair's cheeks burned all the more at the King's generous compliment.

"Milord, I dinna think —" he started. The Bruce held up his hand to interrupt him.

"Lad, I just have one more question for ye."

The crowd quieted to an expectant hush. A shiver slipped over Alistair's backside, and his bowels loosened uncomfortably. The King leaned in close to Alistair, so close that Alistair could smell the haddock the King must have eaten earlier that morn. The King's breath was steamy against his skin, and his shivering increased.

"Are ye a spy, laddie?" Though the words were serious, the King's tone was anything but. With one eyebrow raised in a mocking expression, the King asked a question to which he was already sure of the answer. Alistair dropped to his knee once again.

"Nay, milord," he said as loudly as possible to carry over the din of the crowd. "I have in truth always been your loyal subject."

A few men in the rear of the hall grumbled at this response, and Lioslaith was certain Dougie was one of them. But the King heard Alistair's answer, confirming what he already knew, and laid his hands atop Alistair's head.

"Then rise, ye loyal man of Scotland, embrace your King, and let us celebrate the unity of the isle clans this day!"

The cheering that resulted threatened to bring down the stones of the hall, shaking every rock, every bench, every person gathered. Lachlan jumped atop a nearby bench.

"Here! Here!" his deep voice carried over the cacophony of the room. "Let us celebrate the King! Bring out the mead and ale! To the King! To Scotland!" Lachlan raised his fist and the crowd cheered again.

Alistair leaned close to the King's ear to make himself heard over the noise. "So, I can stay here? I can remain with Lioslaith and her family?"

The King winked at Alistair, that amused look ever-present. "Of course, laddie. Live here with your woman, raise a family, and live the dream that is Scotland."

Raising the King's hand to his lips, Alistair kissed it out of respect and as a show of fealty. He then turned to find Lioslaith. She was standing near the center of the hall, her own face aglow with joy of the King's words and hope that her future with Alistair was secure.

CHAPTER SEVENTEEN

Blessings Upon Blessings

NORTH UIST, EARLY SPRING 1307

As soon as the first snow melt of early spring welcomed the small, creamy faces of primroses near the shores, Muira trekked through the slush and mud to the church near the MacDonald keep. Pale sunlight managed to shine through a smattering of gray clouds and low-lying fog, casting a glow upon the granite house of God.

After her brief conversation with Father Stewart, who was not surprised at the request, he easily acquiesced and began his own planning as soon as Muira left. Both buzzed with excitement of the upcoming nuptials.

Alistair and Lioslaith passed a contented winter with wee Rowan. A smoldering fire burned at the hearth, a warmth reflected in the hearts and faces of the family in the wee cottage. The new year was a celebratory event with Lioslaith's sister and Alisa, all of them having a cheery meal with an exchange of necessary, considerate gifts. Lioslaith knitted woolen socks for Alistair, whose current, overly mended stockings were not expected to last out the season.

Alisa and Muira gave gifts of honey and preserves to Lioslaith and Alistair, with a small jar of honey just for Rowan. The lass squealed with delight at her very own jar. She peeled the waxen cloth off the top and poked a tiny finger to scoop a dollop of the viscous, amber sweetness into her mouth.

Alistair had made several more feathery wind catchers for Rowan. Many were sleek, gray-brown owl feathers, gathered from the short ear owl that recovered in the barn. The owl was more than friendly and enjoyed his warm home in the barn as his wing healed. He was flapping it regularly, and Lioslaith had claimed he would fly soon. They all dearly hoped the owl, that Rowan named *Beag Laith*, meaning "little brown one," would remain. Alisa seemed confident that, if they keep his space clear in the rafters of the lean-to, his residency would continue. He had already done a fair job keeping the mice at bay, for which they were all grateful.

Finally, Alistair handed Lioslaith a slender gift, wrapped in an old scrap of scarlet tartan. She unwound the fabric to find a slim, iron hair pin, topped with a circle of deeply burnished agate. In her whole life, she had never received so beautiful a gift. Her mouth fell open at how it sparkled, but she was speechless.

Muira, however, spoke words for her. "Alistair! Where have ye found such a thing? 'Tis far too lovely!"

Alistair could not prevent the blush that stained his lightly bearded cheeks a deep rose. He pointed to Muira's hair, then to Lioslaith's matching platinum tresses.

"'Twas the first thing I saw of her, bending over me. Her hair was like a halo. I thought she t'be an angel. I thought 'twould look nice, aye?"

He stumbled over his words, trying to explain how he wanted to see the agate in her hair catch the dancing firelight. That she was all things beautiful to him, and this small bauble was only a shadow of the beauty she brought to his life. But those words could not be spoken aloud. At least, not at the supper table.

Later that night she asked him where he could have found such a beautiful stone — agate is a precious red. Alistair only smiled at her; this was his secret he was not ready to share.

A fortnight before the wedding, after making Lioslaith quiver with delight under the wool coverings, he pulled her face to his. She pressed her delicate skin to his, trying to touch as much of him as she could. His mossy green gaze caught her eyes with an intensity that made her chest quiver, as did her loins. She raised one pale, quizzical eyebrow.

"'Tis coming onto spring, lass," he observed. "Have ye decided?"

Her full lips pulled to one side in a teasing grin.

"What if I have no'?" she retorted.

"Weel, then your sisters will have much t'complain of with ye," he teased back.

Lioslaith pressed her lips to his as she spoke into him, talking into his mouth.

"Then 'tis fortunate I want ye, *husband*."

'Twas the first time she said the word aloud since their frightening affair at the MacDonald keep, and Alistair's heart fair burst out of his chest. He pulled her under him again, ready to love her once more.

The early spring wedding itself was direct and endearing. Lioslaith's gown was a skirt of woven bright red and green MacRuaidhrí plaid, a gift from Alisa and Christina, with a creamy shift and forest green girdle. Several ribbons fastened one side of the skirt up near her slender waist, displaying an underskirt of the same creamy hue as her shift. Extra ribbons were tied along her waist, for the wedding guest to pull on or "tear away" from the bride as good luck tokens.

Lioslaith's hair, the long, flaxen mane that matched her sister's, was braided into several small plaits from the front and side, then wrapped around her head to form a golden coronet. The rest of her hair hung down her back, brushing at her waist. Muira pressed the agate hair pin into the braids to hold the braided coronet in place. They stepped back, and Alisa clapped her hands with delight, like a small child, at Lioslaith's appearance.

Rowan, who sat playing on the pallet across the room, came to investigate and clapped her hands over her mouth. She had no voice, not a sound, so in awe she was over her mother. Alisa spoke for her.

"Ye look like an angel," she whispered in reverent tones.

The priest, the good man he was, had instructed Alistair to spend the evening before the wedding at the MacDonald church. His excuse was to "prepare" Alistair, but in truth it was to bathe and dress the lad proper as a surprise to the young couple.

Several of the women Lioslaith assisted with her healing worked together to weave a stunning tartan of bright reds and thin lines of black, a color Alistair wore well. Father Stewart gifted the lad with a new, gray tunic with dramatic billowing sleeves that tapered to his wrists. His woolen trews, which were freshly laundered, tucked into his leather boots, completing his wedding attire.

Father Steward admired the lad, as he looked all that he should as the nephew of a Laird and a man on his wedding day. He then helped pick knots and several small twigs from Alistair's hair, brushing it thoroughly with a bone comb, and the lad was ready to stand on the steps of the kirk with his new bride.

While Angus Og and his faithful Roderick appeared for the event, few from the MacDonald stronghold attended. The MacDonald families that Lioslaith and Alisa had helped over the years where present, ecstatic even, that Lioslaith would now be a woman of good repute.

Lachlan MacRuaidhrí also made his appearance known, standing close to the base of the granite steps near his half-sister Alisa. Rudy decided Lachlan was a staunch enough representative, and even though Christina chastised him for it, Rudy stayed at the MacRuaidhrí keep, sleeping off his drinking from the previous eve. Lachlan nodded respectfully to Alisa's fair woman, Muira, recognizing the importance of this woman in his sister's life. There was only so much he wanted to control in his clan, and his beloved little sister would never be something he could control.

To the surprise of everyone gathered before the church, a lone piper began to play his rich tones that carried across the damp moorland. Heads and necks craned to see who the piper heralded. Three riders on two horses approached from the north, a man and woman, with a second woman riding behind the man.

'Twas the King Robert the Bruce returning to MacDonald lands again. This time his regalia rivaled that of any King in history. His deep black velvet tunic and black braes bespoke his importance, his own Bruce tartan thrown casually around his shoulders in a bright scarlet and green cape. His black cap set off his light brown hair that shimmered in the dappled sunlight, casting a light about his head as though God himself were commanding all to know the Bruce as King.

Christina rode next to him, with Lioslaith, the exquisite bride, seated behind the King. Once they neared the church, the King dismounted and held his hand up to assist the bride, then waved away the MacDonald who moved to assist Christina from her horse. He helped her down, holding her for a few heartbeats as Lioslaith stepped past the admiring crowd that laughed and cheered — whether for her or for the King, she didn't know or care. All Lioslaith could focus on was the handsome Highlander waiting at the top of the steps.

Robert the Bruce pressed through the crowd to walk beside Lioslaith, taking her arm and escorting her up the stairs where the priest stood. He bowed to Father Stewart, kissed Lioslaith's hand, then stepped next to Alistair, who watched the scene with his eyebrows raised to his hairline.

The King smiled at the lad, noting his bewilderment. Shifting close to Alistair's ear, he whispered, "I ken ye could use a man here t'ensure we see this through t'the end, aye?"

An expression of wry humor passed over Alistair's face — better to have the support of the King than risk an outburst from an errant MacDonald. He nodded his thanks to the King, then turned his attention to his bride, who lifted her shockingly clear blue eyes to his face. A soft smile settled into her lips, and she took Alistair's outstretched hand in her dainty one. Rowan peeked around her mother to watch the pair, and Alistair gave her a wink. Then they faced the priest, and it was time.

Father Stewart blessed their union, marking it as a holy sacrament, then called for the rings. Muira had given Lioslaith a silver circlet for Alistair, a most generous gift, to be sure. Alistair surprised Lioslaith when he removed his own silver ring for her, this one with another setting of agate in the silver. The pale lashes of her eyes popped up wide, and a soft gasp escaped her.

"Alistair," she whispered, trying not to distract the priest's prayer over the rings, "It matches the hair pin! Where did ye find such finery?"

Once again, he did not answer and slipped it onto her finger in one fluid move, holding his fingers over hers as though to sear the ring onto her hand.

The priest removed a swath of cloth from his Bible and asked for Alistair's knife. He pulled the short dirk from his sporran, the silver handle set with pieces of agate. Lioslaith noted two of the pieces were missing, and her gaze flew to Alistair, who only looked at her in a sidelong glance. Her heart throbbed at knowing he destroyed the beauty of one of his only belongings that remained from his Highland home to create finery for her. She blinked back tears as Father Stewart gently clasped her hand. And just as Muira did for them when they were handfast, the priest flicked a quick, shallow cut into the base of her palm. Pressing their hands together, the priest wrapped the cloth around their hands as their blood mixed together, marking Alistair and Lioslaith as eternally joined.

Cheers and celebratory calls rose from the crowd as Alistair kissed his new wife. The King, not a man to miss an opportunity, moved past Alistair and planted his own kiss on her surprised lips. Robert chuckled and shot a look to Alistair.

"The King also blesses this marriage," he said, then skipped down the steps to the awaiting arms of Christina.

As the wedded pair descended the stairway, Alisa watched the interaction between the King and her own dear sister. She noted the way Christina kept one hand across her belly and how her breasts seemed to pull at her gown. Biting her lower lip, Alisa looked away, back to the bride, happy for her sister and the new bairn, most likely the King's bairn, growing inside her. She was certain Christina would keep this news to herself for a while more and that she would have to be patient until her sister shared this joyous development with her.

The MacDonald Laird's generosity extended to his main hall, where he had Mistress Maddy and her kitchen maids present a simple feast in celebration. As the patrons enjoyed spiced mead, lean rabbit stew, and warm bread, the King rose, lifting his tankard at the couple.

"I ken we are all impressed at the lengths Alistair has gone through t'end up here, at this table, with this woman, today!" His statement elicited an undercurrent of laughter. The Bruce smiled at his own cleverness and continued. "And 'tis with pride that Lioslaith has found a man worthy of her in all ways. I wish ye all the best!"

'Twas a simple toast, but heartfelt, and from the mouth of the King himself. Who could have a better blessing for a wedding than Alistair and Lioslaith?

The King set down his mug, his expression more somber. "'Tis also a fair opportunity to proclaim the time has come for me to return t'Scotland, take my throne, and conquer these English weasels once and for all! Who will come with me?"

Men scrambled over tables and other people, racing to be the first to volunteer to fight on behalf of the King. He announced he would depart in a fortnight, once the wintry winds of the Minch calmed.

After the excitement died down, the King and Christina made to leave. Alistair caught him as they exited the doorway of the hall.

"I dinna ken what ye would have of me, milord," Alistair spoke honestly as they stepped outside. "Would ye have me accompany ye t'Scotland?"

While the idea intrigued Alistair, to return to the Highlands with King Robert the Bruce in the flesh — *what an impression that would make!* — he did not want to leave this rocky outpost, nor his new wife, and return to a life he despised.

The King threw his head back and let loose a great peal of laughter. Had they been inside the hall, surely everyone would have turned to stare. Fortunately, outside on the stony steps, no one but Christina could see Alistair's cheeks inflame with embarrassment.

"I dinna doubt your fealty, man," the King spoke in an earnest voice. "But I will say nay. No' for the supposition of ye as a spy or whatnot, ye ken?" he asked. Alistair nodded. "Ye have a new life here, a new wife, a family. 'Twould no' do ye well t'leave all that now."

The King clapped him on the shoulder with a heavy hand. "Plus, bad luck seems to follow ye lad. I would do well to try to avoid having it follow me as well, aye?"

At this, Alistair joined in the King's rich laughter, for the man was not wrong. Better for Alistair to remain behind and not stain the King's efforts with any occasion of failure against the English.

"If ye please, I would bring a missive to your family, so they ken your well-being?" the King offered graciously. Alistair startled at the offer — few in the Highlands would believe the King of Scotland offering to serve as a messenger for Alistair.

"Aye. 'Twould be a kindness. Thank ye, milord."

He already knew what the message would read. For his uncle, he would write but two words: *Thank you.* To his mam and da, he would have one brief statement: *I have found my home.*

Alistair bowed to the King, who made a nickering sound at his horse and ambled away, chasing his own destiny.

Another burst of cheering drew his attention back to the hall. Alistair rounded through the doorway and caught sight of Lioslaith at the table, an easy smile dancing across her fair face as she sat with a laughing Rowan.

Aye, Alistair agreed. Better to remain here with this new life, this new path, where he was blessed with this new future.

THE END

Read More!

Want a bonus ebook about Gavin and learn what happened before he and Jenny met? Click the image below to receive *The Heartbreak of the Glen*, the free Glen Highland Romance short ebook, in your inbox!

    Click here: https://view.flodesk.com/pages/5f74c62a924e5bf828c9e0f3

Excerpt from The Jewel of the Glen

His feet sunk into the sandy bottom of the unforgiving Little Minch, icy waves lapping against his boots as he strode to shore. Months had passed since he last laid his doe-brown eyes on his beloved Highlands, but his time in hiding had to come to an end. 'Twas time to return, face down his enemies, and secure the sanctity of his crown.

Robert the Bruce hated that he had to secrete his kingship on a rock in the middle of the sea after the death of Comyn. He feared his following may have waned, that the English could have gained a stronger foothold in Scotland, or, God-forbid, managed to usurp his crown altogether.

The desire to safeguard his position as king and create a unified Scotland burned deeply in him, heating him against the cold waters. His water-logged boots left footprints on the sand, as though he was a mysterious Blue man, emerging from the sea, ready to command the life and death of men. The Bruce watched as the stony-gray waves washed ashore, rolling over his footsteps as if he had never been there.

That would not be his legacy in Scotland. His strength as King, and thus the strength of Scotland, would not be denied.

His men shivered as they walked up the narrow beach, while the rest of his coterie pulled the boats to the shore. Many men from North Uist, including several from both the MacDonald and MacRuaidhrí clans, rallied to his call, shoving each other aside to be the first in the boats heading to the Highlands. Pride swelled in the Bruce's chest as their eagerness. How could he refuse these men the leadership, the Scotland, for which they fought so long and hard?

He had been surprised at the sheer number of men who volunteered to join him on his trek over the Minch. There was an excellent chance they may never see their beloved island again, yet they convened, nonetheless. Dougie of Clan MacDonald was one of the first to join the Bruce, an action that did not surprise the Bruce in the least. After his troubles on North Uist, trying unsuccessfully to have a beloved local woman and her sisters tried as witches, he needed an escape. Taking up the banner of the King of Scotland was a strong option. And though Dougie had a modicum of power on the isle, he was a man too large for such a small island — a voyage to the Highlands would do the man well.

Once the Bruce reached the dry grasses of Malliap, just south of the Highlands proper, he paused. The sight of the grass in the glens, the snowcapped mountains, the expanse of pristine land to which none other could compare, filled his sights. Scotland was God's land on earth, Robert the Bruce was certain, and he would defend it to the death. He inhaled the crisp air, collecting his thoughts. 'Twas time to institute his strategy, rout the English, and unite his country.

His men collected on the rocky beach behind him, wiping at their wet breeches with handfuls of dry grass. The Bruce had no patience for such trivialities as wet pants.

"My good countrymen! 'Tis time to take back our country from the English and those who would support them. For Scotland!" he called, and a rousing cheer erupted from the men. "I need five men to volunteer, messengers to run in each direction across Scotland to make all the clans aware that their King has returned."

Continue the series with *The Jewel of the Glen*!

An Excerpt from Before the Glass Slipper

A different type of series, this fairy tale adaptation series sweep you into the world of fairy tales and villainy and asks the question – What happened before?

Chapter One

"Mother, please. Don't make me do this," I begged.

Over and over, I had begged, pleaded, even tried bribing, but to no avail. I was going to have to wed the miserable Seigneur Dubois in a fortnight, and no recourse had made itself known. From the tight lines around my mother's eyes, she was tired of hearing my protests.

"Corinne, I'll not have you behaving like this. I'm finished with this conversation, and so is your father. You will marry Seigneur Andre Dubois and be grateful. So many girls your age would be ecstatic to wed as accomplished a man as Andre."

Accomplished. That was a code word for old. And wealthy. Those were the sole concerns my parents had for my future. Marrying for love? They'd scoffed at the idea and sent me to my room. Then they had accepted the old man's offer on my behalf.

I understood their concerns. Father had worked hard as a merchant, buying rugs, furs, and fabrics from the docks and selling them to upscale lords, *comptes*, and even a few dukes, but local wars and pirating had plagued the shores of La Rochelle to the bustling town of Poitiers, and fewer goods had become available. Father's financial well-being had started to fall down the path to ruin. Plus, to hear Father tell it, the King's taxes had made his finances worse. They needed a solution, something to keep them in their home for the rest of their lives.

So they were *selling* me. No matter what pretty packaging they tried to wrap the news in, that was the ugly truth.

"Mother," I tried once more. Mother angrily waggled a finger at me.

"I'm finished. Now, go to your chambers and have Elise finish helping you pack. The seamstress will be here this afternoon to complete your gown. And your bridegroom is generous and sent you a fine wedding gift. I'll show you when you try on your dress." Here, her face brightened, the first time I'd seen such a look in longer than I cared to think on. "It is the most refined gift. You'll love it."

She may have been trying to sweeten the pot, but I knew it was nothing more than additional bows on the horrible present I was set to unwrap. I shuddered; the idea of unwrapping anything with regards to my bridegroom made my gorge rise.

When I entered my room, Elise gave me a gentle, closed-mouth smile. She was the only one in the house who commiserated with my plight. A plain, silver-edged glass hung near my water table, and I looked away. Since the announcement of my impending nuptials, I had avoided seeing reflections of myself anywhere, because it was my dark, ethereal beauty that put me into this position to begin with.

Start the Before series today!

A Note on History

As mentioned in previous books, I do try to remain loyal to the history, but I also bend historical elements for many reasons: to create a stronger setting, to make the story more vivid . . . In the case of *Exile*, there are several strong historical points that I used to craft the tale.

First, Robert the Bruce did go into hiding for almost a year, and only supposition exists as to where he actually went. Most of my research indicated North Uist and that Christina did help hide him. The suggestion that their son was supposedly "illegitimate" just gave me more fun history to play with. There is no research I can find that actually indicates it was her son by Robert the Bruce, but there is a lot of insinuation!

Thank You!

A Thank You to My Readers

I WOULD LIKE TO extend a heartfelt thank you to all of you who continue to read this series. Be sure to grab *The Jewel of the Glen* and continue the saga!

I cannot write a book without thanking my family, my children, and especially my hubby who is so supportive of this writing endeavor. I would also like to thank the amazing writing communities I have had the opportunity to become more involved with. Their continued cheerleading helps on the dry days!

If you liked this book, please leave a review! Reviews can be bread and butter for an author, and I appreciate your comments and feedback.

About the Author

MICHELLE DEERWESTER-
DALRYMPLE

Michelle Deerwester-Dalrymple is a professor of writing and an author. She started reading when she was 3 years old, writing when she was 4, and published her first poem at age 16. She has written articles and essays on a variety of topics, including several texts on writing for middle and high school students. She has written over seventy books under a variety of pen names and is also slowly working on a novel inspired by actual events. Her Glen Highland romance series books have won *The Top Ten Academy Awards* for books, *Top 50 Indie Books for 2019,* and the *2021 N.N. Light Book Awards*. She lives in California with her family of seven.

Find Michelle on your favorite social media sites and sign up for her newsletter here: https://linktr.ee/mddalrympleauthor

Also By Michelle

The Christmas in the Glen — Book 9

<u>The Celtic Highland Maidens</u>

The Maiden of the Storm

The Maiden of the Grove

The Maiden of the Celts

The Roman of the North

The Maiden of the Stones

Maiden of the Wood
The Maiden of the Loch - coming soon

<u>The *Before* Series</u>

Before the Glass Slipper

Before the Magic Mirror

Before the Cursed Beast

Before the Mermaid's Tale

<u>Glen Coe Highlanders</u>

Highland Burn – Book 1

Highland Breath– Book 2

Highland Beauty — Book 3 coming soon

<u>Historical Fevered Series – short and steamy romance</u>

The Highlander's Scarred Heart

The Highlander's Legacy

The Highlander's Return

Her Knight's Second Chance

The Highlander's Vow

Her Knight's Christmas Gift

Her Outlaw Highlander

Outlaw Highlander Found

Outlaw Highlander Home

<u>As M.D. Dalrymple - Men in Uniform</u>

Night Shift – Book 1

Day Shift – Book 2

Overtime – Book 3

Holiday Pay – Book 4

School Resource Officer – book 5

Undercover – book 6

Holdover – book 7

<u>Campus Heat</u>

Charming – Book 1

Tempting – Book 2

Infatuated -- Book 3

Craving – Book 4

Alluring – Book 5

<u>*Men In Uniform: Marines*</u>

Her Desirable Defender – Book 1

Her Irresistible Guardian — Book 2